A 21ST CENTURY MODERNIZATION

ALSO BY WESTON OCHSE

CYCLE OF THE AEGIS SERIES

Recalled to Life (Delirium Books, 2007)
The Golden Thread (Delirium Books, 2008)

PREACHER'S DAUGHTER SERIES

A Hole in the World (Solaris, 2021)

SEAL TEAM 666 SERIES

SEAL Team 666 (Thomas Dunne Books / St. Martin's Press, 2012)
Age of Blood (Thomas Dunne Books / St. Martin's Press, 2013)
Reign of Evil (Thomas Dunne Books / St. Martin's Press, 2014)

SKY SERIES

Burning Sky (Solaris, 2018)
Dead Sky (Solaris, 2019)

TASK FORCE OMBRA SERIES

Grunt Life (Solaris, 2014)
Grunt Traitor (Solaris, 2015)
Grunt Hero (Solaris, 2017)

OTHER NOVELS

Scarecrow Gods (Delirium Books, 2005)
Blaze of Glory (Morning Star, 2009)
Empire of Salt (part of the *Tomes of the Dead* universe) (Abaddon, 2010)
Velvet Dogma (Crossroad Press, 2011)
Blood Ocean (part of the *Afterblight Chronicles* universe) (Abaddon, 2012)
Babylon Smiles (Crossroad Press, 2013)
Ghost Heart (with Yvonne Navarro) (Dark Regions Press, 2014)
Halfway House (JournalStone, 2014)
Red Palm (part of the *Apocalypse Weird* universe) (Red Sky, 2015)
Bone Chase (Saga Press/ Simon & Schuster, 2020)
Aliens: Infiltrator (part of the *Aliens* universe) (Titan Books, 2021)
AVP: Rift War (with Yvonne Navarro) (part of the *Alien vs. Predator* universe) (Titan Books, 2022)

SHORT FICTION COLLECTIONS

Scary Rednecks and Other Inbred Horrors (with David Whitman) (Prime Books, 2000)
Appalachian Galapagos (with David Whitman) (Medium Rare Books, 2003)
Multiplex Fandango (Dark Regions Press, 2011)
FUBAR: A Collection of War Stories (Cohesion Press, 2015)

A 21st CENTURY MODERNIZATION

by Weston Ochse

Based on the Translation by Jessie L. Weston

Interior Illustrations by Yvonne Navarro

Afterword by Jason S. Ridler, PhD

DARK MOON BOOKS
Los Angeles, California

Sir Gawain and the Green Knight: A 21st Century Modernization

Edited by Eric J. Guignard
Interior layout by Eric J. Guignard
Cover design by Eric J. Guignard
www.ericjguignard.com

Cover art by Moe Balinger: *Bercilak: The Green Knight* (2016)
www.moebalingerillustration.com

www.wikipedia.org/wiki/Yvonne_Navarro

www.jasonridler.com

First edition published in July, 2021

Library of Congress Cataloging-in-Publication Data
Sir Gawain and the green knight: a 21st century modernization /
by Weston Ochse.

Library of Congress Control Number: 2021940325

ISBN-13: 978-1-949491-44-9 (hardback)
ISBN-13: 978-1-949491-42-5 (trade paperback)
ISBN-13: 978-1-949491-43-2 (e-book)

Dark Moon Books
Los Angeles, California
www.DarkMoonBooks.com

Made in the United States of America
DMB 10 9 8 7 6 5 4 3 2 1

(V021322)

I dedicate this book to my father and mother, who both taught English and encouraged me to read anything and everything I wanted, except for the *Playboys* under my father's bed, which they never really appreciated for the fiction.

TABLE OF CONTENTS

"The romantic chivalric tradition can be very good since it takes fidelity and self-denial, service, courtesy, honor, and courage. Its weakness is, of course that it takes the eye off of women as they are, companions in a shipwreck, not guiding stars."

—J.R.R. Tolkien, Letter 43 (abridged)
sent to his son who was fighting in World War II

PREFACE

BY WESTON OCHSE

I THOUGHT ABOUT SEVERAL WAYS TO WRITE THIS preface, mostly wondering how scholarly I should make it, as an entrée to something spectacular and life-changing. Perhaps pontificate on all that I have learned and, like the post-grad in the bar who confronts Matt Damon's character in the Academy Award-winning movie *Good Will Hunting*, say something that has been repeated over and over to make myself appear smart. Or should I be flat-out pop culture kaiju and challenge all those that came before me to a rubber glow-in-the-dark sword fight regarding beliefs about the version of my text vs. theirs. I'm talking a Texas Cage Match with The Rock, Rick Flair, Randy Savage, Ernest Hemingway, Robert Heinlein, Josh Homme, Stephen King, Clive Barker, Theodore Roethke, and myself, sitting on metal chairs instead of hitting each other with them and chatting late into the night about *Sir Gawain and the Green Knight* with too much great wine. Because you can skip this and go right onto the text, or you can hang out for a few moments and let me give you some things to look for that might make the read a little more exiting and educational.

I'm not necessarily a scholar, although I strive to be. I have a Master of Fine Arts, or MFA, which is essentially a teaching degree. My goal is to provide information in such a way that you, the reader, can enjoy it on multiple levels. This is why we have three versions of the story included in this edition. One for initial reference, the next for first-translation reference, and lastly my own, for enjoyment and accessibility for those who prefer the prose and elegance of storytelling.

Sir Gawain and the Green Knight was believed to have been written in 1348 (Ingledew) by an unknown (i.e. yet-to-be identified) poet. The poem is 2,530 lines long and organized into 101 stanzas and chopped into four sections. The original document containing the poem is referred to as MS Cotton Nero A.X and is found in the British Library. It originated from the estate of Sir Robert Bruce Cotton (1571–1631) who was not only a

Member of Parliament, but also a well-known bibliophile and collector in his day. Had it not been for his efforts, *Sir Gawain and the Green Knight* and *Beowulf* would be lost to time because he held the only copies known to exist (Ingledew). He was much sought after by scholars and opened his library to them. For a complete inventory of what Cotton saved and made available, fellow bibliophiles will find this easy to research.

Much scholarship has been accomplished with regards to the epic poem, *Sir Gawain and the Green Knight*. From Ackerman to Benson to Burrough to Englehart to Hills, Howard, Malarky, Silverstein, and Tolkien, the themes and motifs of the epic poem have been trammeled and excavated to a point where I don't feel it necessary to add my own. So much has been accomplished, if every work was to be an edifice, an entire city has been built as an aspiration to the ideas of this unknown Middle English poet who will never know that his or her one-hundred-and-one-stanza poem fueled hundreds if not thousands of PhD theses on the various aspects of the narrative and its symbolism. If I were to attempt the same, my voice would be but a whisper to these scholars because I lack the credentials and acumen to realistically add something new to the canon.

Therefore I approach the poem for two other reasons and those two reasons only.

The first is the name.

Let's talk about Weston.

Because at the end of the day it's all about me, right?

Weston Ochse and Jesse Weston.

You can't make this up.

Jessie L. Weston translated the poem into then-modern prose in 1898. Known for her translation abilities and lauded by luminaries such as T.S. Elliot, she translated many an Arthurian romance, making them accessible to the public, thus retelling stories that had been lost in a language no longer spoken.

Although my modernization of her modernization is a mere one hundred and twenty-three years hence, it stands as a retelling that is as accessible now, as hers was accessible at the height of the Victorian Era. That we share the name Weston seems no irony or mischance.

Weston is an Anglo-Saxon word for "west enclosure," so it was commonly used by locals to refer to a town or fencing west of their location. My *paterfamilias*'s family can be traced to South Wales where many a town has Weston in its name, to include those towns along the very same literary path taken by Sir Gawain as he followed the almost invisible trail to find the

Green Chapel and the Green Knight. They then traveled across the Atlantic and finally settled in Wyoming in the shadow of Devil's Tower, where there's a county named Weston and a town of the same name.

That Jessie and I share a name is a delight, since *Sir Gawain and the Green Knight* has been a favorite of mine since I attended high school. I don't know of anyone else in my high school class in Chattanooga, Tennessee who read it for enjoyment, but once I saw that Tolkien had done a translation back in the day, and freshly finished with the *Lord of the Rings* trilogy, *The Hobbit*, and *The Silmarillion*, I was eager to experience more Tolkien. Little did I know that his introduction and scholarship for *Sir Gawain and the Green Knight* would open in me a doorway I would pass through again and again.

The other reason I wanted to approach this poem is as a creative writing professional and published author. I've written my share of horror fiction and dark fantasy, but even seven hundred years removed, the unnamed poet who created this epic poem created a darkness that can hardly be matched. But like all great authors, he or she also gave us a protagonist who, when faced with his hero's journey, had as rough a time of it as anyone would.

One of the main reasons I've loved the poem is because it tells the timeless tale of "Zero to Hero." I've told versions of this archetypical tale many times in my own fiction, not the least being the eponymous story that appeared in *Aliens: Bug Hunt* in 2018. The tale of a weak man rising to the challenge and overcoming obstacles is a tale of our society. Although she isn't anymore, America saw herself as the underdog going against England, France, Spain, Germany, Japan, and Russia, in different parts of history. The idea of the underdog is prevalent in western fiction and promises that no matter where one came, they have the chance to become as powerful and as successful as they desire.

And not that Gawain was a weak man, but he certainly was the least of Knights of the Round Table at the moment of this poem. Yet he rose to the task. All of the other knights blanched at the idea of encountering the Green Knight, their deeds already stories to be told to the young and old alike. Sure, Gawain would become the icon of virtue, but he began as a mere mortal who strived to be able to sit as high at the Round Table as the others, earned by deed and not by kinship.

As any educator, I had choices in how I wanted to present the poem in all its modernity. The original format was in what was called the Bob and Wheel—a rhyming device created by the anonymous author.

> "The Bob and Wheel is a short sequence of rhymed lines that concludes the larger unrhymed strophes of *Sir Gawain and the Green Knight* and some other Middle English romances. It consists of one short line (the bob) with a single stress, followed by four three-stress lines (the wheel) of which the second and fourth lines rhyme with the bob" (Baldick).

Perhaps William Marshal describes it best, when he demonstrates the Bob and Wheel from Tolkien's work:

> "While each stanza takes a different shape there is a distinct pattern that connects the last four lines of the poem, often called a 'bob-and-wheel,' a structural device used by the author (Baldick). The rhyme scheme found in the last lines of the poem actually begin with a single line consisting of one or two words followed by four lines offset by the rest of the stanza, making an ABABA rhyme scheme. Here is an example from the 38th stanza:
>
> *When blissful men at board for His birth sing blithe*
>
> *at heart [A]*
>
> *what manners high may mean [B]*
>
> *this knight may now impart. [A]*
>
> *Who hears him will, I ween, [B]*
>
> *of love-speech learn some art. [A]*
>
> This structure continues at length in the poem, giving it structure where there appears to be none . . . This structured but seemingly random use of literary techniques sets the pace for the poem and the bob spins the wheels of a narrative that works both as poetry and as fiction" (Wheeler).

As intriguing as it seemed to reuse the Bob and Wheel, I felt that if I did, I wouldn't add anything new to the canon. I'd just be redoing what has been done before by those with far more Arthurian intellectual acumen. As a creative writing professional and professor, I felt that a new approach would be more beneficial and might be a proper and excited juxtaposition to Jessie

L. Weston's translation. My goal was to make the work even more accessible, especially to those who had trepidation about the accessibility of such a work with a consistent rhyming construct in a language more than a hundred and twenty-five years old.

Poetic prejudice notwithstanding, and although I often prefer the original ingenious rhyming sequences, I needed to treat the epic more like prose than poem. I hearken back to some of the great works of the last part of the twentieth century that could be read aloud to both children and adults. *Something Wicked This Way Comes* by Ray Bradbury is such a story that allows us to gather at imagined feet as we hear the tale of Jimmy Knightshade and Billy Holloway, as Mr. Dark and his carnival come to town. Or Bradbury's *Dandelion Wine* which illuminated the awe of summer and the strength of wanting as a young Douglas Spalding would do anything for the Royal Crown Cream-Sponge Para Litefoot shoes in the window of the local store. Or even Clive Barker's *The Thief of Always* where Harvey Swick encounters the Holiday House and realizes that what he wants is *not* what he wants, and he has to give much of himself to get there.

All of these, like *Sir Gawain and the Green Knight* are timeless tales with timeless ideas that remind us of what it means to be human. Perhaps turning Bradbury and Barker into Bob and Wheel rhyming conventions would make them even more amazing and thrill lovers of them all. If they'd offer me the chance, I'd give it a try.

The original poem has been lost to time, but rewritten versions by those who heard it have become the source documents. As an example of what the Middle English was to Victorian English, I'm providing the original as it stands, with what Jessie L. Weston provided. I'm gleeful in the comparison and find myself trying and failing to speak the Middle English that is my heritage.

MIDDLE ENGLISH VERSION (lines #1–19)	VICTORIAN ENGLISH VERSION
Siþen þe sege and þe assaut watz sesed at Troye, Þe borȝ brittened and brent to brondeȝ and askez, Þe tulk þat þe trammes of tresoun þer wroȝt Watz tried for his tricherie, þe trewest on erthe:	After the siege and the assault of Troy, when that burg was destroyed and burnt to ashes, and the traitor tried for his treason, the noble Æneas and his kin sailed forth to become princes and patrons of well-nigh all the Western Isles.

<table><tr><td>Hit watz Ennias þe athel, and his highe kynde,
Þat siþen depreced prouinces, and patrounes bicome
Welneȝe of al þe wele in þe west iles.
Fro riche Romulus to Rome ricchis hym swyþe,
With gret bobbaunce þat burȝe he biges vpon fyrst,
And neuenes hit his aune nome, as hit now hat;
Tirius to Tuskan and teldes bigynnes,
Langaberde in Lumbardie lyftes vp homes,
And fer ouer þe French flod Felix Brutus
On mony bonkkes ful brode Bretayn he settez
wyth wynne,
Where werre and wrake and wonder,
Bi syþez hatz wont þerinne,
And oft boþe blysse and blunder
Ful skete hatz skyfted synne.</td><td>Thus Romulus built Rome (and gave to the city his own name, which it bears even to this day); and Ticius turned him to Tuscany; and Langobard raised him up dwellings in Lombardy; and Felix Brutus sailed far over the French flood, and founded the kingdom of Britain, wherein have been war and waste and wonder, and bliss and bale, ofttimes since.</td></tr></table>

Notice the Bob and Wheel at the end, *wynne*, then *wonder*, *þerinne*, then *blunder*, then finally *synne*. The Middle English is beautiful, and I've provided a link to an audio translation of the above text in the citations for those who care to listen (Weiskott). Likewise, Jessie L. Weston spent considerable time giving the text justice and providing as accurate a translation as she could.

That is not my goal.

As a creative writer, I feel my profession encourages me to push the limits of creativity. My technique in approaching an eight-hundred-year-old epic poem was simple: I put myself into the head of the unnamed author and asked him or her to speak through me using the vernacular of 2021. Did I take liberties? I don't think so. I believe that what I've produced is as authentic as any other versions produced. Without the original poet to disagree, there's nothing to challenge that opinion. Given the inclusion of so many more words into the English language since the 1400s, one has to wonder if such a renowned poet wouldn't have used them if the vocabulary had been available.

In some places I used fewer words, and in other places I used more. The subtraction or addition was decided entirely to ensure that the narrative flowed more naturally than the seven-hundred-year-old translations. I often checked Jessie L. Weston's translations, as well as comments from other scholars, to make sure I understood the meaning of a particular word, many of which don't have direct descendants in Modern English.

I annotated many of these in my footnotes for anyone who cares to see my reasoning. The work can just as easily be read without referring to them, so if you see a stray number here or there, feel free to ignore it. Additionally, if you are a purist, then I can anticipate you probably not liking my free and unadulterated hand at modernizing this work for twenty-first century readers. You can either run away now, or give me a chance. After all, I might have something to add to the canon.

Now, a note on religious virtue signaling (or, moral viewpoints) in the text.

Much has also been made about the ideas of Christian virtue in the text. Regardless of one's personal beliefs, knowing ahead of time some of the issues at play makes for a more interesting read, especially when we decide to read the poem less as a simple epic and more of a treatise on the rights and wrongs of the fourteenth century.

One could argue that *Sir Gawain and the Green Knight* could easily be an American story as well. Much of the plot of the anonymous author is virtue-scolding. From the opening scene of debauchery, pride, and immaturity displayed by Arthur and his retinue, we are shown how the wealthy live without consideration of their own virtues. The quality of their lives are represented by the material goods itemized in great detail, not the religious ideals that form an amorphous cloud around them. Is there any doubt that any other knight might have taken the lady of the castle to bed given her repeated offerings? But Gawain stands as the epitome of moral and religious rectitude, even in the Middle Ages, urging those who would listen that it is the upright and upstanding who will be the hero of their journey.

Puritan and noted American colonist John Winthrop's covenant with his people who sailed across the Atlantic to the New World brought with it similar ideas of the "City on the Hill":

> "For we must consider that we shall be as a city upon a hill. The eyes of all people are upon us. So that if we shall deal falsely with our

God in this work we have undertaken, and so cause Him to withdraw His present help from us, we shall be made a story and a by-word through the world" (Winthrop).

England wanted to be city on the hill.

Camelot was sold to us as that very city. But as England found herself trying to grow from the long shadow of the Romans and the constant attacks from those across the sea, she attempted to turn a land of embattled and embittered people into a zombie horde of virtue-signaling Gawains. For who better to have as a role model than the young knight who everyone wanted to be.

Feudal England also had its hierarchical challenges. All men weren't created equally, as America espouses in her Constitution. In England, some men were more equal than others. It is in this fuedalocracy upon which the English nobles balance their principles.

Once again, John Winthrop in his *A Model of Christian Charity* explains to those newly arriving in the New World that mankind should restrain evil so that the "rich and mighty should not eat up the poor" and the downtrodden should not rise up against their oppressors. Everyone has their place in the Kingdom of God (Winthrop).

But for all the virtue signaling and righteous writing, let's not forget the erotic nature of Gawain's greatest trophy—the Holy Garter. In modern Great Britain, The Order of the Garter is one of the most coveted royal awards available. Only awarded to senior knights, the origin of the order begins in the year 1348. Does that date make your head itch? It's the same year that *Sir Gawain and the Green Knight* was created. Although the poet-author is unknown, theories have been put forth to ascribe the work to either John of Gaunt, 1st Duke of Lancaster, or to Enguerrand de Coucy, 7th Sire de Coucy (Ingledew). These men weren't part of the twenty-five founding knights, but they were heralded soon after and became members of the sacred order.

The dates and symbology are almost too curious to be called accidental. That said, I've always found it interesting that at the end of Gawain's ontological quest there isn't a holy grail, but instead a garter, meant to contain a woman's pieces underneath layers and layers of clothing.

The closing lines of the poem are similar to the motto for the Order.

Honi soit qui mal y pense, which is Middle French to mean: "Shame on him who thinks evil of it" (Ingledew).

Lines 2374 of Sir Gawain state, "Cursed be ye, cowardice and covetousness, for in ye is the destruction of virtue."

The whole idea of the Girdle or Garter is not as a trophy, but as a reminder. A reminder of one's devotion to the virtues of a woman and the idea that things often displayed should really be hidden, and it is by the hiding that real virtue is realized. On Garter Day in Great Britain, knights wear their garters on the outside of clothing to indicate each member's affiliation, but all other days the undergarment is kept hidden, as it should be if they want to make a country a City on the Hill.

Another major theme in the narrative is the Beheading Game, although the game isn't original to Gawain. Dr. Joseph Turner PhD, currently a professor at the University of Louisville (who has given me permission to use his chart), provided an interesting comparison, for all of us visual learners, to another story, "The Feast of Bricriu," which comes from the Ulster Cycle of Irish mythology, an oral tradition with roots dating back to the first century A.D.

	The Feast of Bricriu	**Sir Gawain and the Green Knight**
1. An outsider, in both outward appearance and social status, comes to the court and challenges.	At the court of Ulster in Ireland, a hideous creature called a "Bachlach" challenges the court. He carries "a great spreading club-tree the size of a shed" (40).	The Green Knight, a huge "half-etayn" clad entirely in green enters the court. He wears no armor, carries an axe and a holly bob, as a symbol of non-aggression.
2. The hero accepts the challenge, usually after others pass off the responsibility.	After 'Fat Neck', Loigaire, and Conall skirt the return blow, Cuchulainn accepts. Note that all four characters give a blow to the Bachlach.	Arthur accepts, but Gawain asks for the responsibility to be shifted to him. He claims that his relationship to Arthur is the cause for his praise (354-57).
3. The hero gives the outsider a blow, cutting off his head.	"Cuchulainn sprang towards him and dealt him a blow with the axe, hurling his head to the top rafter" (43).	Gawain hits the Green Knight, "schyndered þe bones . . . and schade hit in twynne" (424-5).

4. Hero journeys to the court of the outsider.	None. The Bachlach makes a return visit in this story.	Without knowledge of the location of the Green Chapel, Gawain rides through Wales searching for the Green Knight.
5. Outsider tests the hero, who is a symbol of the court.	The Bachlach makes Cuchulainn stretch his neck entirely across the cutting block, "as long as a crane" (44).	A 'Bed Test' ensues between Bertilak's wife and Gawain; Gawain refuses her advances, but accepts the green girdle that will protect his life.
6. Hero accepts the return blow, and returns to court.	The Bachlach gives Cuchulainn a blow with the blunt side of his axe, and then praises Cuchulainn's courage.	After flinching, Gawain accepts the blow; the Green Knight gives another fake blow, before finally hitting him. "with pe barbe of pe bitte bi pe bare nek" (2310).

Gawain's ontological journey across western England was predicated and framed by what was known as The Beheading Game. The first known evidence of this in literature was the aforementioned *The Feast of Bricrue*. As seen in the chart above, there are major similarities. Not that the poet was guilty of any plagiarism, but the Beheading Game was a well-known trope in Medieval Romances. Although the twelfth century Irish story cycle featuring Finn McCool (modernization) might have been an elder relative of the game depicted in Sir Gawain, the Irish lacked the chivalric tradition that had been introduced by the French. More on that later. But at the root of the game was the idea that one must trust in his opponent to play fairly.

Modern warfighters would laugh at such a thing, but the English had created such a hierarchical structure of rules, even those who could own a sword were codified in common law. This beheading game was a way for the Green Knight to demonstrate his superiority over the members of the famed Round Table without having to draw blood.

And in many cases, it is the fear of the blow that makes for greater terror. Just look at the slapping game in American schools where one young man holds out his hands face down and the other attempts to slap. Like Gawain's flinch, to move is a culpable act and makes it so that you have to be slapped again.

Am I saying that American school children are chivalric?

Hardly. But our culture, which is largely originally based on Anglo-Saxon ideals, has inculcated the idea that games represent victories, be it baseball, basketball, or football. No one really gets slapped anymore, but they can get tackled.

But chivalry was definitely a budding notion in the time of Sir Gawain, especially with the influence of French ideas.

Chivalry was a grouping of rules developed in the twelfth century to dictate how those of noble blood should act. Ideas of honesty, courage, courtesy, justice, and honor were at its core. The origins can be traced back to Charlemagne and his horse soldiers, or *chevaliers*. French authors, however, tried consistently to downplay Gawain and portray Lancelot as the true hero (Bornschein). Whether or not either existed or was an actual hero, it's interesting that the French would want to redefine who were the Arthurian heroes based on their Frenchness.

A final note.

As a Master of Fine Arts, I have a responsibility to creativity and accessibility. My fellow scholars with research degrees can provide much more in-depth examination and evaluation of the text. Mine is a teaching degree (as mentioned earlier), and as such, I want to illuminate and elucidate to make the reading more enjoyable. My goal is and has always been to make this story as reachable as possible. That includes this preface, which if read ahead of time, provides a Rand McNally literary atlas of some of the more important themes and ideas the unknown poet wanted to convey, or perhaps *did* convey despite his or her bad self.

Many critics view the Green Knight as evil, but I differ in that regard. In the beginning, when the Green Knight arrives as the challenger and mocks Arthur and his knights, what reader can't help but think him evil. He comes across as a bully, plain and simple. But as the story progresses and the truth of the magic and who he really is unfolds, one comes to know that he really represents the ideals that Gawain wishes to espouse. For as bad as the Green Knight is supposed to be, it is Gawain who fails the test in the end because he never told his host about the garter—the same host who has been magically transformed into the Green Knight by Arthur's half-sister, Morgan le Fay.

And if anything, I'd like the readers to imagine themselves in the fourteenth century in the celebrations and on the hunts and in the wilds. Imagine the bears and the dire wolves and the giants and all the hideous creatures Gawain encountered. Imagine the wonderful celebrations going on for days at a time where you party and awaken and drink and party and sleep and awaken and reboot like the universe is one immense drafty frat party. More importantly, imagine the essence of the Green Knight. Because at the end of the day, he is you and you are him. The Green Knight represents progress and those things we most desire.

Don't you want change?

Don't you want to challenge the status quo?

Don't you want to make a difference in the world?

Then become the Green Knight and become the agent of change.

Most people believe that Sir Gawain is the hero of his eponymous tale. But don't you think that honor might fall to the Green Knight?

Think about it.

Even more, believe that Morgan le Fay is evil.

Think about *that.*

Then read.

And enjoy.

Weston Ochse, MFA
Desert Grotto
2021

WORKS CITED

Baldick, Chris. *The Oxford Dictionary of Literary Terms*. 3rd ed., Oxford University Press, 2008.

Bornschein, Anne N. "Heirs of the Round Table: French Arthurian Fiction from 1977 to the Present." 2013. University of Pennsylvania, PhD dissertation. https://repository.upenn.edu/edissertations/836/.

Ingledew, Francis. *Sir Gawain and the Green Knight and the Order of the Garter*. University of Notre Dame Press, 2006.

Weiskott, Eric. "Sir Gawain and the Green Knight stanza 1 in Middle English." [2016?]. https://soundcloud.com/ericweiskott/sir-gawain-and-the-green-knight-stanza-1-in-middle-english?in=ericweiskott/sets/middle-english-pronunciation.

Wheeler, L. Kip, PhD. "Bob-and-Wheel." 24 Spr. 2018. https://web.cn.edu/kwheeler/lit.bob-and-wheel.html.

Winthrop, John. "A Model of Christian Charity." *A Library of American Literature: Early Colonial Literature, 1607-1675*, edited by Edmund Clarence Stedman and Ellen Mackay Hutchinson, Charles L. Webster & Company, 1892, pp. 304-307.

If you will listen to me, I'll tell you the story ...

I.

SIR GAWAIN AND THE GREEN KNIGHT: A 21ST CENTURY MODERNIZATION IN NARRATIVE PROSE

BY WESTON OCHSE

AFTER THE SIEGE OF THE GREAT CITY OF TROY, WHEN it was destroyed and burned to ashes along with the hopes of a forgotten age, the noble Aeneas (son of the goddess Aphrodite and Prince Anchises, and being ancestor to Romulus and Remus) and his companions sailed to the Western Islands to become princes and patrons of the many lands.

First came Romulus who built Rome. Then Ticius who built Tuscany. Then after, Longobard who built Lombardy. And finally, Felix Brutus, who sailed past France and founded the Kingdom of Britain, where war and wonder and good and evil found themselves to be day-to-day companions.

And in this Kingdom of Britain there have been more gallant deeds than in any of the other kingdoms. Of all the deed makers, King Arthur was the most valiant, and set out for a wondrous adventure that has all but been lost to time and memory.

If you will listen to me, I'll tell you the story, steadfast, part of the land and one of the components of what it is meant to be British.

So, hush.

Sit back.

And imagine.[1]

IT WAS A Christmas long long ago when King Arthur with his gallant lords and ladies and noble brotherhood gathered around his most famed Round Table. They partied and jousted and sang and ate for fifteen straight days with all the joy of life man could devise. Halls and chambers were crowded with beautiful dignified guests, knights, and their ladies bedecked in finery, and Arthur himself the most handsome of them all.

On New Year's Day, a double portion was served on the high table to the noble guests, while the king and his knights held service in the chapel and sang until the end. Once done, they all welcomed each other to the New Year, giving rich gifts and glorifying in their prosperity.

When it was time to feast, Queen Guinevere sat first on her high dais, a canopy above her head studded with gems and embroidered with silk. A more beautiful woman no man could pretend to know as she sat regal, the queen with shining grey eyes and an entire country as her admirer.

Arthur waited until all were served, so full of joy and happiness he could have been a child. As was his custom on high days, he let his mind wander wild, eschewing the dinner, waiting until a knight of his, or another, might come to entertain him with a gallant deed. He'd even look forward to being challenged to a joust or fight, anything to get his blood going by way of lives in jeopardy, for fortune favors the bold.

Thus the king sat on this New Year's Day on his throne before the high tables and spoke of many things. Sir Gawain sat nearest the queen and on her other side, Agravain, the Hand of the Queen,[2] both being the king's sister's sons. At the table's other end were Bishop Bawdewyn and Ywain, King Urien's son. And at the lower tables sat many valiant knights, each eager to please the king and queen on this bright new day.

Then trumpets blared, announcing the first course as banners waved, and pipes and drums played. Many a lute matched with song to lift heart and soul with melodies new and old. Many were the special dishes, served with meats from the rarest animals, so much so that the tables were in danger of flowing over. The gathered helped themselves and feasted, turning two dishes into twelve, and so on, until the beer and wine flowed greatly.

But at the end of the first course when the music died and the voices hushed, there came from the hall door a figure terrible to behold. His size was greater than any upon the earth, his muscles building from neck to loin, and arms and legs thick as trees. So great he was, he seemed to be a giant. And yet he was but a man, broad of chest and shoulders and thin of waist, riding the mightiest of steeds. But the most marvelous of it all was his color, for the knight, as mighty as he appeared, was also completely and utterly green.

Green straight coat and mantle, thrown back to reveal a chiseled face. His green hose ran to golden spurs with richly worked green silk fastenings. Around his waist and saddle were bands of fair stones embroidered in silk and of all the trifles bound there, only birds and insects were recognizable in the earthen tones.

All the trappings of his steed were likened to his own, and even the stirrups and saddle blinked with green stones. The horse was also green, great and strong and hard to hold, with a darker mane and tale, but all as green as the hues from a deadly forest.

The green knight was dressed for a celebration.[3] He also had green hair and a green beard, each falling upon his shoulders and chest. The lower part of his sleeves were fastened with clasps as if he were a king. The horse's mane was knotted with golden thread, woven through the green, and the tail was bound the same. With all the gold and green and gems, no one other could have ridden it except for this same green knight who looked large enough to be able to take down anyone in the hall.

The knight bore no helmet nor armor about his shoulders, chest, or arms.[4] He hid behind no shield, but in one hand he held a holly bow, green with red berries to frame the season, and in the other held an immense axe whose mere sight was of cruel murder. Its head was six hand-breadths wide[5], blade shined to a wicked edge as sharp as any razor. The steel was set into a strong staff and bound with iron. All of it, from end to end, engraved in cunning green work, as if it were a part of him, and not an accoutrement of death.

All this was seen in a heartbeat as the knight rode through the entrance of the hall, hooves echoing in the shocked silence, straight to the raised dais of the king.[6] He looked neither left nor right, but rode straight on until he was close enough for the breath of the horse to spin the locks of Arthur's hair, wherein the Green Knight asked, "Where is the ruler of these people? I would gladly enjoin this hero and have words with him."

His eyes cast about the knights and inventoried each of their weaknesses, judging which among them might be their greatest. And in turn, they looked upon him, wondering who he might be, for none of them had seen such a marvel. Besides his size, it was the color—so much green mixed with gold that he might have been produced by the fairies as a phantasm death-bringer. This made the knights slow to answer as they stood astounded, locked in their own wonder, stone-still silence throughout the recently gaudy hall as if a great sleep had fallen upon it, and dread came home to bed.

Arthur would have none of it, however. He beheld the newcomer and proclaimed, "Sir, you are welcome to this place. I am the lord here. Men call me Arthur. Come down from your horse and stay awhile and we shall see why it is you have come."

"No," said the Green Knight. "I do not mean to stay more than necessary. But I have come to see the source of the praise of the people of this land and to discover why the warriors here are considered the best and the most valiant, wise, and worthy in knightly sports. So, I have come here in peace, which is why I carry this branch, seeking no quarrel. Had I decided to come fight, I would have worn my armor and brought a shield and spear and any other weapon I might have desired to bring forth. But since I seek no war, my presence is one of peace. In this spirit, I come, hoping that you will grant a simple favor I must ask."

King Arthur, still filled with the dreams of gallant deeds said, "Sir Knight, if you crave a battle, I have the knights who can provide it."

And the knight answered, "No, again I ask for no fight. Your knights to me are but beardless children. Had I come prepared to fight, none of them could match me. So I ask in this court for but a Christmas gift. After all, this is Yuletide and New Year, and it is the time to pleasure ourselves with sport. If anyone in your hall believes himself brave enough as to strike me, I will give him the first strike, if I can have the next. To do so, I will give him the gift of this axe. Although it is heavy and ponderous, I will allow one of your knights to wield it, and I will take the first blow, unarmed, and unflinching. So I say, that if there is any knight who believes himself bold, come to me, take my weapon, keep it as his own, then strike me, and I shall do nothing but take it. Then, once struck, you will give me the right to strike back, but only after I give my would-be attacker a year and a day to prepare."

The Green Knight grinned for the first time and said, "Show me if there is any knight brave[7] enough to accept my challenge."

Although the knights had been surprised by the appearance of this great green martial creation, they were now astounded by his words.

The Green Knight sat taller in the saddle, his gaze taking in and dismissing each of the knights in the hall. He frowned and twisted his beard, waiting to see who would take him up on his offer.

But no knight moved.

Seeing this, he cried, "Is this not Camelot? Is this not the throne of a great king? Are these not the knights whose renown is spoken of throughout the realm? Do you have no pride? Where are you now after talk of conquests and wrath and mighty fighting words?"[8]

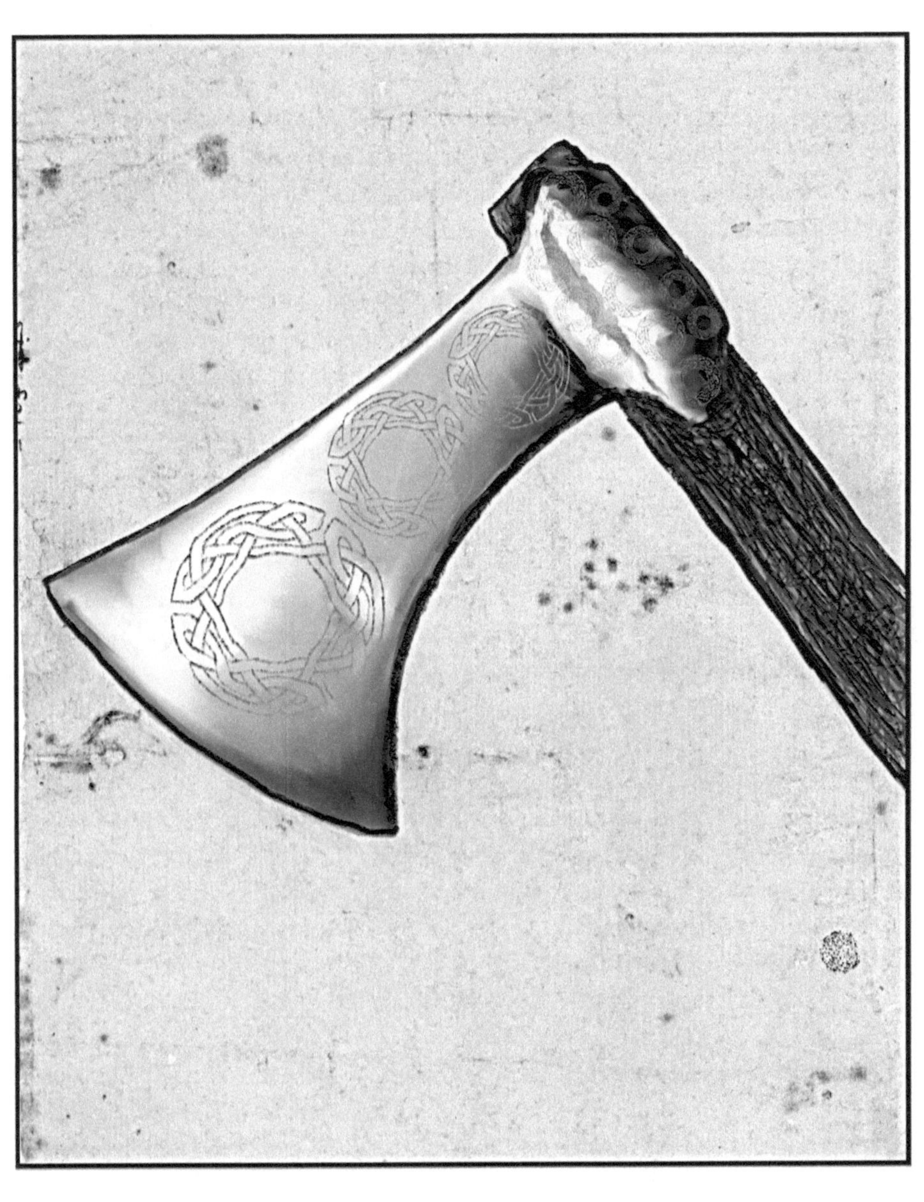

Its blade shined to a wicked edge as sharp as any razor …

The knights began to murmur among themselves.

"Is the Round Table spit asunder by the speech of one man? Does everyone remain silent because they so fear me?"

With that, the Green Knight laughed loud and long.

Blood rushed to the face of the king, and his knights stood in anger and frustration. King Arthur sprang to his feet and approached the Green Knight, unafraid, unabashed, and unmoving.

"You are foolish to come here with such words and will get what you so desire. None of my men are in fear of your words, for they are as such, mere *words*." He held out a hand. "Give me your axe and I shall deliver you the gift you seek."

The knight descended from his charger and handed Arthur the mighty weapon.

The king took it, gripped the haft, and swung it in practice, preparing to strike.

The knight stood before him, taller by a head than anyone in the hall, unmoving, stroking his beard, no more concerned by the aspect of the king than he would be a goblet of wine.

Then Gawain, still beside Queen Guinevere, leaned forward and said, "Please, my lord. Let me do this. Give me the chance, and I shall rise and come to your side. Although your valiance is unquestioning, it is not right for such a challenge to come unknown to the hall and you be the one to take it when there are so many of us worthy knights waiting to defend you. I am the weakest of them all, and to lose me would be nothing for the realm. So allow me to take up the axe and, if I lose, then the court will have lost no one except the feeblest of wit."

The knights pounded the table, and all agreed that it should be Gawain who take up the venture for their king.

Arthur commanded the knight to rise from the table and Gawain did so, soon kneeling before his king, who handed him the axe. Then Arthur lifted his head to the heavens and gave blessing. "Keep thee well, nephew. Give him only the single blow he asks for and if you redden[9] him correctly, to survive his return blow shall be an easy feat to achieve."

Gawain then approached the stranger, axe in hand.

The Green Knight showed no fear, but said, "Let's make a deal before we begin. First, what is your name? Tell me, so that I might know who you are."

"I am Gawain, who offers himself to you," the young knight said, biting the inside of his cheek and lifting his chin. "Whatever happens, I will allow you to strike me in twelve months and one day with the weapon of your choice. This, I swear."

"Sir Gawain, I am pleased that it is you who will offer himself to me. But first, you shall wield the axe just as we have spoken, and you shall swear to me that you will seek me out wherever you believe me to be found so that I may win the award I have negotiated this day."

"Where shall I find you?" Gawain asked. "I know not where you are from, nor do I know your name, or your court. Allow me to know and I will do everything I can to be there, that I do swear and pledge."

"In the New Year you will know," said the Green Knight. "I shall tell you after you have struck me. Only then will I reveal my home and my name. And if you kill me, I shall have no words to give and you do not have to seek me any further." He grinned again, like a father to a child. "So let's begin and see if you can do anything other than speak."

"I am happy to," said Gawain, gripping the axe.

The Green Knight bowed his head and moved his hair out of the way so that his green skin could be seen.

Gawain lifted the axe high, then brought it upon the bare neck, the sharp edge sundering bones, cleaving the head from the body so that it struck the ground and rolled where the gathered knights kicked it with their feet to spin it away.

Blood spurted and glistened over the green clothing, but the giant knight neither staggered nor fell. He moved forward and grabbed his head from the floor by the hair and lifted it high. The Green Knight slid back into his saddle, took ahold of the bridle, and shoved his boots in the stirrups. He sat tall on his steed, blood still spurting from the neck. He made sure the face was turned to the dais.

The eyes of the severed green head lifted their lids and looked upon those present. "Gawain, good slice. Now you must be ready to return the promise that you have sworn in this hall in front of all of your fellow knights. I charge you to come to the Green Chapel and, such a stroke that has been dealt to me, I shall deal to you. To be promptly paid on next New Year's morning."

The Green Knight paused as he watched the gathered staring at him in horrified wonder, then continued. "Many men know me as the Knight of the Green Chapel and if you shall ask, you will not fail to find me. Your choice is simple. Obey your promise or be a coward."

With that, he turned his horse and galloped out the hall door, head in hand. Sparks flew from the horse's hooves as he departed, but everyone stared at his afterimage: Green Knight, warrior, beheaded, alive, and waiting for his own piece of flesh.

Where he went, no one knew.

And the king and Gawain and the others looked at each other, then at the empty space where the Green Knight had just been, and then back to each other, and they had to laugh at the incredulity of the situation. Had it even been real?

The king turned to his queen. "Fear not, my lady. Be not dismayed. Such crazy craft is suited for the holidays when we seek to jest and laugh and sing all the fair carols of the knights and ladies. Now that I have finally seen such a marvel, it is time for meat, and I shall finally sit and dine with the rest of you."

After a moment when he'd been served, the king looked upon Gawain and said, "Fair nephew. Hang up your axe. It has done its job."

The servants took the axe and hung it above the king's dais on a backdrop of regal material.

Once the axe was hung, the king said, "May all men look upon it in marvel because it's a true token of mystery. That another knight might bring it and ask to be struck down by it only to make his leave still alive, demonstrates a reality beyond our perception. But for now, let us celebrate."

Then the pair sat together, the king and the good knight, and they were served with a heroes' portion, with all manner of pomp and circumstance. And all those in the hall spent the day happy, each thrilled to be alive, enjoying a new year, looking forward to what it may bring, except for Gawain who wondered about the idea of a year hence and what it might be like to fight a man who lost his head but was still alive and awaiting his chance to retaliate.

ALTHOUGH ARTHUR HAD been ready to hear of adventures far and wide, he sat back with the other knights, stunned at what had transpired. Seeing his liege so worried, Gawain joked about the entire event, saying that no one should be troubled about anything.

But then when the party was over and the drink had stopped and sober minds prevailed, Gawain realized what he had to do. The months passed quickly, one after the other, seasons turning to the next. Once the chill of winter lost interest in the land, and the spring rains urged forth flowers, optimism grew. Birds returned as did the animals of the forest and glen.

Then came summer with the sweetness of first harvest, and hedgerows filled with lush flowers. Dew dripped from leaves in blissful ignorance of the sun, but happy for the brotherhood.

After summer, with the soft winds and siroccos casting their breath upon the fields for a second harvest, more dew and more sun and more grain, came promise of an honest harvest. But there was no honesty that year. The winds flared and the sun burned and the wind dried and the seeds became dust. Angry winds wrestled with sunlight, and leaves dove for cover to the ground, and what could have been great was instead struck low, the seasons ending until another year was ready to begin.

Then at Michaelmas[10], the end of the harvest season, the moon came as a cold iron harbinger of winter. Only then did Sir Gawain think of the perilous journey he must take. Yet he waited. Hallowe'en came and went, and still he lingered. Arthur's court made a great feast that day for his sake and gave him the hero's portion. Although all were courteous to him, none would speak, even the other knights, whether it be from their own embarrassment or their sorrow.

After the meat was consumed, Sir Gawain turned to his uncle and said, "Lord of my life, I must be gone. You know well the promise I made, and I am bound by my words. Tomorrow I shall set forth and search out the Green Knight."

Then came the noblest of knights, Ywain and Eric, and many another. Sir Dodinel le Sauvage, the Duke of Clarence, and Lancelot and Lionel, and Lucan the Good, Sir Bors and Sir Bedivere, and Sir Mador de la Porte, all valiant knights of renown. They gathered about the youngest and weakest of them and openly weeped, not only for their shame in not stepping forth like Gawain had, but in anticipation of the inevitable death of such a worthy young soul. That he would travel to a place where he could not fight, but must stand and take a blow was a death sentence.

But Gawain laughed true and said, "Do not worry. Although I might die, what a worthy cause I have to perform."

He stayed all day in the main hall, sometimes thinking, sometimes taking counsel, sometimes lamenting, for he was as human as any of them except for the Green Knight. He wouldn't allow his fellow knights to grieve, instead reminding them of their own glories.

The next morning, he arose and asked for his armor, which squires brought to him. First, a rich carpet was stretched upon the floor filled with the luxuriance of the kingdom. Clad only in silk, Gawain strode upon it and was then dressed in steel. Shoes. Legs. Greaves. Kneecaps. All fastened with knots of gold to fit a king. Then his thighs in polished chain, braces for his

And therefore Gawain was suited to his armor and arms ...

arms, elbow pieces, and gloves to protect his hands. They clad him in a shiny hauberk of chainmail.[11] Then a rich surcoat went over that, and golden spurs were set on his heels, and lastly a sword placed about his waist with a silken knot. Once clad in such gaudy formality, he went to the altar and held Mass, praying and offering himself to God.

Once complete, he went to his king and the knights of the Round Table and embraced each of them, kissing their cheeks as true brothers, even as they in turn commended him to Christ.

His steed Gringalet was ready, saddled with golden fringes and enriched for the adventure. The bridle was striped with bright gold buttons, and the hood and the skirt gleamed with a rich silk interlaced with gold, the sun causing it to sparkle like magic popping in cadence.

Then Gawain called for his helmet, lined with fur, and set it high on his head. The clasp was from behind and a light length of silk studded with gems and embroidered with colorful birds covered his visor,[12] worried and knotted by many a maiden for many winters. But it was the circlet which crowned his helmet that was the most precious, adorned with diamonds that sought to blind. Lastly, squires brought his shield, which was a bright red with a pentangle painted gleaming in gold.

Many wondered at Gawain's choice of the pentangle, and had they asked, he would have told them he had chosen such an image because of Solomon, the "broker of truth," as being five points, overlapping, with neither a beginning nor an end, in what the English came to call the Endless Knot. And therefore Gawain was suited to his armor and arms, faithful fivefold, for he was as pure as gold, void of any villainy and owning all virtues.

He wore the Endless Knot on his shield and his surcoat as the truest of heroes and the gentlest of knights, for he was faultless in his five senses:

i. His five senses that will allow him to live.

ii. His five fingers that had never failed him.

iii. The five wounds of Jesus on the Cross.

iv. The five joys when the Queen of Heaven held Her child, and for this he had Her image also on his shield.

v. And the last were the virtues he wore on his soul—frankness, fellowship, purity, courtesy, and compassion.

In these five virtues, the hero was wrapped and clothed. Where each virtue met the other, there was no end, the five points that never failed, folded, or waned. For each had no beginning, so none could ever get in the way of the other. Thus on his shield was the endless knot shaped in gold upon red, as pure as a pentangle there ever was.

Now that Sir Gawain was ready, he took his lance, and bade them farewell. He struck the steed with his spurs and they sprang away, sparks flying magically from the stones after him.

All that saw him were saddened at heart and said to one another:

"By Christ, it's a great pity that one of such noble life should be lost."

"It will not be easy to find his equal upon the Earth."

"The king should have treated him better and made him a duke, a gallant leader of men."

"Of all the knights, Gawain seemed the smallest, put together with pieces of elflings, yet there he goes to do battle."

"Who ever knew a king to risk his knights' lives on a Christmas jest?"

Many were the tears that flowed from their eyes when the good knight rode from the hall.

Gawain made no delay. He took the wild road, his hair flying in the wind like the mane of his horse. He rode through the realm of Logre. Often he lay alone at night by the fire, not seeking companionship nor offering it. No comrade would he have except for his steed, and he took no counsel except from God.

Soon, he arrived in North Wales, leaving the Isles of Angelelsy, crossing over river and vale until he reached Holyhead.[13] Then without a moment's trepidation crossed into the Wilderness of Wirral, where few live who love God and men of true hearts. He asked the wild men he met if they had heard about the Green Knight or the Green Chapel. All answered him that never in their lives had they seen such a man of that hue. The knight continued on, winding his way through many strange roads and rugged paths.

His mood turned dark as the days grew shorter, waiting for the chapel to be seen. He climbed many a cliff in that strange land, and he rode as a foreigner, far from friends, always a stranger to those he might encounter. Never did he come to a stream or a ford where he did not have to fight. So many wonders did he behold that there isn't enough space in the poem to tell a tenth of them.

Sometimes he fought with dragons and wolves. Sometimes with wild men who dwelt in the rocks. And others with bulls and bears and boars. He even encountered the giants of the high moors. Had he not been such a man of valor and a high knight, he might have been slain, for he was too often introduced to death.

Sometimes he fought with wild men who dwelt in the rocks . . .

Yet he cared not for strife, though what was worse was the weather. Cold clear water cascaded from the clouds, often turning to ice before it even struck the ground. And more nights than not, he slept wrapped in his blankets in bare rocks, nearly killed by the sleet and the cold, waking to hard icicles hanging over his head.

Thus, in peril and pain, and many a hardship, the knight rode along until Christmas Eve. Then he made his prayer to the Blessed Virgin that she would guide him in his steps and lead him to a place of comfort. On that morning, he rode by a hill and came into a forest thick with woods of great hoar oaks, wild and dreary. On each side were high hills where hazel and hawthorn trailed through the boughs, intertwining with the ragged moss that spread everywhere. Birds chirped piteously for pain of the cold. The knight rode Gringalet lonely beneath them, clomping through marsh and mire, worried desperately that he might fail in his duty to his god and king. Therefore, he said, sighing, "I beg of you, Lord and Mary thy Gentle Mother, for some shelter where I may hear Mass and say Mattins this morning. This I ask meekly and thereto I pray my Pater Noster, Ave Maria, and Credo." So he rode praying, and regretting his mistakes, and he crossed himself and said, "May the Cross of Christ speed me."

Once he crossed himself three times as being the Holy Trinity, he became aware, in the woods, of a dwelling surrounded by a moat. Many mighty trees surrounded what he came to call the fairest castle ever a knight might own, built in a meadow, with grasses and flowers around it, and a spiked palisade that was firmly driven and as sure a deterrence for attack as anything.

Gawain caught a glimpse through a gap in the oaks and lifted free his helmet and thanked Christ and Saint Julian for so courteously granting his prayers. Then he raised his voice and cried, "Now, I ask of you, grant me a fair lodging," as way of announcement. He urged Gringalet on with his golden spurs and rode happily for the great gate, but was forced to stop because the road came to a swift and deadly end.

The bridge had been drawn up and the gate closed. The walls were strong and thick so that they might never fear the strongest of storms. The knight contemplated all this from his steed, while staring at the moat that surrounded the castle. The castle's walls were set deep in the water and rose to an impressive height up to the corbels, which were adorned beneath the battlements with many carvings. Turrets were set between arrow slits as far as the eye could see.

Sir Gawain had never seen a more impressive castle. Within surely held a high hall with its tower and many windows and carved cornices, chalk white chimneys on the turreted roofs that glistened in the sun. And everywhere were pinnacles, too many to count it seemed, as if they were created from paper because of their intense white.

The knight decided that this was the sort of place he would like to be sheltered come the Holy Day. So he called aloud, and soon there came a porter who greeted Gawain and then asked him his errand.

"Good sir," said Gawain, "will you ask the lord of the castle if I might stay here a while."

The porter left and then returned swiftly, with many retainers to receive the knight. They lowered the drawbridge and knelt on their knees before Gawain to provide him a worthy welcome.

He bowed to them, asked them to rise, then rode past across the bridge and into the castle.

Once inside, he was helped to dismount and squired to the great hall. There were many attendants to receive his helmet, and sword and shield, which they took from him to hold safely. Gawain greeted each and every one of these men. Then, when he arrived in the hall clad in his shining armor, he was led to where a great fire burned brightly from a pit in the center of the room.

The lord of the castle came from his chamber to greet the arriving hero. He said, "You are welcome to do here as you wish. All that is ours to share is at your will and disposal."

"By all means," said Gawain. "May Christ reward you."

As friends afraid to engage with each other, Gawain appraised the knight who had greeted him so kindly and thought him to be such a bold warrior to rule this castle. Getting on in the years, but still of mighty stature, his beard was broad and flowing. His limbs seemed strong and his stride confident. His face was fiery red, and he spoke freely as one would who is a leader of valiant men.

The lord led Sir Gawain to a chamber and commanded his retinue to wait on him in an elegant room. The noble bedding was contained between curtains of pure golden with coverings made from rich embroideries. The curtains ran on ropes with rings of gold, and Asian carpets hung on the walls and lay upon the floor.

They laughed among each other as they removed his coat of mail and all his shining armor. Then they brought him rich robes of the best materials they had to offer. When Gawain tried them on, he noted they were long and flowing and made him look like a hero favored by God. All in all, he seemed like a prince without peer in a field where men strive for battle.

Sir Gawain had never seen a more impressive castle ...

Before the hearth where the fire burned, a chair was set aside for Gawain with plush cushions and draped with cloth. For warmth, they offered him a mantle and hood woven with silken threads on the outside and lined within by the softest fur. He accepted the offer and sat before the fire, relishing in the moment.

While he sat, a serving man placed a trestled table before him, covered with a white cloth and salt, silver spoons, and a napkin. Gawain allowed his hands and feet to be washed, then prepared for his meal.

The folk served him considerably, bringing perfectly seasoned dishes, and even offering him double a knight's allotment of food, including all kinds of fish, some baked in bread, some broiled in the embers, some simmered in liquid, some stewed, all savored with enough spices to invigorate and excite his tastes.

Finally, they asked him from where he came.

He explained he'd come from the court of Arthur, the rich king of the famed Round Table, and that he was Sir Gawain and would stay for Christmas with them.

When the lord of the castle realized this, he laughed aloud at the news. All of the men in the castle were impressed that they would spend the holiday with the one for whom belonged such fame, and valor, and courtesy, and whose honor had been praised above all men's.

Each remarked to their fellows, "Now we shall see courteous bearing and the manner of speech befitting the courts. God has surely shown us his grace for sending Gawain into our midst. We will learn the manners of the court and know how they speak so that those of us in the wilds may come to emulate them."

By the time Gawain had risen for dinner it was nearly nightfall. The chaplains rang loudly for the high feast. The lords and ladies of the manor entered the great hall. Gawain was seated beside the castle's lord who kissed him and bade him be his friend.

Then came the lady of the castle with her retinue of maidens. Her beauty was such that it even eclipsed Queen Guinevere. She was led by an older woman whose absence of beauty was a juxtaposition to the lady of the manor. Where red were the cheeks of one, wrinkled were the other. Where one wore kerchiefs embroidered with glistening pearls, her soft neck bare and beckoning and whiter than the snow that capped the mountains, the other was covered by a gorget with a white headdress over her black and stubbled chin. The elder's forehead was wrapped in silk and worked with knots so that nothing of her was seen except her black brows, her reddened eyes, her wet nose, and dry lips. As ill as she was to look upon, her lady was the perfection of health.

When Sir Gawain finally saw the fair lady, he bowed low, greeted the elder with a nod, but took the younger into his arms and kissed her courteously.

She acknowledged him and he vowed to be her servant.

Then they sat, her at the left of the lord and him at her left, and the older woman mysteriously at the right of the lord as if she were also royalty. Gawain raised an eyebrow at this but let the question lay, hoping to know the answer without pressing.

The food and drink began to flow. The lord stood, removed his hood, and placed it on a spear. He challenged his men in various deeds, and the night flowed well, with much laughter and happiness. When the night ended, they all returned to their rooms, happy to have been part of such an event.

The next morning, after prayers to Christ who was born on Earth to die for humanity, they resumed the celebration with cookies and cakes and crumbles of all sort.

The noblemen sat on the dais, clad in their best. The old woman once again sat beside the lord. Gawain and the fair lady sat together. And throughout the hall, others of the court sat according to their rank until even the least of them had a plate. Then the meat was served along with all the other food, and the day became night with joy.

Gawain enjoyed his companionship with the beautiful lady, often laughing, at times nodding, at the length and depth of her conversation. Her words were as sweet as her demeanor, and he found himself enthralled by her presence.

Amidst trumpets and drums and merry piping, the feast continued from one day to the next until the Feast of Saint John when the guests finally prepared to depart on the next morning.

Gawain was also eager to bid farewell and continue on his journey, but the lord took his hand and led him to his own chamber and thanked him for appearing at the castle and sharing in the great feast.

He said, "I wish, sir, that while I live, I shall be held more worthy because Gawain was my guest at God's own feast."

"I appreciate you," Gawain said. "You deserve all honor that the High King will grant you, but I am at your disposal for such a glorious feast and if there is anything I can do, all you have to do is ask."

The lord did his very best to persuade Gawain to stay, but the knight knew he had to be once again on his quest. The lord asked him what the quest was that would drive him from his own king's castle in such a time of seasonal feasts.

"It is a high quest that has banished me from my normal happiness," Gawain said. "I have been summoned to a place I do not know for a deed I do not understand. I don't know where I might find this place. I would give away all the Kingdom of Logres if I might find it my New Year's morn. In such, I must ask, have you ever heard of the Green Chapel, where it might be found, and the Green Knight who calls it home? For I have pledged a solemn oath to meet the knight on the New Year. Anticipating that you don't know what I am talking about, I must be gone because I only have three days left before I fail at my pledge."

The lord laughed and clapped his hands. "Now you *have* to stay. I will show you where the Green Chapel is before time runs out. Have no fear. Take it easy and relax, and then on the first day of the New Year we shall go to this place. It is a mere two miles from here. Nothing to worry about."

Sir Gawain laughed loudly. "I could not have wished for better reply! Now that my quest is almost achieved, I will stay with you and be at your disposal."

The lord bade him sit even as he called for the ladies to join them. "You have said you will do what I ask. Is this true?"

"Certainly," Gawain said. "While I am in your castle, I do what you wish."

"You have traveled more than I and are far from home. Tomorrow I shall go on a hunt, but I ask of you to rest and relax. Greet my wife and the pair of you can sit together and have a fine time until I return."

Gawain, being an agreeable man, said as much.

"Then that's how it shall be," the lord said. "And we shall make a pact. Whatever I chase down in the woods shall be yours, and whatever you achieve, we will make an exchange for it. Let us swear on this, friend, from one exalted man to another. For better or for worse."

Gawain was joyed to agree for he saw no demons in the details.

They each grabbed a cup of wine and drank to seal the bargain, and the lord claimed, "The bargain is made."

They laughed again and drank more wine and partied throughout the night. The lords and ladies who resided in the castle joined them in the festivities and the night became late with wine and wildness, until finally, each of them so drunk they needed help getting to their beds, repeated the bargain, their covenant whether drunk or sober, solid in the embrace of righteousness.

JUST BEFORE DAWN, the castle was called to wake. Everyone rose groggily. The grooms readied the guests' horses and made about getting the knights into their armor. Finally appareled, the knights leaped atop their horses, took their bridles, and each rode the way that best pleased him.

The lord of the land wasn't concerned. He took time to eat bread soaked in milk[14] with a host of his men after Mass. Only when he heard the hunter's horn indicating that they had spotted something, he urged everyone to join him on the hunt.

The huntsmen released the hounds, blowing three loud blasts from their horns. The hounds barked like mad. Three more blasts of the horns and they were off, hunting, searching with scent what had been seen by man, long leashes held by the trackers.

A hundred hunters followed, each one better than the other and known far and wide for his skill. Then the trackers found the spot where the spoor was greatest and released the hounds from their leads and the forest sang with dogged music.

At the first sounds of the hunt, all the game in the forest quaked and fled, trembling across the vale. They tried to escape, but the hunters waved their arms and turned them back. The only thing they let past were the does and stags, which the lord forbid to be slain. All else was turned back into the killing fields, where arrows descended like rain, and the deer became their targets, falling and bleeding across the valley floor.

The hounds continued with the hunters following right after them, shouting and driving the beasts before them. What lived was driven to the hills and stopped by the confluence of waters where the men did their nasty work. The mastiffs[15] were so great and swift that they ran down the prey as fast as any hunter could slay them. This is how the lord passed his day, joyous for the hunt, mirthful for the companionship, on and on until nightfall.

The lord continued to roam the woods, but Gawain bid him a good night and retired to his tent, where a costly bed and coverlets had been made for him. He slumbered and then sometime near morning, as the daylight lit the canvas, he heard a sound at the door.

He raised his head, and from the bed pulled back a corner of the entry curtain to see who it might be. The lord's wife was there and, swift as she could, she let herself in, silently shutting the door behind her. Then she turned toward the bed where lay Gawain.

But Gawain would have none of it. He closed his eyes and pretended to sleep. Still, she came to him and sat on the bed beside him to await his awakening. He lay there as uncomfortable as one might in such a circumstance, trying to figure a way out.

His idea was one of surprise. He feigned awakening, pretended to notice her for the first time, and crossed himself as any Christian knight might in such a moment.

She stared at him, her face made up so her cheeks were blush upon pale white and lovely to behold. Through smiling lips she said, "Good morning, Sir Gawain. You can have me. I want you. I pray that you do with me what you must."

He blinked in astonishment and said with a voice not wholly his own,[16] "Good morning to you, my fair lady. I give myself to you and pray that you will do with me what you want." Then he chuckled. "But would you allow me to rise, for I feel like a prisoner beneath you. I would like to change clothes and clean myself so we might talk in more civilized comfort."

"I don't think so," she said. "I shall keep you here. You are my prisoner knight and I have captured you so you will talk to me. Sir Gawain is venerated all over the world. Your honor and courtesy are praised by all who live. Now that I have you here, and alone, with my lord and his men on the hunt, the serving men in their beds, my maidens dreaming of knights, and the door shut behind us, I must tell you that I am pleased to be with a man that all men love. I shall speak my wishes, although I beg to be your servant."

"I can't be all that," Gawain said. "I am a mere knight and unworthy of accepting your offer. It's true, if I deserved it, I would be more than happy to be with you, my lady."

"Of course you can. Although I have been praised for my beauty and my abilities, I am not without my wiles. Far gentler women have snatched the virtue of knights in their grasp. You and I have been nothing but courteous to each other, yet each of us desire the same. It's through the grace of God that I have you now in my power and I should not insult the opportunity."

"May Mother Mary bless you, because I have found in no other than you an equal amount of honesty. Your people have shown me so much respect, that to ignore it would make us both look bad."

"By Mary, I think otherwise," she said. "Were I worth all the women alive and had all the wealth of the world with the ability to choose which lord I most wanted, it would be you, for your beauty and your courtesy and your majesty and for all you hold true. I cannot imagine choosing any knight before you."

"I wish you would choose better," he said. "But I am proud of the way you prize me and, as your servant, know that I am your knight and may Christ reward you."

And so they spoke of all matters through the morning, he the lord and she the lady, him continually turning her passionate offers aside.

Finally, she begged her leave. She teased him and blushed while doing it and said, "You are such a knight, Gawain, and so true to yourself, would you deny one such as I who spent so much time with you a single kiss?"

Gawain nodded and said, "I am at your service and will indeed kiss you for fear of displeasure."

Then she leaned in and kissed him.

He kissed her back.

And she left, softly, through the back door.

After a few moments, Gawain called his attendant and picked out his clothes. Then he went to Mass, ate heartily, and spent a glorious day relaxing with the ladies.

By evening, the hunt was finally over. With a great blowing of horns and barking of dogs, they returned.

Eventually, the lord and Gawain were once again in the great hall for a feast. But this one was after an epic hunt and the lord said, "What do you think of all this game, Sir Gawain? Do you not think of me as a tremendous hunter?"

Gawain nodded. "This is the most game I have seen in the last seven years after a winter hunt."

"All of this I give to you," said the lord.

"Then I will give you what I have won while in your great walls," Gawain said. With that, he reached over and kissed the lord as one man might kiss another. "Accept this," Gawain added. "It is but a taste of what I was offered, but it is all I received."

"Well received," said the lord. "But I would know from whom you received this gift."

"That was not part of the deal," Gawain said. "And please don't ask me anymore. Know only that I have given to you what is yours by right and be content with that."

They laughed and bantered, and they ate more and drank more, and after dinner, the lord spread out by his fire. Wine was served and they jokingly promised that the same bargain they'd made this day, they would make for tomorrow. They partied late into the night, enjoying each other's company. At last, they renewed their promise, drank a last drink, then each went to their bed.

By the time the rooster crowed three times, the lord of the castle woke and dressed. Mass was sung and breakfast served. The hunters returned to the woods just as the sun crested the horizon. Hound and horn bellowed, and a cheer went up. The dogs were released into the thorns and they soon found a scent.

Forty of them, slavering, drooling, barking and baying, following an invisible scent. The rocks rang with their excitement. The huntsman blasted horns and shouted for them to go faster, but the hounds were vexed by a thicket, a rush of water, and a high cliff. They milled about in momentary confusion.

Yet the knights sensed[17] that a beast was within. They forced the hounds to continue, despite the animals' reticence. And then, as they beat the bushes, screaming for the animal to come forth, came a great boar, wonderous in size and magnificent to behold.

The towering beast rushed into the middle of the hounds' pack and threw many to the ground. Snorting and pawing at the earth, the boar used its tusks to shred and hurl those who would hunt it to their own graves.

The men shouted and blew horns to urge on the hounds to follow the boar that had plowed through their pack. The hounds turned to follow, and the huntsmen followed on horse. Many times the boar spun about and fought its attackers, only to turn once again and run. Two more times it did this, killing so many of the hounds that the hunters began to pull forth their bows.

Soon, the air was filled with arrows that found their target in the beast's side, though barely piercing its thick hide. Yet when it felt the pain of the arrow tips, the boar screamed with a rage unheard of. Not only did the boar now turn on the hounds, but it also turned on the hunters, and gave so fierce an approach that many of the hunters fled in terror.

But the lord himself, on a swift steed, pursued the monstrous beast, blowing his bugle. He set a regal statue as the sun slung low, his sword high in one hand, his bugle pressed to his lips in the other, chasing the creature who would kill his own.

And while that singular battle raged on, Sir Gawain lay in his bed, richly clothed, as the lady of the house approached. She looked upon him. He greeted her and she him.

She sat by his side, and said, "I think it a wonder that you are so stoic and care not for my friendly courtesies. I'm afraid as soon as I might teach you one of them, you might forget my lesson. You have already forgotten what I taught you yesterday."

"What is that?" he asked. "I trust[18] I do not know, but if you say the truth, then it was my fault for forgetting."

"But I taught you to kiss," she said. "Whenever someone fair is near, a knight should seek a kiss."

"No, my dear.[19] Be easy with me. I should not be the one to seek such a wonder and find it impossible to ask."

"In faith," she laughed. "It is not impossible to ask. You are strong enough to make anyone kiss you if they were so discourteous as to deny you."

"Oh, my heaven. You speak so well, but I'm not the sort to give any threat to a woman. If they desire to kiss me, then I am happy, if not, then I am still happy. I will not force myself upon someone."

Then the lady kissed him.

"I want to know how you have become so knightly. Your chivalry is unbounded. I have always heard how pure knights adventure for their true love, and avenge her with their valor, and ease her sorrow and bring joy to her home. Yet, you are the most beautiful knight of our time and I have sat by you twice, and never have I heard you speak about love. You, who are so skilled and courteous about the subject, surely could teach one so young and unskilled in the art of love."

She saw him demure and look away, so she pressed, "You pretend to not know the art, but really you find me unworthy of it. For shame, Sir Knight, I come to you in your bed chamber to learn your skill and beg for it while my lord is far from home."

"Trust me," Gawain began carefully, "great is my joy that such a wonder as you should bother with this knight, troubling yourself with such a poor man. You are so beautiful it is not right of me to ignore your desires, but I believe that you are more skilled than you say, maybe even by a hundredfold. I am but a poor knight and bound by my oaths, so help me in Christ."

But she would not be dismayed.

She tried and tried again.

And he defended himself as the gentleman he wanted to be, their sexual jousts and jests no more than a flirtatious conversation.

Finally, whether or not she gave up, or she grew tired of the ripostes, she kissed him once more and went on her way.

Once she was gone, Gawain rose and went to Mass, and afterward, had dinner with the ladies. He sat enjoying himself while the lord of the castle hunted, over hill, across raging waters, through wicked thickets.

There, the battle with the beast continued.[20] Men died. Dogs died. The wounded animal howled. Then finally it came to a great rock and could run no farther. It turned, ready, knowing of its certain demise, but more than willing to take as much other life with it as possible. The boar stood there, white tusks and mouth foaming with exertion.

She slipped into his chamber and closed the door ...

Yet the huntsman stood back, unwilling to approach.

The dogs as well, content to bark tiredly, hoping the beast would not charge once more.

That was the moment when the lord sprang to the ground and held out his bright blade. He crossed the stream and approached the boar alone.

When the beast saw the lord, its bristles tightened and it snorted with fury, as if wondering, *how dare a mere mortal might kill me.*

Many of the men feared for their lord as the boar leaped. But the beast had the worst of it. The lord's sword pierced its chest to the hilt, splitting the heart in two. The boar fell snarling, then kicked once, twice, before turning the groundwater pink as its lifeblood poured out.

The celebration began as the tenor of the horns changed and the barking came differently. The beast was finally dead, and the huntsman cut off the boar's head and put it on a pole. Then they tied the body to a larger pole so that many a strong hand could carry it. The lord himself carried the head, proudly in front of the entire entourage back to the castle.

Before long, he came upon Gawain in the hall and invited him to come and look. Then the lord called the ladies and the rest of the household together, showed them the trophy, and recounted the heroic take of how they hunted the wild boar through the woods. He described the enormity of the beast and relayed how men and dogs had died, and many others nearly so.

Gawain praised the lord of the castle for his valor, because he had never seen a boar of that size.

The lord then said, "Gawain, just as we promised, this is yours. What now shall you give me?"

"It is true," Gawain said. "I shall give you all that I have gained." Then he took his host and kissed him twice on the face. "Now we are done," Gawain said. "Of all of the promises we have made."

"By Saint Giles, you are the best that I know. You will be rich in no time if you continue to drive such bargains."

Attendants set up tables and trestles and covered them with elegant cloths and lit candles along the walls. The knights sat and were served the game. Happiness reigned and the halls rang with song, both during supper and after. They sang of Christmas and new carols, thrilled to be together.

The fair lady sat on the other side of Gawain and stole looks of love in his direction, attempting over and over to please him.

Gawain was angry with himself for putting himself in this position. He returned a few courteous glances, but that was all he would do, such was his cunning to keep her from spoiling the moment.

When they'd spent enough time in the hall, Gawain and his host decided to move to the inner chamber. Before the wide fireplace they drank wine.

The lord desired to renew their agreement for New Year's Eve, but the knight said he could not. He had to leave in the morning for it was near the time he must fulfill his pledge.

But the lord was reluctant to let him go. "As I am a true knight," the lord said, "I swear that I will take you to the Green Chapel on New Year's morning so you can achieve your promise. Meanwhile, stay a bit longer. Enjoy my hospitality. I will go once more into the wood and hunt, and when I bring my spoils back to the castle, you can exchange with me once more."

Gawain seemed about to say something, but the lord waved him silent.

"Let's enjoy the moment while we can and remember how misfortune can so often take a man."

Sir Gawain sighed in defeat.

He was given more to drink, then showed to bed, where he slept soft and long.

Early the next morning, after Mass, the lord and his men ate a quick breakfast, then mounted their horses before the hall gates. The morning air was filled with frost, so when the sun rose, it cast everything in a red glow, and the sky was clear of clouds.

The hunters moved in line into the forest, steadily forward and diligent. Then a horn blasted, followed by the bellowing of dogs. They'd scented a fox.

The little creature ran away from them, but was never out of sight.

The hunters and hounds pursued with shouts of excitement and barks of determination.

The fox found a hole in the thicket and dodged into it. Thinking itself free, it ran on straight, only to run into more dogs. It twisted and took off in the other direction, dogs scampering after, and hunters after that. The fox doubled back and now led the lord and his men over hills and dale, while Sir Gawain slept through the cold morning behind thick curtains.

The castle's lady was on a hunt herself.

She rose and put on her best dress, but made sure to leave her throat provocatively bare, while bordering it with rich fur. She wore no golden circlet upon her head, instead a network of precious stones that cast twinkles of light upon the trusses of her dress.

She slipped into his chamber and closed the door. She opened the window and said to him in a cheerful voice, "My knight, how can you sleep? It is such a nice morning."

Sir Gawain was deep in sleep and amidst a dream about his destiny tomorrow when he would finally go to the Green Chapel and let the Green Knight deliver a blow upon his neck that would must assuredly kill him.

But when the lady spoke, the dream dissolved; he opened his eyes and sat up on an elbow.

She came to him and kissed him, and he welcomed it, pleased to be with her and not in his ominous dream.

He noticed how beautiful she was and her immaculate dress. He felt his body warm and tingle.

They spoke and enjoyed each other's company, but no matter what she tried, he manage to deflect her advances. It was infuriating for her, really. He wouldn't outright refuse her love, but he wouldn't accept it either.

God forbid, he thought to himself, *what price would be paid if he slipped?*

But she wouldn't be deterred. She said, "You are to blame if you will not at least hold a lady who sits by you—a lady whom I know you love and have sworn to her not to ever lose that love. So, I have to ask, why is it that you continue to try and hide this love?"

"By Saint John," he said, smiling, "I don't love like that, nor do I think I ever will."

She feigned upset and said, "That is the worst thing I have ever heard. But I have my answer. Kiss me and I will leave so that I may mourn as a maiden who has loved too much."

Sighing, he leaned forward and kissed her.

The fair lady said, "Give me something to remember you by, so that when we part, I will have a memento of you. Even if it were but a glove, I would think of my gallant knight, and it would lesson my agony."

"I wish I had something precious enough to give you," he said. "You deserve a love token, great or small, something worthwhile to reflect my devotion. But a glove is too simple a reward. I am here on a strange mission. I have no squire to assist me nor earthly things to give. It's embarrassing, really."

"Oh, no, my knight. I am highly honored. Although you have nothing to offer me, I have something to give you." Then she handed him a ring of red gold with a sparkling stone.

But the knight refused. "I will take no gift, my lady, because I have none to give in return."

She begged him to take it, but he still refused.

This irritated[21] her, and she didn't try and hide it. "If you are going to refuse my ring because it is too costly, as if you might be afraid that the value will make you owe me, then let me give you a lesser gift. My girdle."

She unloosened a lace that was fastened at her side, opened her outer dress, hitched up her inner dress, and removed the garment in question. It was handmade and braided of green silk and gold.

She offered it to him.

But still he shook his head. "I can neither touch this nor take it until my adventure is over. And please, I don't want to make you angrier, but don't ask me anymore. I am beholden to you as you say, and no matter the heat or the cold, I will be your fair servant."

She looked at him, all mirth aside. "You can't refuse this silk. I know it seems simple enough. It is small to look at and of less value. But if you knew the virtue that is knit within the girdle, you would value it more highly."

Gawain sat straighter.

"Whatever knight is girded with this green lace is impervious to any man under Heaven, and there can be no magic on Earth that may slay him."

Gawain couldn't believe the opportunity this provided. He might be able to go to the Green Chapel, receive the blow, and escape without dying. He let her have her say, listening intently to every word. Then she passed him the girdle, and he granted her a prayer.

She told him, however, never to reveal what it can do and to definitely hide it from her husband, the lord.

Gawain agreed that it was between them and them alone. He thanked her profusely, arose and dressed, hid the girdle beneath his robes, and left the room.

Then he went to the priest, asking to pray and give confession.[22] Gawain asked how better he could save his soul with his journey to the Green Chapel. He admitted to his errors, both great and small, and sought the ultimate mercy, craving absolution for all of his misdeeds.

Because of his honesty, the priest blessed him and made him as clean as if the End of the World was tomorrow.

Afterward, Gawain tried to push all his worries aside, and embraced the seemingly never-ending party of the castle and its inhabitants. He laughed and danced and made jokes all the way until the sun rested in the west.

All of those present said that they had never seen a man as Gawain so filled with joy and so eager to share it.

During all of this, the lord himself was still chasing the fox. He'd lost the creature for a time, and rode in circles[23] until the hounds once again found the scent and howled fiercely, driving the wily beast through a thick grove.[24]

Only by the quickest of reactions, was the lord able to swivel and aim at the fox as it tried escaping the snare of closing hounds. In one fluid motion, he thrust his spear into it and skewered it to the earth. The dogs came and fell on it, but the lord leaped from his saddle and scattered them lest they ruin the beautiful fur coat.

He grabbed the fox by the jaws and held it aloft and hallooed loudly. The joy of the hunt, regardless of the hunted, brought them all together. The hounds bayed. The hunters blew their horns. Those without horns shouted.

It was the merriest of moments, regardless if it was but a single fox. It was all of the men and animals together in a single enterprise. The lord rubbed the heads of the hounds gladly. Soon, they were all heading back to the castle, eager to get there before nightfall.

The lord was happy to return. He found Gawain already warming himself at the fire, having spent his day with the ladies. The lord wore a blue robe and a furred surcoat with a hood that lay about his shoulders.

The knight met the host and greeted him. "Now I will be able to fulfill my promise," he said. Then he embraced the lord and kissed him solemnly three times.

"Definitely,"[25] said the lord. "You have had good luck in the matter of this agreement, if you make a fair trade."

"It does not matter the trade," said Gawain, "since what I owe is so swiftly paid."

The lord looked down. "I am behind in my trade. I hunted all day and all I have to show for it is a foul fox skin, which is poor payment for the three kisses you have given me."

"By the cross[26], I thank you," Gawain said.

Then the lord told the tale of his hunting and how the fox had been slain. With laughter and song, the story flowed until everyone had a part in it. Then the knight took leave and thanked him.

"For the fair relaxation you have provided me with your high feasts and fanfare, may the High King give you honor," Gawain said. "I count myself as one of your servants if you desire. But as you know, I must go this next morning and if you will give me a guide as you promised, someone to show me to the Green Chapel, I might meet my destiny in God's eyes."

"Why, of course," said the lord. "All that I have ever promised I shall happily keep."

Then he provided Gawain a servant to set him on his way and lead him through the low places, so he needn't have to cross a winter's stream, and who would also show him the shortest road through the forests.

Gawain thanked the lord for all the honor provided, and then went among the ladies and kissed each of them courteously, giving them also his thanks.

All the court did not want him to leave, but they understood his passion for the mission and blessed him in Christ.

Each man of the court he met, Gawain shook their hands and thanked them for their service and all the efforts they had made to make him comfortable.

Then they led him with torches to his chamber and brought him to his bed to rest. He slept soundly, even though what was to happen on the morrow gave him much to think upon.

But he was near what he most wanted and if you will listen to me, I will tell you the rest of the story.

DAY CHASED AWAY night into a bright new year. Like a lion, the weather roared, and cold clouds transformed the earth into a snow-packed land. Whistling winds blew from the heights, making great drifts in the valleys.

Gawain, lying in his bed, listened, hoping he might sleep just a little more before the day officially started. Because this was the day where all of his hopes and dreams and fears would collide and he did not know what would happen.

He rose at dawn, called to his attendant, and asked him to bring his armor and to saddle his steed. Gawain was helped into his clothes and armor, piece by piece, latched, snapped, and affixed.

First he had his clothes to keep off the cold. Then the harness above those. Both his chainmail and plates were well shined, the rings free of rust, and all like it was new, so the knight made sure to thank them for the care they showed.

Once armored, he told them to bring his steed, while he put the fairest attire on himself. His coat with his own symbol, adorned with precious stones upon velvet, with embroidered seams, and all fur-lined with expensive skins.

Gawain did not forget the gift the lady had given him. When he had placed the sword around his waist, he wrapped the girdle twice about him, over the sword belt. The gift of green silk looked magnificent upon the royal red cloth and rich to behold. But the knight did not wear it for pride of the pendants, gleaming brightly at the ends, but to save himself from sword or knife if the legend be true.

Day chased away night into a bright new year ...

Once dressed, he went to the people of the court and thanked them.

Then they brought Gringalet his steed to him, who was great and strong and had been well cared for. The knight looked at his horse's coat and said, "I honor the people of this place and the lord who watches over them. May good betide the lovely lady all of her long life. I have been so honored by you all, I wish may God reward you and love you for it. If I were to survive my quest and live anywhere on this wide earth, I would give you all that I might have, readily, of this I swear."

Then he sat foot in his stirrup and mounted his steed. His squire gave him a shield, which he laid on his shoulder. Then he clocked Gringalet with golden spurs and his steed danced down the stones.

The guide mounted also, who carried his spear and lance. As promised, he would show Gawain the way to the Green Chapel.

Gawain proclaimed loudly, "I commend this castle to Christ, may He give it forever fortune."

Then the drawbridge was let down, the broad gates unbarred and opened on both sides.

He crossed himself and passed through the gateway. He nodded to the porter, who knelt before Gawain and wished him a good bye, commending him to God.

This is how Sir Gawain left, with one man who would guide him to the dread place where he would receive his awful payment.

They traveled by hedges where the limbs had been winter-stripped of leaves and up cliffs with icy protrusions. Nothing fell from the sky, but it was freezing just the same. Mist hung heavy over the moors and grabbed at the mountains. The hill was capped with a great cloak of mist. The streams foamed and bubbled, sparkling ice on the shore away from the tumult that ran downward.

Rugged and dangerous was the way through the woods until the sun began to rise. Then they were upon a high hill. The snow lay white all around them. The guide who rode with Gawain reigned his horse.

He said, "I have brought you here and you are not far from the place you've so long sought. But I will tell you, since I love you well, and you are such a knight to be loved, that if you were to follow my counsel you would fare better. The place where you go is dangerous, because the man who lives there is the worst on Earth. He is strong and fierce and loves to fight. He is taller than any man and greater of frame than any four men of King Arthur's court, much less any other.

"It is the custom of the Green Chapel that no man may pass that place. However proficient he is at arms, be it regular folks or a chaplain, or a monk, or a priest, all will be slain by the Green Knight. So, I tell you as you sit in your saddle, even if you had twenty lives you too will be slain. He has been at the Green Chapel a long time and he is so expert at fighting that you cannot defend yourself.

"So I say, Sir Gawain, leave him alone and take another road—seek another land. I will return home and promise by God and all of his saints, or any oath you please, that I will never let anyone know what transpired here today on this hill, nor what decision you make."

"Many thanks," said Gawain, not at all pleased. "Good fortune to those who wish me well and that you would never tell a soul what I might do. But also know that if I were to pass here and flee from fear, that I would be a cowardly knight and couldn't be guiltless in my own soul. So, I will go to the chapel and let chance fall where it may. I will speak with that man, even if I might die doing so. As fierce as he may fight, God knows how to save his servants, so I still have a chance."

"Now that you have decided to kill yourself, I won't try and stop you," said the guide. He passed to Gawain his spear and his helmet, then pointed, "Ride down this same road beside the rock until you come to the bottom of the valley and there, on the left side, you will see the chapel and inside the grim man who keeps it."

With that, the lord spurred his horse, spun about, and galloped back hard to the castle.

Sir Gawain bowed his head, then looked to the heavens. He said, "I commend myself to God."

Then he spurred Gringalet forward and down the path along a bank beside a grove of trees. He wound his way through a rough thicket and suddenly found himself in an open space where he halted. The place seemed wild enough, but there was no sign of a chapel—only high burned banks on either side of the clearing and rugged rock crags with great stones above.

It seemed an evil place.

Then he saw a large mound marring the level space of the clearing. He turned his steed toward it and leaped down. He tied the reins to a branch, then moved to the mound. He walked around it, examining the curious bulge in the earth, wondering what it might be, until he found a hole at the end. On either side it was overgrown with clumps of grass. It appeared to be hollow within, like an old cave, or a crevice. He nodded to himself and allowed himself a tight smile. He knew what this had to be.

"Can this be the Green Chapel?" he asked himself. "Here might be where the devil says his prayers at midnight. There is definite wizardry here. It is a dread hole overgrown with grass and would be the perfect place for a devil to reside. I know the idea is to destroy me here, for this is a chapel of mischance. No luck will live here. This is the most cursed house of God I have ever seen, much less come to enter."

Helmet and spear in hand, he went to the rough place. He heard a fierce sound from the far side of the high hill, an ominous foreboding of something in preparation to be cleaved in two—like the reaper's scythe scraping against a mill wheel, rushing and ringing, so terrible to hear.

"My god," said Gawain to himself. "I know that weapon is meant for me. Although nothing may help me and my life is to be forfeit, I will not retreat."

With that, he called aloud, "Who waits to meet me here? I am Gawain come now. If any man is there, come now or don't come ever."

Silence reigned for a solid moment where nothing seemed to move.

Then a voice boomed, "Stay!" from the bank above his head. "And you shall soon see what I have promised."

For a while, the sound of sharpening continued, growing even fiercer, until it stopped and a giant of a man appeared from a cave in the crag with a fell weapon—a Danish axe newly sharpened. It bore an evil head that was four feet across and bound at the massive handle with a brightly gleaming lace.

The knight, himself, was all green as before, face, foot, locks, and beard. When he came to the water, he leaped over it rather than walk through, using the pole of his axe to propel himself. He landed upright and strode across the ground that was white as snow.

Sir Gawain went to meet him, but he made no low bow.

The other said, "Now, fair sir, one may trust you to keep your appointment. You know the agreement between us. At this time, twelve months before you did give your blow, and now I shall give mine. We are alone in this valley. There are no knights to come between us, so we can do what we want. Feel free to take off my head again if it suits you like you did a year ago with a single blow."

"No," said Gawain. "By the God that gave me life, I will not complain about the agreement. So make yourself ready to strike, and I shall make myself ready in return."

With that he bent his head and made his neck bare as if he had no fear and would not be seen to be afraid.

The Green Knight prepared. He grasped his grim weapon in order to smite Gawain. With all of his force, he bore it aloft and was poised to slay the knight. But when he swung down, he curved the heavy blade away at the last. Had it dropped straight, Gawain's head surely would have been rolling along the ground.

But Gawain had swerved aside at the last moment.

The Green Knight was furious. "You are not Gawain, who is held so valiant—Gawain who never feared a man from high or low, but now you shrink away for fear you might feel pain? Such cowardice I cannot believe. Did I flinch from your blow when you struck me with the axe in Arthur's hall? You struck. My head fell at my feet, and even then I did not flee. But you—you flinched before even being struck, so that makes me definitely the greater knight."

"I did jerk away once," Gawain admitted. "But I will not do it again. Hurry, Green Knight, by my faith, bring back the blade and send me to my destiny for I will let you strike once more and won't move a muscle—my truth on it."

"Then you shall have it," the Green Knight said. He heaved the axe once more, and his face became fierce. Then he brought the blade down, but stopped it a hair's breadth lest it strike Gawain.

Gawain was ready for the strike and did not flinch, but stood instead as still as a stone or the stump of a tree deeply rooted in rocky ground.

Then Gawain said angrily, "Why do you pretend this way? I thought you were going to strike? Come on!"

"Fine then," said the Green Knight. "You speak so forcefully. I will wait no more."

Then he readied to strike, his face ugly with concentration.

He lifted the axe as if it were a feather, then let if fall with the edge of the blade on the bare neck. Although he'd struck quickly, the sharp blade cut into Gawain's flesh only barely enough so that blood dripped into the snow.

When Gawain saw this, he sprang forth, swift-footed, more than a spear's length away, seized his helmet and set it on his head, cast his shield over his shoulder, drew his bright sword, and shouted, "Stop, Sir Knight. Thou shalt not strike me again. I have stood a stroke without flinching and if you try and strike me again, we shall do battle. By the promise made between us at Camelot, you have struck your blow, so lower your axe."

The Green Knight stepped back and leaned on his axe, setting the shaft on the ground, and admired Gawain and his fearlessness.

Then he said in a friendly voice, "Bold sir, there's no need to be so fierce. Neither of us has done anything wrong, nor will we, saved by the agreement we made at Camelot. I promised you a blow and you took it. Well paid. And as such, I release you of all other claims."

To this Gawain stood taller and tilted his head.

"If I had decided to continue," the knight said, "I would have. You see, first I menaced you with a feigned one and didn't hurt you because of the agreement we made that first night. The other deceit I offered the next day when my fair wife kissed you, and you did return those kisses. Both of those days, I have you two blows without mark—true man, true return."

Then he shook his head. "But the third time, you did fail and therefore had to receive the blow that caused you blood. Because it is my cloth you wear—the same woven girdle I gave my wife. I know well of the kisses and conversation and whispered words of love you exchanged with her, because I sent her to you as the purest knight who has ever roamed the earth. Just as a pearl among white peas is worth more, so is Gawain worth more than other knights."[27]

Then the Green Knight laughed. "But you did lack a little, fair knight, and was found wanting in loyalty. Yet because it was for no evil purpose, nor for trying to love my wife, but for the love of your own life that you did it, I blame you less."

Sir Gawain felt the blood rush to his face. He couldn't move and was locked in his own embarrassment. To himself he said, "Curse you cowardice and covetousness, for in you is the destruction of virtue."

When he finally could move, he grabbed the girdle and held it out. "Here! Take this fake thing and may it burn in Hell. It was my own fear of your blow that caused me to befriend covetousness and ignore my own custom of largess and loyalty, which befits all knights."

Gawain shook his head savagely slinging tears of anger. "Here I stand, full of fault and falseness. From treachery and lies come sorry and care. I vow to you, Sir Knight, if I have insulted you by my actions, do with me what you will."

The Green Knight grinned and laughed gently. "You have made so free a confession of your misdeeds and received penance from the edge of my axe, I absolve you of any sin and, even further, purge you of any sin you might have committed since you have been born. And this girdle, which is like my own attire, chased with gold and green, I return to you, so that you can go forth among the princes of renown and keep it as a token of your adventure at the Green Chapel and this meeting between two chivalrous knights."

Then the lord placed a hand on Gawain's shoulder. "I'd like you to return to the castle so that we may have one last feast. I want to ensure that you are able to make peace with my wife, who was your enemy."

"Of course," Gawain said, removing his helm. "I have fared badly. May bliss be between you and may the Lord look favorably upon you. Please bring me to your lovely wife and the other honored ladies of the court.

"It is nothing new how women can make fools of men. Adam was so beguiled, as was Solomon, then of course Sampson was led to his doom by his dear Delilah. David's matrimony with Bathsheba brought him nothing but sorrow. Since all of them were tricked by women, less fault of mine for falling victim to the same.

"But as for your girdle, I will indeed take it, but not for the gold or the silk or the pendants, but as a reminder to my frailty. I shall look upon it when I ride in renown and remind myself of the fault and faintness of the flesh; so when pride uplifts me for prowess of arms, the sight of this lace shall humble my heart. But one thing I would pray, if it is okay to ask, since you are lord of the land in which I stayed, what is your name?"

"Of course, I will share," the lord said, shrugging his shoulders. "I am Bernlak de Hautdesert. You have met my wife. She is controlled by Morgan le Fay, who has taken residence in my castle. Much of the old woman's guile was learned while she was the mistress of Merlin, who is no stranger to your court. She is also known as Morgain the Goddess, and there is none so high that she can't bring low.

"It was she who sent me in this guise to Camelot to test the truth of the Knights of the Round Table. She taught me how to make you confused in what you see and to frighten Queen Guinevere half to death when she saw a dead man grab his own head and speak.

"That is who is at my castle, the ugly juxtaposed to my beautiful. She's even your aunt, Arthur's half-sister, the daughter of the Duchess of Tintagel, who afterward married King Uther. So, I ask you to come to your aunt and have dinner with me. My people truly love you, and I wish you as well as any man on the earth."

Upon learning of this great truth, Sir Gawain had a change of heart and declined the invitation, feeling it better that he not truck anymore with the evil magic of Morgan le Fey.

So they embraced and kissed and commended each other to Christ and left each other in that cold glen. Gawain rode swiftly back to his king, before anyone, including the Green Knight, could stop him.

Sir Gawain had thus won the gift of his life. He rode Gringalet through many wild ways. Sometimes he lodged in houses, sometime he did not, and many adventures did he have on the way home that it would be fodder for yet another story.

By the time he arrived safely to Camelot, the cut in his neck had healed, and he carried the curious green girdle at his side, across his chest, and beneath his left arm.

Joy awakened that morning in the castle. King Arthur kissed his returning knight, as did the queen, and many valiant knights came to embrace him. They all asked him how it turned out, and he told them absolutely everything—the adventure of the chapel, how the Green Knight came to be, and the nature of the lady who'd pretended to love him. He then showed them the scar from the wound on his neck, which he'd won by disloyalty, and shame filled his face once more as he told the story.

"Here. My lady," he said, touching the lace around him. "This is the blame I bear around my neck, this is the harm and loss I have suffered, the cowardness and covetousness in which I have been caught, and a token of the agreement which was fulfilled. I must wear this as long as I live for none may hide his harm; forever it will stay with me and never be left apart."

Then the king comforted the knight, and the court laughed loudly at the tale and proclaimed that all of the lords and ladies who belonged to the Round Table should thereafter wear a baldric of bright green.

Thus it was agreed for all of the honor of the Round Table, and those who wore it were honored even more. And it is testified in the best book of romance that in Arthur's days, this adventure befell, the book of Brutus bears witness that nothing so wonderful and great had occurred since the siege and assault of Troy.

Many a venture herebefore
Hath fallen such as this:
May He that bare the crown of thorn
Bring us unto His bliss.

AMEN.[28]

HONY SOYT QUI MAL PENCE.[29]

Forever it will stay with me and never be left apart …

NOTES

1. Like all setups for great stories, there needs to be an introduction. The poet created one of his own, but I updated it so that it reads like something we know.

2. From original Jessie L. Weston's text "*à la dure main*" translates from French to "the hand." As in the Hand in *Game of Thrones* (George R. R. Martin's *A Song of Ice and Fire*), only in this case, Agravain is the hand for Guinevere and not Cersei.

3. From J.L.W.'s text, "gaily dressed in green": I take this use of "gaily" to mean for a celebration and not as the Green Knight would dress entering battle.

4. From J.L.W.'s text, "neither gorget nor breast-plate": The use of each of these was the same to me, so they cancelled each other out. They all fall under the category of army, though.

5. Six times the width of the knight's hand.

6. The dramatic entrance of the horse is important to the narrative and needed to be played up.

7. From J.L.W.'s text, "fain": I chose to translate it to brave.

8. His challenge was so complete and the effect of him so terrifying that no one wanted to fight the Green Knight, despite Arthur's offerings.

9. From J.L.W.'s text, "redest": I changed to became "redden," which I took to mean causing to bleed, as in beheading.

10. Michaelmas is the end of September and marks the beginning of winter in many parts of the Christian world.

11. From J.L.W.'s text, "byrny": a hauberk or chainmail, which is a heavy shirt made from hundreds of tiny interlocking rings of metal.

12. From J.L.W.'s text, "vintail": a grated visor found in a helmet that sits atop a figure adorned in plate mail.

13. Gawain's path has been mapped by many. For fun, search them out and you will find he did not travel as far as one would have thought.

14. From J.L.W.'s text, "sop": a piece of bread soaked usually in milk, but could also be broth.

15. In the original translation, J.L.W. used greyhounds, but these were not in fashion as we know them in the Middle Ages. Rather, mastiffs were used as hunting dogs, great jowled beasts with long lean muscles.

16. This section begins one of the greatest verbal sword fights in history, where the lady wants to bed Gawain, but his honor won't allow it. I spent

much time on this section, modernizing, but trying to keep the genius strokes alive.

17. From J.L.W.'s text, "wist": to sense or have a sense of here.

18. From J.L.W.'s text, "trow": to trust.

19. This is the perfect example of refrain that I spent a lot of time with. One of many. Trying to parse the 130-year-old translation into something that modern readers could appreciate. Here's J.L.W.'s original and you can see my quandary: "Nay, my dear," said Sir Gawain, "cease that speech; that durst I not do lest I were denied, for if I were forbidden I wot I were wrong did I further entreat."

20. Notice the juxtaposition of the lord battling the beast and Gawain battling the woman who wants to be in his bed.

21. From J.L.W.'s text, "vexed": This can translate to many things. I decided irritation, and I wanted her to be visibly so.

22. From J.L.W.'s text, "shrive": confession.

23. From J.L.W.'s text, "spinney": This was an interesting translation. It meant "crazy," but you can see how I used it, which I felt might work best in the context of the paragraph.

24. From J.L.W.'s text, " . . . and Reynard came creeping through a thick grove": The proper name of Reynard the Fox was part of a medieval literary convention dating back to the twelfth century, attributing all manner of human traits and actions to a wily fox as subject of adventure tales or voice of satire, often taking anthropomorphic (human-like) form.

25. From J.L.W.'s text, "*Of a sooth*": definitely.

26. From J.L.W.'s text, "rood": Old Germanic for cross and also used in M.E. for rod or staff.

27. "A pearl among white peas" is a linked narrative with another poem titled "The Pearl," credited to the same unknown poet who wrote the original "Sir Gawain and the Green Knight" circa 1348.

28. I left the last "bob and wheel" just as J.L.W. translated out of homage to her.

29. Also seen as *Honi soit qui mal y pense*: French for "Shame on him who thinks evil of it."

II.

SIR GAWAIN AND THE GREEN KNIGHT: THE ORIGINAL 1898 TRANSLATION FROM MIDDLE TO MODERN ENGLISH

BY JESSIE L. WESTON

PREFACE TO FIRST EDITION

THE POEM OF WHICH THE FOLLOWING PAGES OFFER a prose rendering is contained in a MS., believed to be unique, of the Cottonian Collection, Nero A.X., preserved in the British Museum. The MS. is of the end of the fourteenth century, but it is possible that the composition of the poem is somewhat earlier; the subject-matter is certainly of very old date. There has been a considerable divergence of opinion among scholars on the question of authorship, but the view now generally accepted is that it is the work of the same hand as *Pearl*, another poem of considerable merit contained in the same MS.

Our poem, or, to speak more correctly, metrical romance, contains over 2500 lines, and is composed in staves of varying length, ending in five short rhyming lines, technically known as a bob and a wheel,—the lines forming the body of the stave being not rhyming, but alliterative. The dialect in which it is written has been decided to be West Midland, probably Lancashire, and is by no means easy to understand. Indeed, it is the real difficulty and obscurity of the language, which, in spite of careful and scholarly editing, will always place the poem in its original form outside the range of any but professed students of mediæval literature, which has encouraged me to make an attempt to render it more accessible to the general public, by giving it a form that shall be easily intelligible, and at the same time preserve as closely as possible the style of the author.

For that style, in spite of a certain roughness, unavoidable at a period in which the language was still in a partially developed and amorphous stage, is really charming. The author has a keen eye for effect; a talent for description, detailed without becoming wearisome; a genuine love of Nature and sympathy with her varying moods; and a real refinement and elevation of feeling which enable him to deal with a *risqué:* situation with an absence of coarseness, not, unfortunately, to be always met with in a mediæval writer. Standards of taste vary with the age, but even judged by that of our own day the author of *Sir Gawain and the Green Knight* comes not all too badly out of the ordeal!

The story with which the poem deals, too, has claims upon our interest. I have shown elsewhere[1] that the beheading challenge is an incident of very early occurrence in heroic legend, and that the particular form given to it in the English poem is especially interesting, corresponding as it does to the variations of the story as preserved in the oldest known version, that of the old Irish *Fled Bricrend.*

But in no other version is the incident coupled with that of a temptation and testing of the hero's honour and chastity, such as meets us here. At first sight one is inclined to assign the episode of the lady of the castle to the class of stories of which the oldest version is preserved in Biblical record—the story of Joseph and Potiphar's wife; a *motif* not unseldom employed by mediæval writers, and which notably occurs in what we may call the *Launfal* group of stories. But there are certain points which may make us hesitate as to whether in its first conception the tale was really one of this class.

It must be noted that here the lady is acting throughout with the knowledge and consent of the husband, an important point of difference. In the second place, it is very doubtful whether her entire attitude was not a *ruse.* From the Green Knight's words to Gawain when he finally reveals himself, "I wot we shall soon make peace with my wife, who was thy bitter enemy," her conduct hardly seems to have been prompted by real passion.

In my *Studies on the Legend of Sir Gawain*, already referred to, I have suggested that the character of the lady here is, perhaps, a reminiscence of that of the Queen of the Magic Castle or Isle, daughter or niece of an enchanter, who at an early stage of Gawain's story was undoubtedly his love. I think it not impossible that she was an integral part of the tale as first told, and her *rôle* here was determined by that which she originally played. In most versions of the story she has dropped out altogether. It is, of course, possible that, there being but a confused reminiscence of the original tale, her share *may* have been modified by the influence of the *Launfal* group; but I should prefer to explain the episode on the whole as a somewhat distorted survival of an original feature.

But in any case we may be thankful for this, that the author of the most important English metrical romance dealing with Arthurian legend faithfully adheres to the original conception of Gawain's character, as drawn before the monkish lovers of edification laid their ruthless hands on his legend, and turned the model of knightly virtues and courtesy into a mere vulgar libertine.

Brave, chivalrous, loyally faithful to his plighted word, scrupulously heedful of his own and others' honour, Gawain stands before us in this poem. We take up Malory or Tennyson, and in spite of their charm of style, in spite of the halo of religious mysticism in which they have striven to enwrap their characters, we lay them down with a feeling of dissatisfaction. How did the Gawain of their imagination, this empty-headed, empty-hearted worldling, cruel murderer, and treacherous friend, ever come to be the typical English hero? For such Gawain certainly was, even more than Arthur himself. Then we turn back to these faded pages, and read the quaintly earnest words in which the old writer reveals the hidden meaning of that mystic symbol, the pentangle, and vindicates Gawain's title to claim it as his badge—and we smile, perhaps, but we cease to wonder at the widespread popularity of King Arthur's famous nephew, or at the immense body of romance that claims him as its hero.

Scholars know all this, of course; they can read the poem for themselves in its original rough and intricate phraseology; perhaps they will be shocked at an attempt to handle it in simpler form. But this little book is not for them, and if to those to whom the tale would otherwise be a sealed treasure these pages bring some new knowledge of the way in which our forefathers looked on the characters of the Arthurian legend, the tales they told of them (unconsciously betraying the while how they themselves lived and thought and spoke)—if by that means they gain a keener appreciation of our national heroes, a wider knowledge of our national literature,—then the spirit of the long-dead poet will doubtless not be the slowest to pardon my handling of what was his masterpiece, as it is, in M. Gaston Paris' words, "The jewel of English mediæval literature."

—J. L.W.
Bournemouth
June, 1898

PREFACE TO SECOND EDITION

IN PREPARING THIS SECOND EDITION I HAVE ADOPTED certain suggestions of the late Professor Kölbing, contained in a review published by him in *Englische Studien xxvi.* In one or two instances, however, I have not felt free to follow his reading—*e.g.*, on page 67, *in þrynne syþe* must certainly mean "*for the third time,*" not "*thrice.*" The lady has already kissed Gawain twice during the interview; Professor Kölbing's suggestion would make him receive five kisses, instead of three, the correct number. Nor do I think the story would gain anything by reproducing the details of the dissection of animals on page 46. This little series is not intended for scholars, who can study the original works for themselves, but for the general public, and I have therefore avoided any digression from the main thread of the story. In the main, however, I have gladly availed myself of the late Professor's learned criticisms.

—J. L.W.
Bournemouth
May, 1900

SIR GAWAIN AND THE GREEN KNIGHT

AFTER THE SIEGE AND THE ASSAULT OF TROY, WHEN that burg was destroyed and burnt to ashes, and the traitor tried for his treason, the noble Æneas and his kin sailed forth to become princes and patrons of well-nigh all the Western Isles. Thus Romulus built Rome (and gave to the city his own name, which it bears even to this day); and Ticius turned him to Tuscany; and Langobard raised him up dwellings in Lombardy; and Felix Brutus sailed far over the French flood, and founded the kingdom of Britain, wherein have been war and waste and wonder, and bliss and bale, ofttimes since.

And in that kingdom of Britain have been wrought more gallant deeds than in any other; but of all British kings Arthur was the most valiant, as I have heard tell, therefore will I set forth a wondrous adventure that fell out in his time. And if ye will listen to me, but for a little while, I will tell it even as it stands in story stiff and strong, fixed in the letter, as it hath long been known in the land.

KING ARTHUR LAY at Camelot upon a Christmas-tide, with many a gallant lord and lovely lady, and all the noble brotherhood of the Round Table. There they held rich revels with gay talk and jest; one while they would ride forth to joust and tourney, and again back to the court to make carols;[2] for there was the feast holden fifteen days with all the mirth that men could devise, song and glee, glorious to hear, in the daytime, and dancing at night. Halls and chambers were crowded with noble guests, the bravest of knights and the loveliest of ladies, and Arthur himself was the comeliest king that ever held a court. For all this fair folk were in their youth, the fairest and most fortunate under heaven, and the king himself of such fame that it were hard now to name so valiant a hero.

Now the New Year had but newly come in, and on that day a double portion was served on the high table to all the noble guests, and thither came the king with all his knights, when the service in the chapel had been sung to an end. And they greeted each other for the New Year, and gave rich gifts, the one to the other (and they that received them were not wroth, that may ye well believe!), and the maidens laughed and made mirth till it was time to get them to meat. Then they washed and sat them down to the feast in fitting rank and order, and Guinevere the queen, gaily clad, sat on the high daïs. Silken was her seat, with a fair canopy over her head, of rich tapestries of Tars, embroidered, and studded with costly gems; fair she was to look upon, with her shining grey eyes, a fairer woman might no man boast himself of having seen.

But Arthur would not eat till all were served, so full of joy and gladness was he, even as a child; he liked not either to lie long, or to sit long at meat, so worked upon him his young blood and his wild brain. And another custom he had also, that came of his nobility, that he would never eat upon an high day till he had been advised of some knightly deed, or some strange and marvellous tale, of his ancestors, or of arms, or of other ventures. Or till some stranger knight should seek of him leave to joust with one of the Round Table, that they might set their lives in jeopardy, one against another, as fortune might favour them. Such was the king's custom when he sat in hall at each high feast with his noble knights, therefore on that New Year tide, he abode, fair of face, on the throne, and made much mirth withal.

Thus the king sat before the high tables, and spake of many things; and there good Sir Gawain was seated by Guinevere the queen, and on her other side sat Agravain, *à la dure main*;[3] both were the king's sister's sons and full gallant knights. And at the end of the table was Bishop Bawdewyn, and Ywain, King Urien's son, sat at the other side alone. These were worthily served on the daïs, and at the lower tables sat many valiant knights. Then they bare the first course with the blast of trumpets and waving of banners, with the sound of drums and pipes, of song and lute, that many a heart was uplifted at the melody. Many were the dainties, and rare the meats, so great was the plenty they might scarce find room on the board to set on the dishes. Each helped himself as he liked best, and to each two were twelve dishes, with great plenty of beer and wine.

Now I will say no more of the service, but that ye may know there was no lack, for there drew near a venture that the folk might well have left their labour to gaze upon. As the sound of the music ceased, and the first course had been fitly served, there came in at the hall door one terrible to behold, of stature greater than any on earth; from neck to loin so strong and thickly made, and with limbs so long and so great that he seemed even as a giant. And yet he was but a man, only the mightiest that might mount a steed; broad of chest and shoulders and slender of waist, and all his features of like fashion; but men marvelled much at his colour, for he rode even as a knight, yet was green all over.

For he was clad all in green, with a straight coat, and a mantle above; all decked and lined with fur was the cloth and the hood that was thrown back from his locks and lay on his shoulders. Hose had he of the same green, and spurs of bright gold with silken fastenings richly worked; and all his vesture was verily green. Around his waist and his saddle were bands with fair stones set upon silken work, 'twere too long to tell of all the trifles that were embroidered thereon—birds and insects in gay gauds of green and gold. All the trappings of his steed were of metal of like enamel, even the stirrups that he stood in stained of the same, and stirrups and saddle-bow alike gleamed and shone with green stones. Even the steed on which he rode was of the same hue, a green horse, great and strong, and hard to hold, with broidered bridle, meet for the rider.

The knight was thus gaily dressed in green, his hair falling around his shoulders; on his breast hung a beard, as thick and green as a bush, and the beard and the hair of his head were clipped all round above his elbows. The lower part of his sleeves were fastened with clasps in the same wise as a king's mantle. The horse's mane was crisp and plaited with many a knot folded in with gold thread about the fair green, here a twist of the hair, here another of gold. The tail was twined in like manner, and both were bound about with a band of bright green set with many a precious stone; then they were tied aloft in a cunning knot, whereon rang many bells of burnished gold. Such a steed might no other ride, nor had such ever been looked upon in that hall ere that time; and all who saw that knight spake and said that a man might scarce abide his stroke.

The knight bore no helm nor hauberk, neither gorget nor breast-plate, neither shaft nor buckler to smite nor to shield, but in one hand he had a holly-bough, that is greenest when the groves are bare, and in his other an axe, huge and uncomely, a cruel weapon in fashion, if one would picture it. The head was an ell-yard long, the metal all of green steel and gold, the blade burnished bright, with a broad edge, as well shapen to shear as a sharp razor. The steel was set into a strong staff, all bound round with iron, even to the end, and engraved with green in cunning work. A lace was twined about it, that looped at the head, and all adown the handle it was clasped with tassels on buttons of bright green richly broidered.

The knight rideth through the entrance of the hall, driving straight to the high daïs, and greeted no man, but looked ever upwards; and the first words he spake were, "Where is the ruler of this folk? I would gladly look upon that hero, and have speech with him." He cast his eyes on the knights, and mustered them up and down, striving ever to see who of them was of most renown.

Then was there great gazing to behold that chief, for each man marvelled what it might mean that a knight and his steed should have even such a hue as the green grass; and that seemed even greener than green enamel on bright gold. All looked on him as he stood, and drew near unto him wondering greatly what he might be; for many marvels had they seen, but none such as this, and phantasm and faërie did the folk deem it. Therefore were the gallant knights slow to answer, and gazed astounded, and sat stone still in a deep silence through that goodly hall, as if a slumber were fallen upon them. I deem it was not all for doubt, but some for courtesy that they might give ear unto his errand.

Then Arthur beheld this adventurer before his high daïs, and knightly he greeted him, for fearful was he never. "Sir," he said, "thou art welcome to this place—lord of this hall am I, and men call me Arthur. Light thee down, and tarry awhile, and what thy will is, that shall we learn after."

"Nay," quoth the stranger, "so help me He that sitteth on high, 'twas not mine errand to tarry any while in this dwelling; but the praise of this thy folk and thy city is lifted up on high, and thy warriors are holden for the best and the most valiant of those who ride mail-clad to the fight. The wisest and the worthiest of this world are they, and well proven in all knightly sports. And here, as I have heard tell, is fairest courtesy, therefore have I come hither as at this time. Ye may be sure by the branch that I bear here that I come in peace, seeking no strife. For had I willed to journey in warlike guise I have at home both hauberk and helm, shield and shining spear, and other weapons to mine hand, but since I seek no war my raiment is that of peace. But if thou be as bold as all men tell thou wilt freely grant me the boon I ask."

And Arthur answered, "Sir Knight, if thou cravest battle here thou shalt not fail for lack of a foe."

And the knight answered, "Nay, I ask no fight, in faith here on the benches are but beardless children, were I clad in armour on my steed there is no man here might match me. Therefore I ask in this court but a Christmas jest, for that it is Yule-tide, and New Year, and there are here many fain for sport. If any one in this hall holds himself so hardy,[4] so bold both of blood and brain, as to dare strike me one stroke for another, I will give him as a gift this axe, which is heavy enough, in sooth, to handle as he may list, and I will abide the first blow, unarmed as I sit. If any knight be so bold as to prove my words let him come swiftly to me here, and take this weapon, I quit claim to it, he may keep it as his own, and I will abide his stroke, firm on the floor. Then shalt thou give me the right to deal him another, the respite of a year and a day shall he have. Now haste, and let see whether any here dare say aught."

Now if the knights had been astounded at the first, yet stiller were they all, high and low, when they had heard his words. The knight on his steed straightened himself in the saddle, and rolled his eyes fiercely round the hall, red they gleamed under his green and bushy brows. He frowned and twisted his beard, waiting to see who should rise, and when none answered he cried aloud in mockery, "What, is this Arthur's hall, and these the knights whose renown hath run through many realms? Where are now your pride and your conquests, your wrath, and anger, and mighty words? Now are the praise and the renown of the Round Table overthrown by one man's speech, since all keep silence for dread ere ever they have seen a blow!"

With that he laughed so loudly that the blood rushed to the king's fair face for very shame; he waxed wroth, as did all his knights, and sprang to his feet, and drew near to the stranger and said, "Now by heaven foolish is thy asking, and thy folly shall find its fitting answer. I know no man aghast at thy great words. Give me here thine axe and I shall grant thee the boon thou hast asked." Lightly he sprang to him and caught at his hand, and the knight, fierce of aspect, lighted down from his charger.

Then Arthur took the axe and gripped the haft, and swung it round, ready to strike. And the knight stood before him, taller by the head than any in the hall; he stood, and stroked his beard, and drew down his coat, no more dismayed for the king's threats than if one had brought him a drink of wine.

Then Gawain, who sat by the queen, leaned forward to the king and spake, "I beseech ye, my lord, let this venture be mine. Would ye but bid me rise from this seat, and stand by your side, so that my liege lady thought it not ill, then would I come to your counsel before this goodly court. For I think it not seemly when such challenges be made in your hall that ye yourself should undertake it, while there are many bold knights who sit beside ye, none are there, methinks, of readier will under heaven, or more valiant in open field. I am the weakest, I wot, and the feeblest of wit, and it will be the less loss of my life if ye seek sooth. For save that ye are mine uncle naught is there in me to praise, no virtue is there in my body save your blood, and since this challenge is such folly that it beseems ye not to take it, and I have asked it from ye first, let it fall to me, and if I bear myself ungallantly then let all this court blame me."

Then they all spake with one voice that the king should leave this venture and grant it to Gawain.

Then Arthur commanded the knight to rise, and he rose up quickly and knelt down before the king, and caught hold of the weapon; and the king loosed his hold of it, and lifted up his hand, and gave him his blessing, and bade him be strong both of heart and hand. "Keep thee well, nephew," quoth

Arthur, "that thou give him but the one blow, and if thou redest him rightly I trow thou shalt well abide the stroke he may give thee after."

Gawain stepped to the stranger, axe in hand, and he, never fearing, awaited his coming. Then the Green Knight spake to Sir Gawain, "Make we our covenant ere we go further. First, I ask thee, knight, what is thy name? Tell me truly, that I may know thee."

"In faith," quoth the good knight, "Gawain am I, who give thee this buffet, let what may come of it; and at this time twelvemonth will I take another at thine hand with whatsoever weapon thou wilt, and none other."

Then the other answered again, "Sir Gawain, so may I thrive as I am fain to take this buffet at thine hand," and he quoth further, "Sir Gawain, it liketh me well that I shall take at thy fist that which I have asked here, and thou hast readily and truly rehearsed all the covenant that I asked of the king, save that thou shalt swear me, by thy troth, to seek me thyself wherever thou hopest that I may be found, and win thee such reward as thou dealest me to-day, before this folk."

"Where shall I seek thee?" quoth Gawain. "Where is thy place? By Him that made me, I wot never where thou dwellest, nor know I thee, knight, thy court, nor thy name. But teach me truly all that pertaineth thereto, and tell me thy name, and I shall use all my wit to win my way thither, and that I swear thee for sooth, and by my sure troth."

"That is enough in the New Year, it needs no more," quoth the Green Knight to the gallant Gawain, "if I tell thee truly when I have taken the blow, and thou hast smitten me; then will I teach thee of my house and home, and mine own name, then mayest thou ask thy road and keep covenant. And if I waste no words then farest thou the better, for thou canst dwell in thy land, and seek no further. But take now thy toll, and let see how thy strikest."

"Gladly will I," quoth Gawain, handling his axe.

Then the Green Knight swiftly made him ready, he bowed down his head, and laid his long locks on the crown that his bare neck might be seen. Gawain gripped his axe and raised it on high, the left foot he set forward on the floor, and let the blow fall lightly on the bare neck. The sharp edge of the blade sundered the bones, smote through the neck, and clave it in two, so that the edge of the steel bit on the ground, and the fair head fell to the earth that many struck it with their feet as it rolled forth. The blood spurted forth, and glistened on the green raiment, but the knight neither faltered nor fell; he started forward with out-stretched hand, and caught the head, and lifted it up; then he turned to his steed, and took hold of the bride, set his foot in the stirrup, and mounted. His head he held by the hair, in his hand. Then he seated himself in his saddle as if naught ailed him, and he were not headless. He turned his steed about, the grim corpse bleeding freely the while, and they who looked upon him doubted them much for the covenant.

For he held up the head in his hand, and turned the face towards them that sat on the high daïs, and it lifted up the eyelids and looked upon them and spake as ye shall hear. "Look, Gawain, that thou art ready to go as thou hast promised, and seek leally till thou find me, even as thou hast sworn in this hall in the hearing of these knights. Come thou, I charge thee, to the Green Chapel, such a stroke as thou hast dealt thou hast deserved, and it shall be promptly paid thee on New Year's morn. Many men know me as the knight of the Green Chapel, and if thou askest, thou shalt not fail to find me. Therefore it behoves thee to come, or to yield thee as recreant."

With that he turned his bridle, and galloped out at the hall door, his head in his hands, so that the sparks flew from beneath his horse's hoofs. Whither he went none knew, no more than they wist whence he had come; and the king and Gawain they gazed and laughed, for in sooth this had proved a greater marvel than any they had known aforetime.

Though Arthur the king was astonished at his heart, yet he let no sign of it be seen, but spake in courteous wise to the fair queen: "Dear lady, be not dismayed, such craft is well suited to Christmas-tide when we seek jesting, laughter and song, and fair carols of knights and ladies. But now I may well get me to meat, for I have seen a marvel I may not forget." Then he looked on Sir Gawain, and said gaily, "Now, fair nephew, hang up thine axe, since it has hewn enough," and they hung it on the dossal above the daïs, where all men might look on it for a marvel, and by its true token tell of the wonder. Then the twain sat them down together, the king and the good knight, and men served them with a double portion, as was the share of the noblest, with all manner of meat and of minstrelsy. And they spent that day in gladness, but Sir Gawain must well bethink him of the heavy venture to which he had set his hand.

THIS BEGINNING OF adventures had Arthur at the New Year; for he yearned to hear gallant tales, though his words were few when he sat at the feast. But now had they stern work on hand. Gawain was glad to begin the jest in the hall, but ye need have no marvel if the end be heavy. For though a man be merry in mind when he has well drunk, yet a year runs full swiftly, and the beginning but rarely matches the end.

For Yule was now over-past[5], and the year after, each season in its turn following the other. For after Christmas comes crabbed Lent, that will have fish for flesh and simpler cheer. But then the weather of the world chides with winter; the cold withdraws itself, the clouds uplift, and the rain falls in warm showers on the fair plains. Then the flowers come forth, meadows and grove are clad in green, the birds make ready to build, and sing sweetly for solace of the soft summer that follows thereafter. The blossoms bud and blow in the hedgerows rich and rank, and noble notes enough are heard in the fair woods.

After the season of summer, with the soft winds, when zephyr breathes lightly on seeds and herbs, joyous indeed is the growth that waxes thereout when the dew drips from the leaves beneath the blissful glance of the bright sun. But then comes harvest and hardens the grain, warning it to wax ripe ere the winter. The drought drives the dust on high, flying over the face of the land; the angry wind of the welkin wrestles with the sun; the leaves fall from the trees and light upon the ground, and all brown are the groves that but now were green, and ripe is the fruit that once was flower. So the year passes into many yesterdays, and winter comes again, as it needs no sage to tell us.

When the Michaelmas moon was come in with warnings of winter, Sir Gawain bethought him full oft of his perilous journey. Yet till All Hallows Day he lingered with Arthur, and on that day they made a great feast for the hero's sake, with much revel and richness of the Round Table. Courteous knights and comely ladies, all were in sorrow for the love of that knight, and though they spake no word of it, many were joyless for his sake.

And after meat, sadly Sir Gawain turned to his uncle, and spake of his journey, and said, "Liege lord of my life, leave from you I crave. Ye know well how the matter stands without more words, to-morrow am I bound to set forth in search of the Green Knight."

Then came together all the noblest knights, Ywain and Erec, and many another. Sir Dodinel le Sauvage, the Duke of Clarence, Launcelot and Lionel, and Lucan the Good, Sir Bors and Sir Bedivere, valiant knights both, and many another hero, with Sir Mador de la Porte, and they all drew near, heavy at heart, to take counsel with Sir Gawain. Much sorrow and weeping was there in the hall to think that so worthy a knight as Gawain should wend his way to seek a deadly blow, and should no more wield his sword in fight. But the knight made ever good cheer, and said, "Nay, wherefore should I shrink? What may a man do but prove his fate?"

He dwelt there all that day, and on the morn he arose and asked betimes for his armour; and they brought it unto him on this wise: first, a rich carpet was stretched on the floor[6] (and brightly did the gold gear glitter upon it), then the knight stepped on to it, and handled the steel; clad he was in a doublet of silk, with a close hood, lined fairly throughout. Then they set the steel shoes upon his feet, and wrapped his legs with greaves, with polished knee-caps, fastened with knots of gold. Then they cased his thighs in cuisses closed with thongs, and brought him the byrny of bright steel rings sewn upon a fair stuff. Well burnished braces they set on each arm with good elbow-pieces, and gloves of mail, and all the goodly gear that should shield him in his need. And they cast over all a rich surcoat, and set the golden spurs on his heels, and girt him with a trusty sword fastened with a silken bawdrick. When he was thus clad his harness was costly, for the least loop or latchet gleamed with gold. So armed as he was he hearkened Mass and made his offering at the high altar. Then he came to the king, and the knights of his court, and courteously took leave of lords and ladies, and they kissed him, and commended him to Christ.

With that was Gringalet ready, girt with a saddle that gleamed gaily with many golden fringes, enriched and decked anew for the venture. The bridle was all barred about with bright gold buttons, and all the covertures and trappings of the steed, the crupper and the rich skirts, accorded with the saddle; spread fair with the rich red gold that glittered and gleamed in the rays of the sun.

Then the knight called for his helmet, which was well lined throughout, and set it high on his head, and hasped it behind. He wore a light kerchief over the vintail, that was broidered and studded with fair gems on a broad silken ribbon, with birds of gay colour, and many a turtle and true-lover's knot interlaced thickly, even as many a maiden had wrought diligently for seven winter long. But the circlet which crowned his helmet was yet more precious, being adorned with a device in diamonds. Then they brought him his shield, which was of bright red, with the pentangle painted thereon in gleaming gold.[7] And why that noble prince bare the pentangle I am minded to tell you, though my tale tarry thereby. It is a sign that Solomon set erewhile, as betokening truth; for it is a figure with five points and each line overlaps the other, and nowhere hath it beginning or end, so that in English it is called "the endless knot." And therefore was it well suiting to this knight and to his arms, since Gawain was faithful in five and five-fold, for pure was he as gold, void of all villainy and endowed with all virtues. Therefore he bare the pentangle on shield and surcoat as truest of heroes and gentlest of knights.

For first he was faultless in his five senses; and his five fingers never failed him; and all his trust upon earth was in the five wounds that Christ bare on the cross, as the Creed tells. And wherever this knight found himself in stress of battle he deemed well that he drew his strength from the five joys which the Queen of Heaven had of her Child. And for this cause did he bear an image of Our Lady on the one half of his shield, that whenever he looked upon it he might not lack for aid. And the fifth five that the hero used were frankness and fellowship above all, purity and courtesy that never failed him, and compassion that surpasses all; and in these five virtues was that hero wrapped and clothed. And all these, five-fold, were linked one in the other, so that they had no end, and were fixed on five points that never failed, neither at any side were they joined or sundered, nor could ye find beginning or end. And therefore on his shield was the knot shapen, red-gold upon red, which is the pure pentangle. Now was Sir Gawain ready, and he took his lance in hand, and bade them all *Farewell*, he deemed it had been for ever.

Then he smote the steed with his spurs, and sprang on his way, so that sparks flew from the stones after him. All that saw him were grieved at heart, and said one to the other, "By Christ, 'tis great pity that one of such noble life should be lost! I'faith, 'twere not easy to find his equal upon earth. The king had done better to have wrought more warily. Yonder knight should have been made a duke; a gallant leader of men is he, and such a fate had beseemed him better than to be hewn in pieces at the will of an elfish man, for mere pride. Who ever knew a king to take such counsel as to risk his knights on a Christmas jest?" Many were the tears that flowed from their eyes when that goodly knight rode from the hall. He made no delaying, but went his way swiftly, and rode many a wild road, as I heard say in the book.

So rode Sir Gawain through the realm of Logres, on an errand that he held for no jest. Often he lay companionless at night, and must lack the fare that he liked. No comrade had he save his steed, and none save God with whom to take counsel. At length he drew nigh to North Wales, and left the isles of Anglesey on his left hand, crossing over the fords by the foreland over at Holyhead, till he came into the wilderness of Wirral[8], where but few dwell who love God and man of true heart. And ever he asked, as he fared, of all whom he met, if they had heard any tidings of a Green Knight in the country thereabout, or of a Green Chapel? And all answered him, Nay, never in their lives had they seen any man of such a hue. And the knight wended his way by many a strange road and many a rugged path, and the fashion of his countenance changed full often ere he saw the Green Chapel.

Many a cliff did he climb in that unknown land, where afar from his friends he rode as a stranger. Never did he come to a stream or a ford but he found a foe before him, and that one so marvellous, so foul and fell, that it behoved him to fight. So many wonders did that knight behold, that it were too long to tell the tenth part of them. Sometimes he fought with dragons and wolves; sometimes with wild men that dwelt in the rocks; another while with bulls, and bears, and wild boars, or with giants of the high moorland that drew near to him. Had he not been a doughty knight, enduring, and of well-proved valour, and a servant of God, doubtless he had been slain, for he was oft in danger of death. Yet he cared not so much for the strife, what he deemed worse was when the cold clear water was shed from the clouds, and froze ere it fell on the fallow ground. More nights than enough he slept in his harness on the bare rocks, near slain with the sleet, while the stream leapt bubbling from the crest of the hills, and hung in hard icicles over his head.

Thus in peril and pain, and many a hardship, the knight rode alone till Christmas Eve, and in that tide he made his prayer to the Blessed Virgin that she would guide his steps and lead him to some dwelling. On that morning he rode by a hill, and came into a thick forest, wild and drear; on each side were high hills, and thick woods below them of great hoar oaks, a hundred together, of hazel and hawthorn with their trailing boughs intertwined, and rough ragged moss spreading everywhere. On the bare twigs the birds chirped piteously, for pain of the cold. The knight upon Gringalet rode lonely beneath them, through marsh and mire, much troubled at heart lest he should fail to see the service of the Lord, who on that self-same night was born of a maiden for the cure of our grief; and therefore he said, sighing, "I beseech Thee, Lord, and Mary Thy gentle Mother, for some shelter where I may hear Mass, and Thy mattins at morn. This I ask meekly, and thereto I pray my Paternoster, Ave, and Credo." Thus he rode praying, and lamenting his misdeeds, and he crossed himself, and said, "May the Cross of Christ speed me."

Now that knight had crossed himself but thrice ere he was aware in the wood of a dwelling within a moat, above a lawn, on a mound surrounded by many mighty trees that stood round the moat. 'Twas the fairest castle that ever a knight owned[9]; built in a meadow with a park all about it, and a spiked palisade, closely driven, that enclosed the trees for more than two miles. The knight was ware of the hold from the side, as it shone through the oaks. Then he lifted off his helmet, and thanked Christ and S. Julian that they had courteously granted his prayer, and hearkened to his cry. "Now," quoth the knight, "I beseech ye, grant me fair hostel." Then he pricked Gringalet with his golden spurs, and rode gaily towards the great gate, and came swiftly to the bridge end.

The bridge was drawn up and the gates close shut; the walls were strong and thick, so that they might fear no tempest. The knight on his charger abode on the bank of the deep double ditch that surrounded the castle. The walls were set deep in the water, and rose aloft to a wondrous height; they were of hard hewn stone up to the corbels, which were adorned beneath the battlements with fair carvings, and turrets set in between with many a loophole; a better barbican Sir Gawain had never looked upon. And within he beheld the high hall, with its tower and many windows with carven cornices, and chalk-white chimneys on the turreted roofs that shone fair in the sun. And everywhere, thickly scattered on the castle battlements, were pinnacles, so many that it seemed as if it were all wrought out of paper, so white was it.

The knight on his steed deemed it fair enough, if he might come to be sheltered within it to lodge there while that the Holy-day lasted. He called aloud, and soon there came a porter of kindly countenance, who stood on the wall and greeted this knight and asked his errand.

"Good sir," quoth Gawain, "wilt thou go mine errand to the high lord of the castle, and crave for me lodging?"

"Yea, by S. Peter," quoth the porter. "In sooth I trow that ye be welcome to dwell here so long as it may like ye."

Then he went, and came again swiftly, and many folk with him to receive the knight. They let down the great drawbridge, and came forth and knelt on their knees on the cold earth to give him worthy welcome. They held wide open the great gates, and courteously he bid them rise, and rode over the bridge. Then men came to him and held his stirrup while he dismounted, and took and stabled his steed. There came down knights and squires to bring the guest with joy to the hall. When he raised his helmet there were many to take it from his hand, fain to serve him, and they took from him sword and shield.

Sir Gawain gave good greeting to the noble and the mighty men who came to do him honour. Clad in his shining armour they led him to the hall, where a great fire burnt brightly on the floor; and the lord of the household came forth from his chamber to meet the hero fitly. He spake to the knight, and said: "Ye are welcome to do here as it likes ye. All that is here is your own to have at your will and disposal."

"Gramercy!" quote Gawain, "may Christ requite ye."

As friends that were fain each embraced the other; and Gawain looked on the knight who greeted him so kindly, and thought 'twas a bold warrior that owned that burg.

Of mighty stature he was, and of high age; broad and flowing was his beard, and of a bright hue. He was stalwart of limb, and strong in his stride, his face fiery red, and his speech free: in sooth he seemed one well fitted to be a leader of valiant men.

Then the lord led Sir Gawain to a chamber, and commanded folk to wait upon him, and at his bidding there came men enough who brought the guest to a fair bower. The bedding was noble, with curtains of pure silk wrought with gold, and wondrous coverings of fair cloth all embroidered. The curtains ran on ropes with rings of red gold, and the walls were hung with carpets of Orient, and the same spread on the floor. There with mirthful speeches they took from the guest his byrny and all his shining armour, and brought him rich robes of the choicest in its stead. They were long and flowing, and became him well, and when he was clad in them all who looked on the hero thought that surely God had never made a fairer knight: he seemed as if he might be a prince without peer in the field where men strive in battle.

Then before the hearth-place, whereon the fire burned, they made ready a chair for Gawain, hung about with cloth and fair cushions; and there they cast around him a mantle of brown samite, richly embroidered and furred within with costly skins of ermine, with a hood of the same, and he seated himself in that rich seat, and warmed himself at the fire, and was cheered at heart. And while he sat thus the serving men set up a table on trestles, and covered it with a fair white cloth, and set thereon salt-cellar, and napkin, and silver spoons; and the knight washed at his will, and set him down to meat.

The folk served him courteously with many dishes seasoned of the best, a double portion. All kinds of fish were there, some baked in bread, some broiled on the embers, some sodden, some stewed and savoured with spices, with all sorts of cunning devices to his taste. And often he called it a feast, when they spake gaily to him all together, and said, "Now take ye this penance, and it shall be for your amendment." Much mirth thereof did Sir Gawain make.

Then they questioned that prince courteously of whence he came; and he told them that he was of the court of Arthur, who is the rich royal King of the Round Table, and that it was Gawain himself who was within their walls, and would keep Christmas with them, as the chance had fallen out. And when the lord of the castle heard those tidings he laughed aloud for gladness, and all men in that keep were joyful that they should be in the company of him to whom belonged all fame, and valour, and courtesy, and whose honour was praised above that of all men on earth. Each said softly to his fellow, "Now shall we see courteous bearing, and the manner of speech befitting courts. What charm lieth in gentle speech shall we learn without asking, since here we have welcomed the fine father of courtesy. God has surely shewn us His grace since He sends us such a guest as Gawain! When men shall sit and sing, blithe for Christ's birth, this knight shall bring us to the knowledge of fair manners, and it may be that hearing him we may learn the cunning speech of love."

By the time the knight had risen from dinner it was near nightfall. Then chaplains took their way to the chapel, and rang loudly, even as they should, for the solemn evensong of the high feast. Thither went the lord, and the lady also, and entered with her maidens into a comely closet, and thither also went Gawain. Then the lord took him by the sleeve and led him to a seat, and called him by his name, and told him he was of all men in the world the most welcome. And Sir Gawain thanked him truly, and each kissed the other, and they sat gravely together throughout the service.

Then was the lady fain to look upon that knight; and she came forth from her closet with many fair maidens. The fairest of ladies was she in face, and figure, and colouring, fairer even than Guinevere, so the knight thought. She came through the chancel to greet the hero, another lady held her by the left hand, older than she, and seemingly of high estate, with many nobles about her. But unlike to look upon were those ladies, for if the younger were fair, the elder was yellow. Rich red were the cheeks of the one, rough and wrinkled those of the other; the kerchiefs of the one were broidered with many glistening pearls, her throat and neck bare, and whiter than the snow that lies on the hills; the neck of the other was swathed in a gorget, with a white wimple over her black chin. Her forehead was wrapped in silk with many folds, worked with knots, so that naught of her was seen save her black brows, her eyes, her nose and her lips, and those were bleared, and ill to look upon. A worshipful lady in sooth one might call her! In figure was she short and broad, and thickly made—far fairer to behold was she whom she led by the hand.

When Gawain beheld that fair lady, who looked at him graciously, with leave of the lord he went towards them, and, bowing low, he greeted the elder, but the younger and fairer he took lightly in his arms, and kissed her courteously, and greeted her in knightly wise. Then she hailed him as friend, and he quickly prayed to be counted as her servant, if she so willed. Then they took him between them, and talking, led him to the chamber, to the hearth, and bade them bring spices, and they brought them in plenty with the good wine that was wont to be drunk at such seasons. Then the lord sprang to his feet and bade them make merry, and took off his hood, and hung it on a spear, and bade him win the worship thereof who should make most mirth that Christmas-tide. "And I shall try, by my faith, to fool it with the best, by the help of my friends, ere I lose my raiment." Thus with gay words the lord made trial to gladden Gawain with jests that night, till it was time to bid them light the tapers, and Sir Gawain took leave of them and gat him to rest.

In the morn when all men call to mind how Christ our Lord was born on earth to die for us, there is joy, for His sake, in all dwellings of the world; and so was there here on that day. For high feast was held, with many dainties and cunningly cooked messes. On the daïs sat gallant men, clad in their best. The ancient dame sat on the high seat, with the lord of the castle beside her. Gawain and the fair lady sat together, even in the midst of the board, when the feast was served; and so throughout all the hall each sat in his degree, and was served in order. There was meat, there was mirth, there was much joy, so that to tell thereof would take me too long, though peradventure I might strive to declare it. But Gawain and that fair lady had much joy of each other's company through her sweet words and courteous converse. And there was music made before each prince, trumpets and drums, and merry piping; each man hearkened his minstrel, and they too hearkened theirs.

So they held high feast that day and the next, and the third day thereafter, and the joy on S. John's Day was fair to hearken, for 'twas the last of the feast and the guests would depart in the grey of the morning. Therefore they awoke early, and drank wine, and danced fair carols, and at last, when it was late, each man took his leave to wend early on his way. Gawain would bid his host farewell, but the lord took him by the hand, and led him to his own chamber beside the hearth, and there he thanked him for the favour he had shown him in honouring his dwelling at that high season, and gladdening his castle with his fair countenance. "I wis, sir, that while I live I shall be held the worthier that Gawain has been my guest at God's own feast."

"Gramercy, sir," quoth Gawain, "in good faith, all the honour is yours, may the High King give it you, and I am but at your will to work your behest, inasmuch as I am beholden to you in great and small by rights."

Then the lord did his best to persuade the knight to tarry with him, but Gawain answered that he might in no wise do so. Then the host asked him courteously what stern behest had driven him at the holy season from the king's court, to fare all alone, ere yet the feast was ended?

"Forsooth," quoth the knight, "ye say but the truth: 'tis a high quest and a pressing that hath brought me afield, for I am summoned myself to a certain place, and I know not whither in the world I may wend to find it; so help me Christ, I would give all the kingdom of Logres an I might find it by New Year's morn. Therefore, sir, I make request of you that ye tell me truly if ye ever heard word of the Green Chapel, where it may be found, and the Green Knight that keeps it. For I am pledged by solemn compact sworn between us to meet that knight at the New Year if so I were on life; and of that same New Year it wants but little—I'faith, I would look on that hero more joyfully than on any other fair sight! Therefore, by your will, it behoves me to leave you, for I have but barely three days, and I would as fain fall dead as fail of mine errand."

Then the lord quoth, laughing, "Now must ye needs stay, for I will show you your goal, the Green Chapel, ere your term be at an end, have ye no fear! But ye can take your ease, friend, in your bed, till the fourth day, and go forth on the first of the year and come to that place at mid-morn to do as ye will. Dwell here till New Year's Day, and then rise and set forth, and ye shall be set in the way; 'tis not two miles hence."

Then was Gawain glad, and he laughed gaily. "Now I thank you for this above all else. Now my quest is achieved I will dwell here at your will, and otherwise do as ye shall ask."

Then the lord took him, and set him beside him, and bade the ladies be fetched for their greater pleasure, tho' between themselves they had solace. The lord, for gladness, made merry jest, even as one who wist not what to do for joy; and he cried aloud to the knight, "Ye have promised to do the thing I bid ye: will ye hold to this behest, here, at once?"

"Yea, forsooth," said that true knight, "while I abide in your burg I am bound by your behest."

"Ye have travelled from far," said the host, "and since then ye have waked with me, ye are not well refreshed by rest and sleep, as I know. Ye shall therefore abide in your chamber, and lie at your ease tomorrow at Mass-tide, and go to meat when ye will with my wife, who shall sit with you, and comfort you with her company till I return; and I shall rise early and go forth to the chase." And Gawain agreed to all this courteously.

"Sir knight," quoth the host, "we shall make a covenant. Whatsoever I win in the wood shall be yours, and whatever may fall to your share, that shall ye exchange for it. Let us swear, friend, to make this exchange, however our hap may be, for worse or for better."

"I grant ye your will," quoth Gawain the good; "if ye list so to do, it liketh me well."

"Bring hither the wine-cup, the bargain is made," so said the lord of that castle. They laughed each one, and drank of the wine, and made merry, these lords and ladies, as it pleased them. Then with gay talk and merry jest they arose, and stood, and spoke softly, and kissed courteously, and took leave of each other. With burning torches, and many a serving-man, was each led to his couch; yet ere they gat them to bed the old lord oft repeated their covenant, for he knew well how to make sport.

FULL EARLY, ERE daylight, the folk rose up; the guests who would depart called their grooms, and they made them ready, and saddled the steeds, tightened up the girths, and trussed up their mails. The knights, all arrayed for riding, leapt up lightly, and took their bridles, and each rode his way as pleased him best.

The lord of the land was not the last. Ready for the chase, with many of his men, he ate a sop hastily when he had heard Mass, and then with blast of the bugle fared forth to the field.[10] He and his nobles were to horse ere daylight glimmered upon the earth.

Then the huntsmen coupled their hounds, unclosed the kennel door, and called them out. They blew three blasts gaily on the bugles, the hounds bayed fiercely, and they that would go a-hunting checked and chastised them. A hundred hunters there were of the best, so I have heard tell. Then the trackers gat them to the trysting-place and uncoupled the hounds, and forest rang again with their gay blasts.

At the first sound of the hunt the game quaked for fear, and fled, trembling, along the vale. They betook them to the heights, but the liers in wait turned them back with loud cries; the harts they let pass them, and the stags with their spreading antlers, for the lord had forbidden that they should be slain, but the hinds and the does they turned back, and drave down into the valleys. Then might ye see much shooting of arrows. As the deer fled under the boughs a broad whistling shaft smote and wounded each sorely, so that, wounded and bleeding, they fell dying on the banks. The hounds followed swiftly on their tracks, and hunters, blowing the horn, sped after them with ringing shouts as if the cliffs burst asunder. What game escaped those that shot was run down at the outer ring. Thus were they driven on the hills, and harassed at the waters, so well did the men know their work, and the greyhounds were so great and swift that they ran them down as fast as the hunters could slay them. Thus the lord passed the day in mirth and joyfulness, even to nightfall.

So the lord roamed the woods, and Gawain, that good night, lay ever a-bed, curtained about, under the costly coverlet, while the daylight gleamed on the walls. And as he lay half slumbering, he heard a little sound at the door, and he raised his head, and caught back a corner of the curtain, and waited to see what it might be. It was the lovely lady, the lord's wife; she shut the door softly behind her, and turned towards the bed; and Gawain was shamed, laid him down softly and made as if he slept. And she came lightly to the bedside, within the curtain, and sat herself down beside him, to wait till he wakened. The knight lay there awhile, and marvelled within himself what her coming might betoken; and he said to himself, "'Twere more seemly if I asked her what hath brought her hither." Then he made feint to waken, and turned towards her, and opened his eyes as one astonished, and crossed himself; and she looked on him laughing, with her cheeks red and white, lovely to behold, and small smiling lips.

"Good morrow, Sir Gawain," said that fair lady; "ye are but a careless sleeper, since one can enter thus. Now are ye taken unawares, and lest ye escape me I shall bind you in your bed; of that be ye assured!" Laughing, she spake these words.

"Good morrow, fair lady," quoth Gawain blithely. "I will do your will, as it likes me well. For I yield me readily, and pray your grace, and that is best, by my faith, since I needs must do so." Thus he jested again, laughing. "But an ye would, fair lady, grant me this grace that ye pray your prisoner to rise. I would get me from bed, and array me better, then could I talk with ye in more comfort."

"Nay, forsooth, fair sir," quoth the lady, "ye shall not rise, I will rede ye better. I shall keep ye here, since ye can do no other, and talk with my knight whom I have captured. For I know well that ye are Sir Gawain, whom all the world worships, wheresoever ye may ride. Your honour and your courtesy are praised by lords and ladies, by all who live. Now ye are here and we are alone, my lord and his men are afield; the serving men in their beds, and my maidens also, and the door shut upon us. And since in this hour I have him that all men love, I shall use my time well with speech, while it lasts. Ye are welcome to my company, for it behoves me in sooth to be your servant."

"In good faith," quoth Gawain, "I think me that I am not him of whom ye speak, for unworthy am I of such service as ye here proffer. In sooth, I were glad if I might set myself by word or service to your pleasure; a pure joy would it be to me!"

"In good faith, Sir Gawain," quoth the gay lady, "the praise and the prowess that pleases all ladies I lack them not, nor hold them light; yet are there ladies enough who would liever now have the knight in their hold, as I have ye here, to dally with your courteous words, to bring them comfort and to ease their cares, than much of the treasure and the gold that are theirs. And now, through the grace of Him who upholds the heavens, I have wholly in my power that which they all desire!"

Thus the lady, fair to look upon, made him great cheer, and Sir Gawain, with modest words, answered her again: "Madam," he quoth, "may Mary requite ye, for in good faith I have found in ye a noble frankness. Much courtesy have other folk shown me, but the honour they have done me is naught to the worship of yourself, who knoweth but good."

"By Mary," quoth the lady, "I think otherwise; for were I worth all the women alive, and had I the wealth of the world in my hand, and might choose me a lord to my liking, then, for all that I have seen in ye, Sir Knight, of beauty and courtesy and blithe semblance, and for all that I have hearkened and hold for true, there should be no knight on earth to be chosen before ye!"

"Well I wot," quoth Sir Gawain, "that ye have chosen a better; but I am proud that ye should so prize me, and as your servant do I hold ye my sovereign, and your knight am I, and may Christ reward ye."

So they talked of many matters till mid-morn was past, and ever the lady made as though she loved him, and the knight turned her speech aside. For though she were the brightest of maidens, yet had he forborne to shew her love for the danger that awaited him, and the blow that must be given without delay.

Then the lady prayed her leave from him, and he granted it readily. And she gave [the text reads "have"] him good-day, with laughing glance, but he must needs marvel at her words:

"Now He that speeds fair speech reward ye this disport; but that ye be Gawain my mind misdoubts me greatly."

"Wherefore?" quoth the knight quickly, fearing lest he had lacked in some courtesy.

And the lady spake: "So true a knight as Gawain is holden, and one so perfect in courtesy, would never have tarried so long with a lady but he would of his courtesy have craved a kiss at parting."

Then quoth Gawain, "I wot I will do even as it may please ye, and kiss at your commandment, as a true knight should who forbears to ask for fear of displeasure."

At that she came near and bent down and kissed the knight, and each commended the other to Christ, and she went forth from the chamber softly.

Then Sir Gawain arose and called his chamberlain and chose his garments, and when he was ready he gat him forth to Mass, and then went to meat, and made merry all day till the rising of the moon, and never had a knight fairer lodging than had he with those two noble ladies, the elder and the younger.

And even the lord of the land chased the hinds through holt and heath till eventide, and then with much blowing of bugles and baying of hounds they bore the game homeward; and by the time daylight was done all the folk had returned to that fair castle. And when the lord and Sir Gawain met together, then were they both well pleased. The lord commanded them all to assemble in the great hall, and the ladies to descend with their maidens, and there, before them all, he bade the men fetch in the spoil of the day's hunting, and he called unto Gawain, and counted the tale of the beasts, and showed them unto him, and said, "What think ye of this game, Sir Knight? Have I deserved of ye thanks for my woodcraft?"

"Yea, I wis," quoth the other, "here is the fairest spoil I have seen this seven year in the winter season."

"And all this do I give ye, Gawain," quoth the host, "for by accord of covenant ye may claim it as your own."

"That is sooth," quoth the other, "I grant you that same; and I have fairly won this within walls, and with as good will do I yield it to ye." With that he clasped his hands round the lord's neck and kissed him as courteously as he might. "Take ye here my spoils, no more have I won; ye should have it freely, though it were greater than this."

"'Tis good," said the host, "gramercy thereof. Yet were I fain to know where ye won this same favour, and if it were by your own wit?"

"Nay," answered Gawain, "that was not in the bond. Ask me no more: ye have taken what was yours by right, be content with that."

They laughed and jested together, and sat them down to supper, where they were served with many dainties; and after supper they sat by the hearth, and wine was served out to them; and oft in their jesting they promised to observe on the morrow the same covenant that they had made before, and whatever chance might betide to exchange their spoil, be it much or little, when they met at night. Thus they renewed their bargain before the whole court, and then the night-drink was served, and each courteously took leave of the other and gat him to bed.

By the time the cock had crowed thrice the lord of the castle had left his bed; Mass was sung and meat fitly served. The folk were forth to the wood ere the day broke, with hound and horn they rode over the plain, and uncoupled their dogs among the thorns. Soon they struck on the scent, and the hunt cheered on the hounds who were first to seize it, urging them with shouts. The others hastened to the cry, forty at once, and there rose such a clamour from the pack that the rocks rang again. The huntsmen spurred them on with shouting and blasts of the horn; and the hounds drew together to a thicket betwixt the water and a high crag in the cliff beneath the hillside. There where the rough rock fell ruggedly they, the huntsmen, fared to the finding, and cast about round the hill and the thicket behind them. The knights wist well what beast was within, and would drive him forth with the bloodhounds. And as they beat the bushes, suddenly over the beaters there rushed forth a wondrous great and fierce boar, long since had he left the herd to roam by himself. Grunting, he cast many to the ground, and fled forth at his best speed, without more mischief. The men hallooed loudly and cried, *"Hay! Hay!"* and blew the horns to urge on the hounds, and rode swiftly after the boar. Many a time did he turn to bay and tare the hounds, and they yelped, and howled shrilly. Then the men made ready their arrows and shot at him, but the points were turned on his thick hide, and the barbs would not bite upon him, for the shafts shivered in pieces, and the head but leapt again wherever it hit.

But when the boar felt the stroke of the arrows he waxed mad with rage, and turned on the hunters and tare many, so that, affrightened, they fled before him. But the lord on a swift steed pursued him, blowing his bugle; as a gallant knight he rode through the woodland chasing the boar till the sun grew low.

So did the hunters this day, while Sir Gawain lay in his bed lapped in rich gear; and the lady forgat not to salute him, for early was she at his side, to cheer his mood.

She came to the bedside and looked on the knight, and Gawain gave her fit greeting, and she greeted him again with ready words, and sat her by his side and laughed, and with a sweet look she spoke to him:

"Sir, if ye be Gawain, I think it a wonder that ye be so stern and cold, and care not for the courtesies of friendship, but if one teach ye to know them ye cast the lesson out of your mind. Ye have soon forgotten what I taught ye yesterday, by all the truest tokens that I knew!"

"What is that?" quoth the knight. "I trow I know not. If it be sooth that ye say, then is the blame mine own."

"But I taught ye of kissing, " quoth the fair lady. "Wherever a fair countenance is shown him, it behoves a courteous knight quickly to claim a kiss."

"Nay, my dear," said Sir Gawain, "cease that speech; that durst I not do lest I were denied, for if I were forbidden I wot I were wrong did I further entreat."

"I' faith," quoth the lady merrily, "ye may not be forbid, ye are strong enough to constrain by strength an ye will, were any so discourteous as to give ye denial."

"Yea, by Heaven," said Gawain, "ye speak well; but threats profit little in the land where I dwell, and so with a gift that is given not of good will! I am at your commandment to kiss when ye like, to take or to leave as ye list."

Then the lady bent her down and kissed him courteously.

And as they spake together she said, "I would learn somewhat from ye, an ye would not be wroth, for young ye bare and fair, and so courteous and knightly as ye are known to be, the head of all chivalry, and versed in all wisdom of love and war—'tis ever told of true knights how they adventured their lives for their true love, and endured hardships for her favours, and avenged her with valour, and eased her sorrows, and brought joy to her bower; and ye are the fairest knight of your time, and your fame and your honour are everywhere, yet I have sat by ye here twice, and never a word have I heard of love! Ye who are so courteous and skilled in such love ought surely to teach one so young and unskilled some little craft of true love! Why are ye so unlearned who art otherwise so famous? Or is it that ye deemed me unworthy to hearken to your teaching? For shame, Sir Knight! I come hither alone and sit at your side to learn of ye some skill; teach me of your wit, while my lord is from home."

"In good faith," quoth Gawain, "great is my joy and my profit that so fair a lady as ye are should deign to come hither, and trouble ye with so poor a man, and make sport with your knight with kindly countenance, it pleaseth me much. But that I, in my turn, should take it upon me to tell of love and such like matters to ye who know more by half, or a hundred fold, of such craft than I do, or ever shall in all my lifetime, by my troth 'twere folly indeed! I will work your will to the best of my might as I am bounden, and evermore will I be your servant, so help me Christ!"

Then often with guile she questioned that knight that she might win him to woo her, but he defended himself so fairly that none might in any wise blame him, and naught but bliss and harmless jesting was there between them. They laughed and talked together till at last she kissed him, and craved her leave of him, and went her way.

Then the knight arose and went forth to Mass, and afterward dinner was served and he sat and spake with the ladies all day. But the lord of the castle rode ever over the land chasing the wild boar, that fled through the thickets, slaying the best of his hounds and breaking their backs in sunder; till at last he was so weary he might run no longer, but made for a hole in a mound by a rock. He got the mound at his back and faced the hounds, whetting his white tusks and foaming at the mouth. The huntsmen stood aloof, fearing to draw nigh him; so many of them had been already wounded that they were loth to be torn with his tusks, so fierce he was and mad with rage. At length the lord himself came up, and saw the beast at bay, and the men standing aloof. Then quickly he sprang to the ground and drew out a bright blade, and waded through the stream to the boar.

When the beast was aware of the knight with weapon in hand, he set up his bristles and snorted loudly, and many feared for their lord lest he should be slain. Then the boar leapt upon the knight so that beast and man were one atop of the other in the water; but the boar had the worst of it, for the man had marked, even as he sprang, and set the point of his brand to the beast's chest, and drove it up to the hilt, so that the heart was split in twain, and the boar fell snarling, and was swept down by the water to where a hundred hounds seized on him, and the men drew him to shore for the dogs to slay.

Then was there loud blowing of horns and baying of hounds, the huntsmen smote off the boar's head, and hung the carcase by the four feet to a stout pole, and so went on their way homewards. The head they bore before the lord himself, who had slain the beast at the ford by force of his strong hand.

It seemed him o'er long ere he saw Sir Gawain in the hall, and he called, and the guest came to take that which fell to his share. And when he saw Gawain the lord laughed aloud, and bade them call the ladies and the household together, and he showed them the game, and told them the tale, how they hunted the wild boar through the woods, and of his length and breadth and height; and Sir Gawain commended his deeds and praised him for his valour, well proven, for so mighty a beast had he never seen before.

Then they handled the huge head, and the lord said aloud, "Now, Gawain, this game is your own by sure covenant, as ye right well know."

"'Tis sooth," quoth the knight, "and as truly will I give ye all I have gained." He took the host round the neck, and kissed him courteously twice. "Now are we quits," he said, "this eventide, of all the covenants that we made since I came hither."

And the lord answered, "By S. Giles, ye are the best I know; ye will be rich in a short space if ye drive such bargains!"

Then they set up the tables on trestles, and covered them with fair cloths, and lit waxen tapers on the walls. The knights sat and were served in the hall, and much game and glee was there round the hearth, with many songs, both at supper and after; song of Christmas, and new carols, with all the mirth one may think of. And ever that lovely lady sat by the knight, and with still stolen looks made such feint of pleasing him, that Gawain marvelled much, and was wroth with himself, but he could not for his courtesy return her fair glances, but dealt with her cunningly, however she might strive to wrest the thing.

When they had tarried in the hall so long as it seemed them good, they turned to the inner chamber and the wide hearthplace, and there they drank wine, and the host proffered to renew the covenant for New Year's Eve; but the knight craved leave to depart on the morrow, for it was nigh to the term when he must fulfil his pledge. But the lord would withhold him from so doing, and prayed him to tarry, and said,

"As I am a true knight I swear my troth that ye shall come to the Green Chapel to achieve your task on New Year's morn, long before prime. Therefore abide ye in your bed, and I will hunt in this wood, and hold ye to the covenant to exchange with me against all the spoil I may bring hither. For twice have I tried ye, and found ye true, and the morrow shall be the third time and the best. Make we merry now while we may, and think on joy, for misfortune may take a man whensoever it wills."

Then Gawain granted his request, and they brought them drink, and they gat them with lights to bed.

Sir Gawain lay and slept softly, but the lord, who was keen on woodcraft, was afoot early. After Mass he and his men ate a morsel, and he asked for his steed; all the knights who should ride with him were already mounted before the hall gates.

'Twas a fair frosty morning, for the sun rose red in ruddy vapour, and the welkin was clear of clouds. The hunters scattered them by a forest side, and the rocks rang again with the blast of their horns. Some came on the scent of a fox, and a hound gave tongue; the huntsmen shouted, and the pack followed in a crowd on the trail. The fox ran before them, and when they saw him they pursued him with noise and much shouting, and he wound and turned through many a thick grove, often cowering and hearkening in a hedge. At last by a little ditch he leapt out of a spinney, stole away slily by a copse path, and so out of the wood and away from the hounds. But he went, ere he wist, to a chosen tryst, and three started forth on him at once, so he must needs double back, and betake him to the wood again.

Then was it joyful to hearken to the hounds; when all the pack had met together and had sight of their game they made as loud a din as if all the lofty cliffs had fallen clattering together. The huntsmen shouted and threatened, and followed close upon him so that he might scarce escape, but Reynard was wily, and he turned and doubled upon them, and led the lord and his men over the hills, now on the slopes, now in the vales, while the knight at home slept through the cold morning beneath his costly curtains.

But the fair lady of the castle rose betimes, and clad herself in a rich mantle that reached even to the ground, left her throat and her fair neck bare, and was bordered and lined with costly furs. On her head she wore no golden circlet, but a network of precious stones, that gleamed and shone through her tresses in clusters of twenty together. Thus she came into the chamber, closed the door after her, and set open a window, and called to him gaily, "Sir Knight, how may ye sleep? The morning is so fair."

Sir Gawain was deep in slumber, and in his dream he vexed him much for the destiny that should befall him on the morrow, when he should meet the knight at the Green Chapel, and abide his blow; but when the lady spake he heard her, and came to himself, and roused from his dream and answered swiftly. The lady came laughing, and kissed him courteously, and he welcomed her fittingly with a cheerful countenance. He saw her so glorious and gaily dressed, so faultless of features and complexion, that it warmed his heart to look upon her.

They spake to each other smiling, and all was bliss and good cheer between them. They exchanged fair words, and much happiness was therein, yet was there a gulf between them, and she might win no more of her knight, for that gallant prince watched well his words—he would neither take her love, nor frankly refuse it. He cared for his courtesy, lest he be deemed churlish, and yet more for his honour lest he be traitor to his host. "God forbid," quoth he to himself, "that it should so befall." Thus with courteous words did he set aside all the special speeches that came from her lips.

Then spake the lady to the knight, "Ye deserve blame if ye hold not that lady who sits beside ye above all else in the world, if ye have not already a love whom ye hold dearer, and like better, and have sworn such firm faith to that lady that ye care not to loose it—and that am I now fain to believe. And now I pray ye straitly that ye tell me that in truth, and hide it not."

And the knight answered, "By S. John" (and he smiled as he spake) "no such love have I, nor do I think to have yet awhile."

"That is the worst word I may hear," quoth the lady, "but in sooth I have mine answer; kiss me now courteously, and I will go hence; I can but mourn as a maiden that loves much."

Sighing, she stooped down and kissed him, and then she rose up and spake as she stood, "Now, dear, at our parting do me this grace: give me some gift, if it were but thy glove, that I may bethink me of my knight, and lessen my mourning."

"Now, I wis," quoth the knight, "I would that I had here the most precious thing that I possess on earth that I might leave ye as love-token, great or small, for ye have deserved forsooth more reward than I might give ye. But it is not to your honour to have at this time a glove for reward as gift from Gawain, and I am here on a strange errand, and have no man with me, nor mails with goodly things—that mislikes me much, lady, at this time; but each man must fare as he is taken, if for sorrow and ill."

"Nay, knight highly honoured," quoth that lovesome lady, "though I have naught of yours, yet shall ye have somewhat of mine." With that she reached him a ring of red gold with a sparkling stone therein, that shone even as the sun (wit ye well, it was worth many marks); but the knight refused it, and spake readily,

"I will take no gift, lady, at this time. I have none to give, and none will I take."

She prayed him to take it, but he refused her prayer, and sware in sooth that he would not have it.

The lady was sorely vexed, and said, "If ye refuse my ring as too costly, that ye will not be so highly beholden to me, I will give you my girdle[11] as a lesser gift." With that she loosened a lace that was fastened at her side, knit upon her kirtle under her mantle. It was wrought of green silk, and gold, only braided by the fingers, and that she offered to the knight, and besought him though it were of little worth that he would take it, and he said nay, he would touch neither gold nor gear ere God give him grace to achieve the adventure for which he had come hither. "And therefore, I pray ye, displease ye not, and ask me no longer, for I may not grant it. I am dearly beholden to ye for the favour ye have shown me, and ever, in heat and cold, will I be your true servant."

"Now," said the lady, "ye refuse this silk, for it is simple in itself, and so it seems, indeed; lo, it is small to look upon and less in cost, but whoso knew the virtue that is knit therein he would, peradventure, value it more highly. For whatever knight is girded with this green lace, while he bears it knotted about him there is no man under heaven can overcome him, for he may not be slain for any magic on earth."

Then Gawain bethought him, and it came into his heart that this were a jewel for the jeopardy that awaited him when he came to the Green Chapel to seek the return blow—could he so order it that he should escape unslain, 'twere a craft worth trying. Then he bare with her chiding, and let her say her say, and she pressed the girdle on him and prayed him to take it, and he granted her prayer, and she gave it him with good will, and besought him for her sake never to reveal it but to hide it loyally from her lord; and the knight agreed that never should any man know it, save they two alone. He thanked her often and heartily, and she kissed him for the third time.

Then she took her leave of him, and when she was gone Sir Gawain arose, and clad him in rich attire, and took the girdle, and knotted it round him, and hid it beneath his robes. Then he took his way to the chapel, and sought out a priest privily and prayed him to teach him better how his soul might be saved when he should go hence; and there he shrived him, and showed his misdeeds, both great and small, and besought mercy and craved absolution; and the priest assoiled him, and set him as clean as if Doomsday had been on the morrow. And afterwards Sir Gawain made him merry with the ladies, with carols, and all kinds of joy, as never he did but that one day, even to nightfall; and all the men marvelled at him, and said that never since he came thither had he been so merry.

Meanwhile the lord of the castle was abroad chasing the fox; awhile he lost him, and as he rode through a spinny he heard the hounds near at hand, and Reynard came creeping through a thick grove, with all the pack at his heels. Then the lord drew out his shining brand, and cast it at the beast, and the fox swerved aside for the sharp edge, and would have doubled back, but a hound was on him ere he might turn, and right before the horse's feet they all fell on him, and worried him fiercely, snarling the while.

Then the lord leapt from his saddle, and caught the fox from the jaws, and held it aloft over his head, and hallooed loudly, and many brave hounds bayed as they beheld it; and the hunters hied them thither, blowing their horns; all that bare bugles blew them at once, and all the others shouted. 'Twas the merriest meeting that ever men heard, the clamour that was raised at the death of the fox. They rewarded the hounds, stroking them and rubbing their heads, and took Reynard and stripped him of his coat; then blowing their horns, they turned them homewards, for it was nigh nightfall.

The lord was gladsome at his return, and found a bright fire on the hearth, and the knight beside it, the good Sir Gawain, who was in joyous mood for the pleasure he had had with the ladies. He wore a robe of blue, that reached even to the ground, and a surcoat richly furred, that became him well. A hood like to the surcoat fell on his shoulders, and all alike were done about with fur. He met the host in the midst of the floor, and jesting, he greeted him, and said, "Now shall I be first to fulfil our covenant which we made together when there was no lack of wine." Then he embraced the knight, and kissed him thrice, as solemnly as he might.

"Of a sooth," quoth the other, "ye have good luck in the matter of this covenant, if ye made a good exchange!"

"Yea, it matters naught of the exchange," quoth Gawain, "since what I owe is swiftly paid."

"Marry," said the other, "mine is behind, for I have hunted all this day, and naught have I got but this foul fox-skin, and that is but poor payment for three such kisses as ye have here given me."

"Enough," quoth Sir Gawain, "I thank ye, by the Rood."

Then the lord told them of his hunting, and how the fox had been slain.

With mirth and minstrelsy, and dainties at their will, they made them as merry as a folk well might till 'twas time for them to sever, for at last they must needs betake them to their beds. Then the knight took his leave of the lord, and thanked him fairly.

"For the fair sojourn that I have had here at this high feast may the High King give ye honour. I give ye myself, as one of your servants, if ye so like; for I must needs, as you know, go hence with the morn, and ye will give me, as ye promised, a guide to show me the way to the Green Chapel, an God will suffer me on New Year's Day to deal the doom of my weird."

"By my faith," quoth the host, "all that ever I promised, that shall I keep with good will." Then he gave him a servant to set him in the way, and lead him by the downs, that he should have no need to ford the stream, and should fare by the shortest road through the groves; and Gawain thanked the lord for the honour done him. Then he would take leave of the ladies, and courteously he kissed them, and spake, praying them to receive his thanks, and they made like reply; then with many sighs they commended him to Christ, and he departed courteously from that folk. Each man that he met he thanked him for his service and his solace, and the pains he had been at to do his will; and each found it as hard to part from the knight as if he had ever dwelt with him.

Then they led him with torches to his chamber, and brought him to his bed to rest. That he slept soundly I may not say, for the morrow gave him much to think on. Let him rest awhile, for he was near that which he sought, and if ye will but listen to me I will tell ye how it fared with him thereafter.

NOW THE NEW YEAR drew nigh, and the night passed, and the day chased the darkness, as is God's will; but wild weather wakened therewith. The clouds cast the cold to the earth, with enough of the north to slay them that lacked clothing. The snow drave smartly, and the whistling wind blew from the heights, and made great drifts in the valleys. The knight, lying in his bed, listened, for though his eyes were shut, he might sleep but little, and hearkened every cock that crew.

He arose ere the day broke, by the light of a lamp that burned in his chamber, and called to his chamberlain, bidding him bring his armour and saddle his steed. The other gat him up, and fetched his garments, and robed Sir Gawain.

First he clad him in his clothes to keep off the cold, and then in his harness, which was well and fairly kept. Both hauberk and plates were well burnished, the rings of the rich byrny freed from rust, and all as fresh as at first, so that the knight was fain to thank them. Then he did on each piece, and bade them bring his steed, while he put the fairest raiment on himself; his coat with its fair cognizance, adorned with precious stones upon velvet, with broidered seams, and all furred within with costly skins. And he left not the lace, the lady's gift, that Gawain forgot not, for his own good. When he had girded on his sword he wrapped the gift twice about him, swathed around his waist. The girdle of green silk set gaily and well upon the royal red cloth, rich to behold, but the knight ware it not for pride of the pendants, polished though they were with fair gold that gleamed brightly on the ends, but to save himself from sword and knife, when it behoved him to abide his hurt without question. With that the hero went forth, and thanked that kindly folk full often.

Then was Gringalet ready, that was great and strong, and had been well cared for and tended in every wise; in fair condition was that proud steed, and fit for a journey. Then Gawain went to him, and looked on his coat, and said by his sooth, "There is a folk in this place that thinketh on honour; much joy may they have, and the lord who maintains them, and may all good betide that lovely lady all her life long. Since they for charity cherish a guest, and hold honour in their hands, may He who holds the heaven on high requite them, and also ye all. And if I might live anywhere on earth, I would give ye full reward, readily, if so I might." Then he set foot in the stirrup and bestrode his steed, and his squire gave him his shield, which he laid on his shoulder. Then he smote Gringalet with his golden spurs, and the steed pranced on the stones and would stand no longer.

By that his man was mounted, who bare his spear and lance, and Gawain quoth, "I commend this castle to Christ, may He give it ever good fortune." Then the drawbridge was let down, and the broad gates unbarred and opened on both sides; the knight crossed himself, and passed through the gateway, and praised the porter, who knelt before the prince, and gave him good-day, and commended him to God. Thus the knight went on his way with the one man who should guide him to that dread place where he should receive rueful payment.

The two went by hedges where the boughs were bare, and climbed the cliffs where the cold clings. Naught fell from the heavens, but 'twas ill beneath them; mist brooded over the moor and hung on the mountains; each hill had a cap, a great cloak, of mist. The streams foamed and bubbled between their banks, dashing sparkling on the shores where they shelved downwards. Rugged and dangerous was the way through the woods, till it was time for the sun-rising. Then were they on a high hill; the snow lay white beside them, and the man who rode with Gawain drew rein by his master.

"Sir," he said, "I have brought ye hither, and now ye are not far from the place that ye have sought so specially. But I will tell ye for sooth, since I know ye well, and ye are such a knight as I well love, would ye follow my counsel ye would fare the better. The place whither ye go is accounted full perilous, for he who liveth in that waste is the worst on earth, for he is strong and fierce, and loveth to deal mighty blows; taller is he than any man on earth, and greater of frame than any four in Arthur's court, or in any other. And this is his custom at the Green Chapel; there may no man pass by that place, however proud his arms, but he does him to death by force of his hand, for he is a discourteous knight, and shews no mercy. Be he churl or chaplain who rides by that chapel, monk or mass priest, or any man else, he thinks it as pleasant to slay them as to pass alive himself. Therefore, I tell ye, as sooth as ye sit in saddle, if ye come there and that knight know it, ye shall be slain, though ye had twenty lives; trow me that truly! He has dwelt here full long and seen many a combat; ye may not defend ye against his blows. Therefore, good Sir Gawain, let the man be, and get ye away some other road; for God's sake seek ye another land, and there may Christ speed ye! And I will hie me home again, and I promise ye further that I will swear by God and the saints, or any other oath ye please, that I will keep counsel faithfully, and never let any wit the tale that ye fled for fear of any man."

"Gramercy," quoth Gawain, but ill-pleased. "Good fortune be his who wishes me good, and that thou wouldst keep faith with me I will believe; but didst thou keep it never so truly, an I passed here and fled for fear as thou sayest, then were I a coward knight, and might not be held guiltless. So I will to the chapel let chance what may, and talk with that man, even as I may list, whether for weal or for woe as fate may have it. Fierce though he may be in fight, yet God knoweth well how to save His servants."

"Well," quoth the other, "now that ye have said so much that ye will take your own harm on yourself, and ye be pleased to lose your life, I will neither let nor keep ye. Have here your helm and the spear in your hand, and ride down this same road beside the rock till ye come to the bottom of the valley, and there look a little to the left hand, and ye shall see in that vale the chapel, and the grim man who keeps it. Now fare ye well, noble Gawain; for all the gold on earth I would not go with ye nor bear ye fellowship one step further." With that the man turned his bridle into the wood, smote the horse with his spurs as hard as he could, and galloped off, leaving the knight alone.

Quoth Gawain, "I will neither greet nor groan, but commend myself to God, and yield me to His will."

Then the knight spurred Gringalet, and rode adown the path close in by a bank beside a grove. So he rode through the rough thicket, right into the dale, and there he halted, for it seemed him wild enough. No sign of a chapel could he see, but high and burnt banks on either side and rough rugged crags with great stones above. An ill-looking place he thought it.

Then he drew in his horse and looked around to seek the chapel, but he saw none and thought it strange. Then he saw as it were a mound on a level space of land by a bank beside the stream where it ran swiftly, the water bubbled within as if boiling. The knight turned his steed to the mound, and lighted down and tied the rein to the branch of a linden; and he turned to the mound and walked round it, questioning with himself what it might be. It had a hole at the end and at either side, and was overgrown with clumps of grass, and it was hollow within as an old cave or the crevice of a crag; he knew not what it might be.

"Ah," quoth Gawain, "can this be the Green Chapel? Here might the devil say his mattins at midnight! Now I wis there is wizardry here. 'Tis an ugly oratory, all overgrown with grass, and 'twould well beseem that fellow in green to say his devotions on devil's wise. Now feel I in five wits, 'tis the foul fiend himself who hath set me this tryst, to destroy me here! This is a chapel of mischance: ill-luck betide it, 'tis the cursedest kirk that ever I came in!"

Helmet on head and lance in hand, he came up to the rough dwelling, when he heard over the high hill beyond the brook, as it were in a bank, a wondrous fierce noise, that rang in the cliff as if it would cleave asunder. 'Twas as if one ground a scythe on a grindstone, it whirred and whetted like water on a mill-wheel and rushed and rang, terrible to hear.

"By God," quoth Gawain, "I trow that gear is preparing for the knight who will meet me here. Alas! naught may help me, yet should my life be forfeit, I fear not a jot!" With that he called aloud. "Who waiteth in this place to give me tryst? Now is Gawain come hither: if any man will aught of him let him hasten hither now or never."

"Stay," quoth one on the bank above his head, "and ye shall speedily have that which I promised ye." Yet for a while the noise of whetting went on ere he appeared, and then he came forth from a cave in the crag with a fell weapon, a Danish axe newly dight, wherewith to deal the blow. An evil head it had, four feet large, no less, sharply ground, and bound to the handle by the lace that gleamed brightly. And the knight himself was all green as before, face and foot, locks and beard, but now he was afoot. When he came to the water he would not wade it, but sprang over with the pole of his axe, and strode boldly over the brent that was white with snow.

Sir Gawain went to meet him, but he made no low bow. The other said, "Now, fair sir, one may trust thee to keep tryst. Thou art welcome, Gawain, to my place. Thou hast timed thy coming as befits a true man. Thou knowest the covenant set between us: at this time twelve months agone thou didst take that which fell to thee, and I at this New Year will readily requite thee. We are in this valley, verily alone, here are no knights to sever us, do what we will. Have off thy helm from thine head, and have here thy pay; make me no more talking than I did then when thou didst strike off my head with one blow."

"Nay," quoth Gawain, "by God that gave me life, I shall make no moan whatever befall me, but make thou ready for the blow and I shall stand still and say never a word to thee, do as thou wilt."

With that he bent his head and shewed his neck all bare, and made as if he had no fear, for he would not be thought a-dread.

Then the Green Knight made him ready, and grasped his grim weapon to smite Gawain. With all his force he bore it aloft with a mighty feint of slaying him: had it fallen as straight as he aimed he who was ever doughty of deed had been slain by the blow. But Gawain swerved aside as the axe came gliding down to slay him as he stood, and shrank a little with the shoulders, for the sharp iron. The other heaved up the blade and rebuked the prince with many proud words:

"Thou art not Gawain," he said, "who is held so valiant, that never feared he man by hill or vale, but *thou* shrinkest for fear ere thou feelest hurt. Such cowardice did I never hear of Gawain! Neither did *I* flinch from thy blow, or make strife in King Arthur's hall. My head fell to my feet, and yet I fled not; but thou didst wax faint of heart ere any harm befell. Wherefore must I be deemed the braver knight."

Quoth Gawain, "I shrank once, but so will I no more, though an *my* head fall on the stones I cannot replace it. But haste, Sir Knight, by thy faith, and bring me to the point, deal me my destiny, and do it out of hand, for I will stand thee a stroke and move no more till thine axe have hit me—my troth on it."

"Have at thee, then," quoth the other, and heaved aloft the axe with fierce mien, as if he were mad. He struck at him fiercely but wounded him not, withholding his hand ere it might strike him.

Gawain abode the stroke, and flinched in no limb, but stood still as a stone or the stump of a tree that is fast rooted in the rocky ground with a hundred roots.

Then spake gaily the man in green, "So now thou hast thine heart whole it behoves me to smite. Hold aside thy hood that Arthur gave thee, and keep thy neck thus bent lest it cover it again."

Then Gawain said angrily, "Why talk on thus? Thou dost threaten too long. I hope thy heart misgives thee."

"For sooth," quoth the other, "so fiercely thou speakest I will no longer let thine errand wait its reward." Then he braced himself to strike, frowning with lips and brow, 'twas no marvel that it pleased but ill him who hoped for no rescue. He lifted the axe lightly and let it fall with the edge of the blade on the bare neck. Though he struck swiftly it hurt him no more than on the one side where it severed the skin. The sharp blade cut into the flesh so that the blood ran over his shoulder to the ground. And when the knight saw the blood staining the snow, he sprang forth, swift-foot, more than a spear's length, seized his helmet and set it on his head, cast his shield over his shoulder, drew out his bright sword, and spake boldly (never since he was born was he half so blithe), "Stop, Sir Knight, bid me no more blows. I have stood a stroke here without flinching, and if thou give me another, I shall requite thee, and give thee as good again. By the covenant made betwixt us in Arthur's hall but one blow falls to me here. Halt, therefore."

Then the Green Knight drew off from him and leaned on his axe, setting the shaft on the ground, and looked on Gawain as he stood all armed and faced him fearlessly—at heart it pleased him well. Then he spake merrily in a loud voice, and said to the knight, "Bold sir, be not so fierce, no man here hath done thee wrong, nor will do, save by covenant, as we made at

Arthur's court. I promised thee a blow and thou hast it—hold thyself well paid! I release thee of all other claims. If I had been so minded I might perchance have given thee a rougher buffet. First I menaced thee with a feigned one, and hurt thee not for the covenant that we made in the first night, and which thou didst hold truly. All the gain didst thou give me as a true man should. The other feint I proffered thee for the morrow: my fair wife kissed thee, and thou didst give me her kisses—for both those days I gave thee two blows without scathe—true man, true return. But the third time thou didst fail, and therefore hadst thou that blow. For 'tis *my* weed thou wearest, that same woven girdle, my own wife wrought it, that do I wot for sooth. Now know I well thy kisses, and thy conversation, and the wooing of my wife, for 'twas mine own doing. I sent her to try thee, and in sooth I think thou art the most faultless knight that ever trode earth. As a pearl among white peas is of more worth than they, so is Gawain, i' faith, by other knights. But thou didst lack a little, Sir Knight, and wast wanting in loyalty, yet that was for no evil work, nor for wooing neither, but because thou lovedst thy life—therefore I blame thee the less."

Then the other stood a great while, still sorely angered and vexed within himself; all the blood flew to his face, and he shrank for shame as the Green Knight spake; and the first words he said were, "Cursed be ye, cowardice and covetousness, for in ye is the destruction of virtue." Then he loosed the girdle, and gave it to the knight. "Lo, take there the falsity, may foul befall it! For fear of thy blow cowardice bade me make friends with covetousness and forsake the customs of largess and loyalty, which befit all knights. Now am I faulty and false and have been afeared: from treachery and untruth come sorrow and care. I avow to thee, Sir Knight, that I have ill done; do then thy will. I shall be more wary hereafter."

Then the other laughed and said gaily, "I wot I am whole of the hurt I had, and thou hast made such free confession of thy misdeeds, and hast so borne the penance of mine axe edge, that I hold thee absolved from that sin, and purged as clean as if thou hadst never sinned since thou wast born. And this girdle that is wrought with gold and green, like my raiment, do I give thee, Sir Gawain, that thou mayest think upon this chance when thou goest forth among princes of renown, and keep this for a token of the adventure of the Green Chapel, as it chanced between chivalrous knights. And thou shalt come again with me to my dwelling and pass the rest of this feast in gladness." Then the lord laid hold of him, and said, "I wot we shall soon make peace with my wife, who was thy bitter enemy."

"Nay, forsooth," said Sir Gawain, and seized his helmet and took it off swiftly, and thanked the knight: "I have fared ill, may bliss betide thee, and may He who rules all things reward thee swiftly. Commend me to that courteous lady, thy fair wife, and to the other my honoured ladies, who have beguiled their knight with skilful craft. But 'tis no marvel if one be made a fool and brought to sorrow by women's wiles, for so was Adam beguiled by one, and Solomon by many, and Samson all too soon, for Delilah dealt him his doom; and David thereafter was wedded with Bathsheba, which brought him much sorrow—if one might love a woman and believe her not, 'twere great gain! And since all they were beguiled by women, methinks 'tis the less blame to me that I was misled! But as for thy girdle, that will I take with good will, not for gain of the gold, nor for samite, nor silk, nor the costly pendants, neither for weal nor for worship, but in sign of my frailty. I shall look upon it when I ride in renown and remind myself of the fault and faintness of the flesh; and so when pride uplifts me for prowess of arms, the sight of this lace shall humble my heart. But one thing would I pray, if it displease thee not: since thou art lord of yonder land wherein I have dwelt, tell me what thy rightful name may be, and I will ask no more."

"That will I truly," quoth the other. "Bernlak de Hautdesert am I called in this land. Morgain le Fay dwelleth in mine house[12], and through knowledge of clerkly craft hath she taken many. For long time was she the mistress of Merlin, who knew well all you knights of the court. Morgain the goddess is she called therefore, and there is none so haughty but she can bring him low. She sent me in this guise to yon fair hall to test the truth of the renown that is spread abroad of the valour of the Round Table. She taught me this marvel to betray your wits, to vex Guinevere and fright her to death by the man who spake with his head in his hand at the high table. That is she who is at home, that ancient lady, she is even thine aunt, Arthur's half-sister, the daughter of the Duchess of Tintagel, who afterward married King Uther. Therefore I bid thee, knight, come to thine aunt, and make merry in thine house; my folk love thee, and I wish thee as well as any man on earth, by my faith, for thy true dealing."

But Sir Gawain said nay, he would in no wise do so; so they embraced and kissed, and commended each other to the Prince of Paradise, and parted right there, on the cold ground. Gawain on his steed rode swiftly to the king's hall, and the Green Knight got him whithersoever he would.

Sir Gawain who had thus won grace of his life, rode through wild ways on Gringalet; oft he lodged in a house, and oft without, and many adventures did he have and came off victor full often, as at this time I cannot relate in tale. The hurt that he had in his neck was healed, he bare the shining girdle as a baldric bound by his side, and made fast with a knot 'neath his left arm, in token that he was taken in a fault—and thus he came in safety again to the court.

Then joy awakened in that dwelling when the king knew that the good Sir Gawain was come, for he deemed it gain. King Arthur kissed the knight, and the queen also, and many valiant knights sought to embrace him. They asked him how he had fared, and he told them all that had chanced to him—the adventure of the chapel, the fashion of the knight, the love of the lady—at last of the lace. He showed them the wound in the neck which he won for his disloyalty at the hand of the knight, the blood flew to his face for shame as he told the tale.

"Lo, lady," he quoth, and handled the lace, "this is the bond of the blame that I bear in my neck, this is the harm and the loss I have suffered, the cowardice and covetousness in which I was caught, the token of my covenant in which I was taken. And I must needs wear it so long as I live, for none may hide his harm, but undone it may not be, for if it hath clung to thee once, it may never be severed."

Then the king comforted the knight, and the court laughed loudly at the tale, and all made accord that the lords and the ladies who belonged to the Round Table, each hero among them, should wear bound about him a baldric of bright green for the sake of Sir Gawain.[13] And to this was agreed all the honour of the Round Table, and he who ware it was honoured the more thereafter, as it is testified in the best book of romance. That in Arthur's days this adventure befell, the book of Brutus bears witness. For since that bold knight came hither first, and the siege and the assault were ceased at Troy, I wis

Many a venture herebefore
Hath fallen such as this:
May He that bare the crown of thorn
Bring us unto His bliss.

AMEN.

HONY SOYT QUI MAL PENCE.

NOTES

1. "The Legend of Sir Gawain," Grimm Library, Vol. VII. (Chapter IX. Sir Gawain and the Green Knight).

2. Dance accompanied by song. Often mentioned in old romances.

3. *Agravain, "à la dure main."* This characterisation of Gawain's brother seems to indicate that there was a French source at the root of this story. The author distinctly tells us more than once that the tale, as he tells it, was written *in a book*, M. Gaston Paris thinks that the direct source was an Anglo-Norman poem, now lost.

4. *If any in this hall holds himself so hardy.* This, the main incident of the tale, is apparently of very early date. The oldest version we possess is that found in the Irish tale of the *Fled Bricrend* (Bricriu's feast) [edited and translated by the Rev. G. Henderson, M.A., Irish Texts Society, vol. ii.], where the hero of the tale is the Irish champion, Cuchulinn. Two mediæval romances, the *Mule sans Frein* (French) and *Diu Krône* (German), again attribute it to Gawain; while the continuator of Chrétien de Troye's *Conte del Graal* gives as hero a certain Carados, whom he represents as Arthur's nephew; and the prose *Perceval* has Lancelot. So far as the mediæval versions are concerned, the original hero is undoubtedly Gawain; and our poem gives the fullest and most complete form of the story we possess. In the Irish version the magician is a *giant*, and the abnormal size and stature of the Green Knight is, in all probability, the survival of a primitive feature. His curious *colour* is a trait found nowhere else. In *Diu Krône* we are told that the challenger changes shapes in a terrifying manner, but no details are given.

5. *For Yule was over-past.* This passage, descriptive of the flight of the year, should be especially noticed. Combined with the other passages—the description of Gawain's journey, the early morning hunts, the dawning of New Year's Day, and the ride to the Green Chapel—they indicate a knowledge of Nature, and an observant eye for her moods, uncommon among mediæval poets. It is usual enough to find graceful and charming descriptions of spring and early summer—an appreciation of *May* in especial, when the summer courts were held, is part of the stock-in-trade of mediæval romancers—but a sympathy with the year in all its changes is far rarer, and certainly deserves to be specially reckoned to the credit of this nameless writer.

6. *First a rich carpet was stretched on the floor.* The description of the arming of Gawain is rather more detailed in the original, but some of the minor points are not easy to understand, the identification of sundry of the pieces of armour being doubtful.

7. *The pentangle painted thereupon in gleaming gold.* I do not remember that the pentangle is elsewhere attributed to Gawain. He often bears a red shield; but the blazon varies. Indeed, the heraldic devices borne by Arthur's knights are distractingly chaotic—their legends are older than the science of heraldry, and no one has done for them the good office that the compiler of the Thidrek Saga has rendered to his Teutonic heroes.

8. *The Wilderness of Wirral.* This is in Cheshire. Sir F. Madden suggests that the forest which forms the final stage of Gawain's journey is that of Inglewood, in Cumberland. The geography here is far clearer than is often the case in such descriptions.

9. *'Twas the fairest castle that ever a knight owned.* Here, again, I have omitted some of the details of the original, the architectural terms lacking identification.

10. *With blast of the bugle fared forth to the field.* The account of each day's hunting contains a number of obsolete terms and details of woodcraft, not given in full. The meaning of some has been lost, and the minute descriptions of skinning and dismembering the game would be distinctly repulsive to the general reader. They are valuable for a student of the history of the English sport, but interfere with the progress of the story. The fact that the author devotes so much space to them seems to indicate that he lived in the country and was keenly interested in field sports. (Gottfried von Strassbourg's *Tristan* contains a similar and almost more detailed description.)

11. *I will give [you] my girdle.* This magic girdle, which confers invulnerability on its owner, is a noticeable feature of our story. It is found nowhere else in this connection, yet in other romances we find that Gawain possesses a girdle with similar powers (cf., my *Legend of Sir Gawain*, Chap. IX.). Such a talisman was also owned by Cuchulinn, the Irish hero, who has many points of contact with Gawain. It seems not improbable that this was also an old feature of the story. I have commented, in the Introduction, on the lady's persistent wooing of Gawain, and need not repeat the remarks here. The Celtic *Lay of the Great Fool* (*Amadan Mor*) presents some curious points of contact with our story, which may, however, well be noted here. In the *Lay* the hero is mysteriously deprived of his legs, through the draught

from a cup proffered by a *Gruagach* or magician. He comes to a castle, the lord of which goes out hunting, leaving his wife in the care of the Great Fool, who is to allow no man to enter. He falls asleep, and a young knight arrives and kisses the host's wife. The Great Fool, awaking, refuses to allow the intruder to depart; and, in spite of threats and blandishments, insists on detaining him till the husband returns. Finally, the stranger reveals himself as the host in another shape; he is also the *Gruagach*, who deprived the hero of his limbs, and the Great Fool's brother. He has only intended to test the *Amadon Mor's* fidelity. A curious point in connection with this story is that it possesses a prose opening which shows a marked affinity with the "Perceval" *enfances*. That the Perceval and Gawain stories early became connected is certain, but what is the precise connection between them and the Celtic *Lay* is not clear. *In its present form* the latter is certainly posterior to the Grail romances, but it is quite possible that the matter with which it deals represents a tradition older than the Arthurian story.

12. *Morgain le Fay, who dwelleth in my house.* The enmity between Morgain le Fay and Guinevere, which is here stated to have been the *motif* of the enchantment, is no invention of the author, but is found in the *Merlin,* probably the earliest of the Arthurian *prose* romances. In a later version of our story, a poem, written in ballad form, and contained in the "Percy" MS., Morgain does not appear; her place is taken by an old witch, mother to the lady, but the enchantment is still due to her spells. In this later form the knight bears the curious name of *Sir Bredbeddle*. That given in our romance, *Bernlak de Hautdesert,*, seems to point to the original French source of the story. (It is curious that Morgain should here be represented as extremely old, while Arthur is still in his first youth. There is evidently a discrepancy or misunderstanding of the source here.)

13. *A baldric of bright green, for sake of Sir Gawain.* The later version connects this *lace* with that worn by the knights of the Bath; but this latter was *white,* not *green*. The knights wore it on the left shoulder till they had done some gallant deed, or till some noble lady took it off for them.

III.

SIR GAWAIN AND THE GREEN KNIGHT: THE ORIGINAL POEM, CA. 1348 WRITTEN IN MIDDLE ENGLISH (AS AN ALLITERATIVE ROMANCE)

BY UNKNOWN

SYR GAWAYN AND THE GRENE KNY3T

PASSUS I

[stanza i]

Siþen þe sege and þe assaut watz sesed at Troye,
Þe borȝ brittened and brent to brondeȝ and askez,
Þe tulk þat þe trammes of tresoun þer wroȝt
Watz tried for his tricherie, þe trewest on erthe:
Hit watz Ennias þe athel, and his highe kynde,
Þat siþen depreced prouinces, and patrounes bicome
Welneȝe of al þe wele in þe west iles.
Fro riche Romulus to Rome ricchis hym swyþe,
With gret bobbaunce þat burȝe he biges vpon fyrst,
And neuenes hit his aune nome, as hit now hat;

11. Tirius to Tuskan and teldes bigynnes,
12. Langaberde in Lumbardie lyftes vp homes,
13. And fer ouer þe French flod Felix Brutus
14. On mony bonkkes ful brode Bretayn he settez

[bob]

15. wyth wynne,

[wheel]

16. Where werre and wrake and wonder,
17. Bi syþez hatz wont þerinne,
18. And oft boþe blysse and blunder
19. Ful skete hatz skyfted synne.

[stanza ii]

20. Ande quen þis Bretayn watz bigged bi þis burn rych,
21. Bolde bredden þerinne, baret þat lofden,
22. In mony turned tyme tene þat wroȝten.
23. Mo ferlyes on þis folde han fallen here oft
24. Þen in any oþer þat I wot, syn þat ilk tyme.
25. Bot of alle þat here bult, of Bretaygne kynges,
26. Ay watz Arthur þe hendest, as I haf herde telle.
27. Forþi an aunter in erde I attle to schawe,
28. Þat a selly in siȝt summe men hit holden,
29. And an outtrage awenture of Arthurez wonderez.
30. If ȝe wyl lysten þis laye bot on littel quile,
31. I schal telle hit as-tit, as I in toun herde,

[bob]

32. with tonge,

[wheel]

33. As hit is stad and stoken,
34. In stori stif and stronge,
35. With lel letteres loken,
36. In londe so hatz ben longe.

[stanza iii]

37. Þis kyng lay at Camylot vpon Krystmasse
38. With mony luflych lorde, ledez of þe best,

Rekenly of þe Rounde Table alle þo rich breþer,
With rych reuel ory3t and rechles merþes.
Þer tournayed tulkes by tymez ful mony,
Justed ful jolilé þise gentyle kni3tes,
Syþen kayred to þe court caroles to make.
For þer þe fest watz ilyche ful fiften dayes,
With alle þe mete and þe mirþe þat men couþe avyse;
Such glaum ande gle glorious to here,
Dere dyn vpon day, daunsyng on ny3tes,
Al watz hap vpon he3e in hallez and chambrez
With lordez and ladies, as leuest him þo3t.
With all þe wele of þe worlde þay woned þer samen,
Þe most kyd kny3tez vnder Krystes seluen,
And þe louelokkest ladies þat euer lif haden,
And he þe comlokest kyng þat þe court haldes;
For al watz þis fayre folk in her first age,

[bob]

on sille,

[wheel]

Þe hapnest vnder heuen,
Kyng hy3est mon of wylle;
Hit were now gret nye to neuen
So hardy a here on hille.

[stanza iv]

Wyle Nw 3er watz so 3ep þat hit watz nwe cummen,
Þat day doubble on þe dece watz þe douth serued.
Fro þe kyng watz cummen with kny3tes into þe halle,
Þe chauntré of þe chapel cheued to an ende,
Loude crye watz þer kest of clerkez and oþer,
Nowel nayted onewe, neuened ful ofte;
And syþen riche forth runnen to reche hondeselle,
3e3ed 3eres-3iftes on hi3, 3elde hem bi hond,
Debated busyly aboute þo giftes;
Ladies la3ed ful loude, þo3 þay lost haden,
And he þat wan watz not wrothe, þat may 3e wel trawe.
Alle þis mirþe þay maden to þe mete tyme;
When þay had waschen worþyly þay wenten to sete,

Þe best burne ay abof, as hit best semed,
Whene Guenore, ful gay, grayþed in þe myddes,
Dressed on þe dere des, dubbed al aboute,
Smal sendal bisides, a selure hir ouer
Of tryed tolouse, and tars tapites innoghe,
Þat were enbrawded and beten wyth þe best gemmes
Þat my3t be preued of prys wyth penyes to bye,

[bob]

in daye.

[wheel]

Þe comlokest to discrye
Þer glent with y3en gray,
A semloker þat euer he sy3e
Soth mo3t no mon say.

[stanza v]

Bot Arthure wolde not ete til al were serued,
He watz so joly of his joyfnes, and sumquat childgered:
His lif liked hym ly3t, he louied þe lasse
Auþer to longe lye or to longe sitte,
So bisied him his 3onge blod and his brayn wylde.
And also an oþer maner meued him eke
Þat he þur3 nobelay had nomen, he wolde neuer ete
Vpon such a dere day er hym deuised were
Of sum auenturus þyng an vncouþe tale,
Of sum mayn meruayle, þat he my3t trawe,
Of alderes, of armes, of oþer auenturus,
Oþer sum segg hym biso3t of sum siker kny3t
To joyne wyth hym in iustyng, in jopardé to lay,
Lede, lif for lyf, leue vchon oþer,
As fortune wolde fulsun hom, þe fayrer to haue.
Þis watz þe kynges countenaunce where he in court were,
At vch farand fest among his fre meny

[bob]

in halle.

[wheel]

Þerfore of face so fere

104. He sti3tlez stif in stalle,
105. Ful 3ep in þat Nw 3ere
106. Much mirthe he mas withalle.

[stanza vi]

107. Thus þer stondes in stale þe stif kyng hisseluen,
108. Talkkande bifore þe hy3e table of trifles ful hende.
109. There gode Gawan watz grayþed Gwenore bisyde,
110. And Agrauayn a la dure mayn on þat oþer syde sittes,
111. Boþe þe kynges sistersunes and ful siker kni3tes;
112. Bischop Bawdewyn abof biginez þe table,
113. And Ywan, Vryn son, ette with hymseluen.
114. Þise were di3t on þe des and derworþly serued,
115. And siþen mony siker segge at þe sidbordez.
116. Þen þe first cors come with crakkyng of trumpes,
117. Wyth mony baner ful bry3t þat þerbi henged;
118. Nwe nakryn noyse with þe noble pipes,
119. Wylde werbles and wy3t wakned lote,
120. Þat mony hert ful hi3e hef at her towches.
121. Dayntés dryuen þerwyth of ful dere metes,
122. Foysoun of þe fresche, and on so fele disches
123. Þat pine to fynde þe place þe peple biforne
124. For to sette þe sylueren þat sere sewes halden

[bob]

125. on clothe.

[wheel]

126. Iche lede as he loued hymselue
127. Þer laght withouten loþe;
128. Ay two had disches twelue,
129. Good ber and bry3t wyn boþe.

[stanza vii]

130. Now wyl I of hor seruise say yow no more,
131. For vch wy3e may wel wit no wont þat þer were.
132. An oþer noyse ful newe ne3ed biliue,
133. Þat þe lude my3t haf leue liflode to cach;
134. For vneþe watz þe noyce not a whyle sesed,

And þe fyrst cource in þe court kyndely serued,
Þer hales in at þe halle dor an aghlich mayster,
On þe most on þe molde on mesure hyghe;
Fro þe swyre to þe swange so sware and so þik,
And his lyndes and his lymes so longe and so grete,
Half etayn in erde I hope þat he were,
Bot mon most I algate mynn hym to bene,
And þat þe myriest in his muckel þat myȝt ride;
For of bak and of brest al were his bodi sturne,
Both his wombe and his wast were worthily smale,
And alle his fetures folȝande, in forme þat he hade,

[bob]

ful clene;

[wheel]

For wonder of his hwe men hade,
Set in his semblaunt sene;
He ferde as freke were fade,
And oueral enker-grene.

[stanza viii]

Ande al grayþed in grene þis gome and his wedes:
A strayte cote ful streȝt, þat stek on his sides,
A meré mantile abof, mensked withinne
With pelure pured apert, þe pane ful clene
With blyþe blaunner ful bryȝt, and his hod boþe,
Þat watz laȝt fro his lokkez and layde on his schulderes;
Heme wel-haled hose of þat same,
Þat spenet on his sparlyr, and clene spures vnder
Of bryȝt golde, vpon silk bordes barred ful ryche,
And scholes vnder schankes þere þe schalk rides;
And alle his vesture uerayly watz clene verdure,
Boþe þe barres of his belt and oþer blyþe stones,
Þat were richely rayled in his aray clene
Aboutte hymself and his sadel, vpon silk werkez.
Þat were to tor for to telle of tryfles þe halue
Þat were enbrauded abof, wyth bryddes and flyȝes,
With gay gaudi of grene, þe golde ay inmyddes.
Þe pendauntes of his payttrure, þe proude cropure,

169. His molaynes, and alle þe metail anamayld was þenne,
170. Þe steropes þat he stod on stayned of þe same,
171. And his arsounz al after and his aþel skyrtes,
172. Þat euer glemered and glent al of grene stones;
173. Þe fole þat he ferkkes on fyn of þat ilke,

[bob]

174. sertayn,

[wheel]

175. A grene hors gret and þikke,
176. A stede ful stif to strayne,
177. In brawden brydel quik—
178. To þe gome he watz ful gayn.

[stanza ix]

179. Wel gay watz þis gome gered in grene,
180. And þe here of his hed of his hors swete.
181. Fayre fannand fax vmbefoldes his schulderes;
182. A much berd as a busk ouer his brest henges,
183. Þat wyth his hiȝlich here þat of his hed reches
184. Watz euesed al vmbetorne abof his elbowes,
185. Þat half his armes þer-vnder were halched in þe wyse
186. Of a kyngez capados þat closes his swyre;
187. Þe mane of þat mayn hors much to hit lyke,
188. Wel cresped and cemmed, wyth knottes ful mony
189. Folden in wyth fildore aboute þe fayre grene,
190. Ay a herle of þe here, an oþer of golde;
191. Þe tayl and his toppyng twynnen of a sute,
192. And bounden boþe wyth a bande of a bryȝt grene,
193. Dubbed wyth ful dere stonez, as þe dok lasted,
194. Syþen þrawen wyth a þwong a þwarle knot alofte,
195. Þer mony bellez ful bryȝt of brende golde rungen.
196. Such a fole vpon folde, ne freke þat hym rydes,
197. Watz neuer sene in þat sale wyth syȝt er þat tyme,

[bob]

198. with yȝe.

[wheel]

199. He loked as layt so lyȝt,

So sayd al þat hym syȝe;
Hit semed as no mon myȝt
Vnder his dynttez dryȝe.

[stanza x]

Wheþer hade he no helme ne hawbergh nauþer,
Ne no pysan ne no plate þat pented to armes,
Ne no schafte ne no schelde to schwue ne to smyte,
Bot in his on honde he hade a holyn bobbe,
Þat is grattest in grene when greuez ar bare,
And an ax in his oþer, a hoge and vnmete,
A spetos sparþe to expoun in spelle, quoso myȝt.
Þe lenkþe of an elnȝerde þe large hede hade,
Þe grayn al of grene stele and of golde hewen,
Þe bit burnyst bryȝt, with a brod egge
As wel schapen to schere as scharp rasores,
Þe stele of a stif staf þe sturne hit bi grypte,
Þat watz wounden wyth yrn to þe wandez ende,
And al bigrauen with grene in gracios werkes;
A lace lapped aboute, þat louked at þe hede,
And so after þe halme halched ful ofte,
Wyth tryed tasselez þerto tacched innoghe
On botounz of þe bryȝt grene brayden ful ryche.
Þis haþel heldez hym in and þe halle entres,
Driuande to þe heȝe dece, dut he no woþe,
Haylsed he neuer one, bot heȝe he ouer loked.
Þe fyrst word þat he warp, 'Wher is', he sayd,
'Þe gouernour of þis gyng? Gladly I wolde
Se þat segg in syȝt, and with hymself speke

[bob]

raysoun.'

[wheel]

To knyȝtez he kest his yȝe,
And reled hym vp and doun;
He stemmed, and con studie
Quo walt þer most renoun.

[stanza xi]

Ther watz lokyng on lenþe þe lude to beholde,
For vch mon had meruayle quat hit mene myȝt
Þat a haþel and a horse myȝt such a hwe lach,
As growe grene as þe gres and grener hit semed,
Þen grene aumayl on golde glowande bryȝter.
Al studied þat þer stod, and stalked hym nerre
Wyth al þe wonder of þe worlde what he worch schulde.
For fele sellyez had þay sen, bot such neuer are;
Forþi for fantoum and fayryȝe þe folk þere hit demed.
Þerfore to answare watz arȝe mony aþel freke,
And al stouned at his steuen and stonstil seten
In a swoghe sylence þurȝ þe sale riche;
As al were slypped vpon slepe so slaked hor lotez

[bob]

in hyȝe—

[wheel]

I deme hit not al for doute,
Bot sum for cortaysye—
Bot let hym þat al schulde loute
Cast vnto þat wyȝe.

[stanza xii]

Þenn Arþour bifore þe hiȝ dece þat auenture byholdez,
And rekenly hym reuerenced, for rad was he neuer,
And sayde, 'Wyȝe, welcum iwys to þis place,
Þe hede of þis ostel Arthour I hat;
Liȝt luflych adoun and lenge, I þe praye,
And quat-so þy wylle is we schal wyt after.'
'Nay, as help me,' quoþ þe haþel, 'he þat on hyȝe syttes,
To wone any quyle in þis won, hit watz not myn ernde;
Bot for þe los of þe, lede, is lyft vp so hyȝe,
And þy burȝ and þy burnes best ar holden,
Stifest vnder stel-gere on stedes to ryde,
Þe wyȝtest and þe worþyest of þe worldes kynde,
Preue for to play wyth in oþer pure laykez,
And here is kydde cortaysye, as I haf herd carp,
And þat hatz wayned me hider, iwyis, at þis tyme.
Ȝe may be seker bi þis braunch þat I bere here

Þat I passe as in pes, and no ply3t seche;
For had I founded in fere in fe3tyng wyse,
I haue a hauberghe at home and a helme boþe,
A schelde and a scharp spere, schinande bry3t,
Ande oþer weppenes to welde, I wene wel, als;
Bot for I wolde no were, my wedez ar softer.
Bot if þou be so bold as alle burnez tellen,
Þou wyl grant me godly þe gomen þat I ask

[bob]

bi ry3t.'

[wheel]

Arthour con onsware,
And sayd, 'Sir cortays kny3t,
If þou craue batayl bare,
Here faylez þou not to fy3t.'

[stanza xiii]

'Nay, frayst I no fy3t, in fayth I þe telle,
Hit arn aboute on þis bench bot berdlez chylder.
If I were hasped in armes on a he3e stede,
Here is no mon me to mach, for my3tez so wayke.
Forþy I craue in þis court a Crystemas gomen,
For hit is 3ol and Nwe 3er, and here ar 3ep mony:
If any so hardy in þis hous holdez hymseluen,
Be so bolde in his blod, brayn in hys hede,
Þat dar stifly strike a strok for an oþer,
I schal gif hym of my gyft þys giserne ryche,
Þis ax, þat is heué innogh, to hondele as hym lykes,
And I schal bide þe fyrst bur as bare as I sitte.
If any freke be so felle to fonde þat I telle,
Lepe ly3tly me to, and lach þis weppen,
I quit-clayme hit for euer, kepe hit as his auen,
And I schal stonde hym a strok, stif on þis flet,
Ellez þou wyl di3t me þe dom to dele hym an oþer

[bob]

barlay,

[wheel]

And ʒet gif hym respite,
A twelmonyth and a day;
Now hyʒe, and let se tite
Dar any herinne oʒt say.'

[stanza xiv]

If he hem stowned vpon fyrst, stiller were þanne
Alle þe heredmen in halle, þe hyʒ and þe loʒe.
Þe renk on his rouncé hym ruched in his sadel,
And runischly his rede yʒen he reled aboute,
Bende his bresed broʒez, blycande grene,
Wayued his berde for to wayte quo-so wolde ryse.
When non wolde kepe hym with carp he coʒed ful hyʒe,
Ande rimed hym ful richly, and ryʒt hym to speke:
'What, is þis Arthures hous,' quoþ þe haþel þenne,
'Þat al þe rous rennes of þurʒ ryalmes so mony?
Where is now your sourquydrye and your conquestes,
Your gryndellayk and your greme, and your grete wordes?
Now is þe reuel and þe renoun of þe Rounde Table
Ouerwalt wyth a worde of on wyʒes speche,
For al dares for drede withoute dynt schewed!'
Wyth þis he laʒes so loude þat þe lorde greued;
Þe blod schot for scham into his schyre face

[bob]

and lere;

[wheel]

He wex as wroth as wynde,
So did alle þat þer were.
Þe kyng as kene bi kynde
Þen stod þat stif mon nere,

[stanza xv]

Ande sayde, 'Haþel, by heuen, þyn askyng is nys,
And as þou foly hatz frayst, fynde þe behoues.
I know no gome þat is gast of þy grete wordes;
Gif me now þy geserne, vpon Godez halue,
And I schal bayþen þy bone þat þou boden habbes.'
Lyʒtly lepez he hym to, and laʒt at his honde.

329. Þen feersly þat oþer freke vpon fote ly3tis.
330. Now hatz Arthure his axe, and þe halme grypez,
331. And sturnely sturez hit aboute, þat stryke wyth hit þo3t.
332. Þe stif mon hym bifore stod vpon hy3t,
333. Herre þen ani in þe hous by þe hede and more.
334. Wyth sturne schere þer he stod he stroked his berde,
335. And wyth a countenaunce dry3e he dro3 doun his cote,
336. No more mate ne dismayd for hys mayn dintez
337. Þen any burne vpon bench hade bro3t hym to drynk

[bob]

338. of wyne.

[wheel]

339. Gawan, þat sate bi þe quene,
340. To þe kyng he can enclyne:
341. 'I beseche now with sa3ez sene
342. Þis melly mot be myne.

[stanza xvi]

343. 'Wolde 3e, worþilych lorde,' quoþ Wawan to þe kyng,
344. 'Bid me bo3e fro þis benche, and stonde by yow þere,
345. Þat I wythoute vylanye my3t voyde þis table,
346. And þat my legge lady lyked not ille,
347. I wolde com to your counseyl bifore your cort ryche.
348. For me þink hit not semly, as hit is soþ knawen,
349. Þer such an askyng is heuened so hy3e in your sale,
350. Þa3 3e 3ourself be talenttyf, to take hit to yourseluen,
351. Whil mony so bolde yow aboute vpon bench sytten,
352. Þat vnder heuen I hope non ha3erer of wylle,
353. Ne better bodyes on bent þer baret is rered.
354. I am þe wakkest, I wot, and of wyt feblest,
355. And lest lur of my lyf, quo laytes þe soþe—
356. Bot for as much as 3e ar myn em I am only to prayse,
357. No bounté bot your blod I in my bodé knowe;
358. And syþen þis note is so nys þat no3t hit yow falles,
359. And I haue frayned hit at yow fyrst, foldez hit to me;
360. And if I carp not comlyly, let alle þis cort rych

[bob]

361. bout blame.'

[wheel]

Ryche togeder con roun,
And syþen þay redden alle same
To ryd þe kyng wyth croun,
And gif Gawan þe game.
Þen comaunded þe kyng þe knyȝt for to ryse;

[stanza xvii]

And he ful radly vpros, and ruchched hym fayre,
Kneled doun bifore þe kyng, and cachez þat weppen;
And he luflyly hit hym laft, and lyfte vp his honde,
And gef hym Goddez blessyng, and gladly hym biddes
Þat his hert and his honde schulde hardi be boþe.
'Kepe þe, cosyn,' quoþ þe kyng, 'þat þou on kyrf sette,
And if þou redez hym ryȝt, redly I trowe
Þat þou schal byden þe bur þat he schal bede after.'
Gawan gotz to þe gome with giserne in honde,
And he baldly hym bydez, he bayst neuer þe helder.
Þen carppez to Sir Gawan þe knyȝt in þe grene,
'Refourme we oure forwardes, er we fyrre passe.
Fyrst I eþe þe, haþel, how þat þou hattes
Þat þou me telle truly, as I tryst may.'
'In god fayth,' quoþ þe goode knyȝt, 'Gawan I hatte,
Þat bede þe þis buffet, quat-so bifallez after,
And at þis tyme twelmonyth take at þe an oþer
Wyth what weppen so þou wylt, and wyth no wyȝ ellez

[bob]

on lyue.'

[wheel]

Þat oþer onswarez agayn,
'Sir Gawan, so mot I þryue
As I am ferly fayn
Þis dint þat þou schal dryue.

[stanza xviii]

'Bigog,' quoþ þe grene knyȝt, 'Sir Gawan, me lykes
Þat I schal fange at þy fust þat I haf frayst here.
And þou hatz redily rehersed, bi resoun ful trwe,

Clanly al þe couenaunt þat I þe kynge asked,
Saf þat þou schal siker me, segge, bi þi trawþe,
Þat þou schal seche me þiself, where-so þou hopes
I may be funde vpon folde, and foch þe such wages
As þou deles me to-day bifore þis douþe ryche.'
'Where schulde I wale þe,' quoþ Gauan, 'where is þy place?
I wot neuer where þou wonyes, bi hym þat me wroȝt,
Ne I know not þe, knyȝt, by cort ne þi name.
Bot teche me truly þerto, and telle me how þou hattes,
And I schal ware alle my wyt to wynne me þeder,
And þat I swere þe for soþe, and by my seker traweþ.'
'Þat is innogh in Nwe Ȝer, hit nedes no more',
Quoþ þe gome in þe grene to Gawan þe hende;
'Ȝif I þe telle trwly, quen I þe tape haue
And þou me smoþely hatz smyten, smartly I þe teche
Of my hous and my home and myn owen nome,
Þen may þou frayst my fare and forwardez holde;
And if I spende no speche, þenne spedez þou þe better,
For þou may leng in þy londe and layt no fyrre—

[bob]

bot slokes!

[wheel]

Ta now þy grymme tole to þe,
And let se how þou cnokez.'
'Gladly, sir, for soþe',
Quoþ Gawan; his ax he strokes.

[stanza xix]

Þe grene knyȝt vpon grounde grayþely hym dresses,
A littel lut with þe hede, þe lere he discouerez,
His longe louelych lokkez he layd ouer his croun,
Let þe naked nec to þe note schewe.
Gauan gripped to his ax, and gederes hit on hyȝt,
Þe kay fot on þe folde he before sette,
Let him doun lyȝtly lyȝt on þe naked,
Þat þe scharp of þe schalk schyndered þe bones,
And schrank þurȝ þe schyire grece, and schade hit in twynne,
Þat þe bit of þe broun stel bot on þe grounde.

Þe fayre hede fro þe halce hit to þe erþe,
Þat fele hit foyned wyth her fete, þere hit forth roled;
Þe blod brayd fro þe body, þat blykked on þe grene;
And nawþer faltered ne fel þe freke neuer þe helder,
Bot styþly he start forth vpon styf schonkes,
And runyschly he raȝt out, þere as renkkez stoden,
Laȝt to his lufly hed, and lyft hit vp sone;
And syþen boȝez to his blonk, þe brydel he cachchez,
Steppez into stelbawe and strydez alofte,
And his hede by þe here in his honde haldez;
And as sadly þe segge hym in his sadel sette
As non vnhap had hym ayled, þaȝ hedlez he were

[bob]

in stedde.

[wheel]

He brayde his bulk aboute,
Þat vgly bodi þat bledde;
Moni on of hym had doute,
Bi þat his resounz were redde.

[stanza xx]

For þe hede in his honde he haldez vp euen,
Toward þe derrest on þe dece he dressez þe face,
And hit lyfte vp þe yȝe-lyddez and loked ful brode,
And meled þus much with his muthe, as ȝe may now here:
'Loke, Gawan, þou be grayþe to go as þou hettez,
And layte as lelly til þou me, lude, fynde,
As þou hatz hette in þis halle, herande þise knyȝtes;
To þe grene chapel þou chose, I charge þe, to fotte
Such a dunt as þou hatz dalt—disserued þou habbez
To be ȝederly ȝolden on Nw Ȝeres morn.
Þe knyȝt of þe grene chapel men knowen me mony;
Forþi me for to fynde if þou fraystez, faylez þou neuer.
Þerfore com, oþer recreaunt be calde þe behoues.'
With a runisch rout þe raynez he tornez,
Halled out at þe hal dor, his hed in his hande,
Þat þe fyr of þe flynt flaȝe fro fole houes.
To quat kyth he becom knwe non þere,

461. Neuer more þen þay wyste from queþen he watz wonnen.
[bob]
462. What þenne?
[wheel]
463. Þe kyng and Gawen þare
464. At þat grene þay laȝe and grenne,
465. Ȝet breued watz hit ful bare
466. A meruayl among þo menne.

[stanza xxi]

467. Þaȝ Arþer þe hende kyng at hert hade wonder,
468. He let no semblaunt be sene, bot sayde ful hyȝe
469. To þe comlych quene wyth cortays speche,
470. 'Dere dame, to-day demay yow neuer;
471. Wel bycommes such craft vpon Cristmasse,
472. Laykyng of enterludez, to laȝe and to syng,
473. Among þise kynde caroles of knyȝtez and ladyez.
474. Neuer þe lece to my mete I may me wel dres,
475. For I haf sen a selly, I may not forsake.'
476. He glent vpon Sir Gawen, and gaynly he sayde,
477. 'Now, sir, heng vp þyn ax, þat hatz innogh hewen';
478. And hit watz don abof þe dece on doser to henge,
479. Þer alle men for meruayl myȝt on hit loke,
480. And bi trwe tytel þerof to telle þe wonder.
481. Þenne þay boȝed to a borde þise burnes togeder,
482. Þe kyng and þe gode knyȝt, and kene men hem serued
483. Of alle dayntyez double, as derrest myȝt falle;
484. Wyth alle maner of mete and mynstralcie boþe,
485. Wyth wele walt þay þat day, til worþed an ende
[bob]
486. in londe.
[wheel]
487. Now þenk wel, Sir Gawan,
488. For woþe þat þou ne wonde
489. Þis auenture for to frayn
490. Þat þou hatz tan on honde.

PASSUS II

[stanza xxii]

491. This hanselle hatz Arthur of auenturus on fyrst
492. In ȝonge ȝer, for he ȝerned ȝelpyng to here.
493. Thaȝ hym wordez were wane when þay to sete wenten,
494. Now ar þay stoken of sturne werk, stafful her hond.
495. Gawan watz glad to begynne þose gomnez in halle,
496. Bot þaȝ þe ende be heuy haf ȝe no wonder;
497. For þaȝ men ben mery in mynde quen þay han mayn drynk,
498. A ȝere ȝernes ful ȝerne, and ȝeldez neuer lyke,
499. Þe forme to þe fynisment foldez ful selden.
500. Forþi þis Ȝol ouerȝede, and þe ȝere after,
501. And vche sesoun serlepes sued after oþer:
502. After Crystenmasse com þe crabbed lentoun,
503. Þat fraystez flesch wyth þe fysche and fode more symple;
504. Bot þenne þe weder of þe worlde wyth wynter hit þrepez,
505. Colde clengez adoun, cloudez vplyften,
506. Schyre schedez þe rayn in schowrez ful warme,
507. Fallez vpon fayre flat, flowrez þere schewen,
508. Boþe groundez and þe greuez grene ar her wedez,
509. Bryddez busken to bylde, and bremlych syngen
510. For solace of þe softe somer þat sues þerafter

[bob]

511. bi bonk;

[wheel]

512. And blossumez bolne to blowe
513. Bi rawez rych and ronk,
514. Þen notez noble innoȝe
515. Ar herde in wod so wlonk.

[stanza xxiii]

516. After þe sesoun of somer wyth þe soft wyndez
517. Quen Zeferus syflez hymself on sedez and erbez,
518. Wela wynne is þe wort þat waxes þeroute,
519. When þe donkande dewe dropez of þe leuez,
520. To bide a blysful blusch of þe bryȝt sunne.
521. Bot þen hyȝes heruest, and hardenes hym sone,

Warnez hym for þe wynter to wax ful rype;
He dryues wyth droȝt þe dust for to ryse,
Fro þe face of þe folde to flyȝe ful hyȝe;
Wroþe wynde of þe welkyn wrastelez with þe sunne,
Þe leuez lancen fro þe lynde and lyȝten on þe grounde,
And al grayes þe gres þat grene watz ere;
Þenne al rypez and rotez þat ros vpon fyrst,
And þus ȝirnez þe ȝere in ȝisterdayez mony,
And wynter wyndez aȝayn, as þe worlde askez,

[bob]

no fage,

[wheel]

Til Meȝelmas mone
Watz cumen wyth wynter wage;
Þen þenkkez Gawan ful sone
Of his anious uyage.

[stanza xxiv]

Ȝet quyl Al-hal-day with Arþer he lenges;
And he made a fare on þat fest for þe frekez sake,
With much reuel and ryche of þe Rounde Table.
Knyȝtez ful cortays and comlych ladies
Al for luf of þat lede in longynge þay were,
Bot neuer þe lece ne þe later þay neuened bot merþe:
Mony ioylez for þat ientyle iapez þer maden.
For aftter mete with mournyng he melez to his eme,
And spekez of his passage, and pertly he sayde,
'Now, lege lorde of my lyf, leue I yow ask;
Ȝe knowe þe cost of þis cace, kepe I no more
To telle yow tenez þerof neuer bot trifel;
Bot I am boun to þe bur barely to-morne
To sech þe gome of þe grene, as God wyl me wysse.'
Þenne þe best of þe burȝ boȝed togeder,
Aywan, and Errik, and oþer ful mony,
Sir Doddinaual de Sauage, þe duk of Clarence,
Launcelot, and Lyonel, and Lucan þe gode,
Sir Boos, and Sir Byduer, big men boþe,
And mony oþer menskful, with Mador de la Port.

556. Alle þis compayny of court com þe kyng nerre
557. For to counseyl þe kny3t, with care at her hert.
558. Þere watz much derue doel driuen in þe sale
559. Þat so worthé as Wawan schulde wende on þat ernde,
560. To dry3e a delful dynt, and dele no more

[bob]

561. wyth bronde.

[wheel]

562. Þe kny3t mad ay god chere,
563. And sayde, 'Quat schuld I wonde?
564. Of destinés derf and dere
565. What may mon do bot fonde?'

[stanza xxv]

566. He dowellez þer al þat day, and dressez on þe morn,
567. Askez erly hys armez, and alle were þay bro3t.
568. Fyrst a tulé tapit ty3t ouer þe flet,
569. And miche watz þe gyld gere þat glent þeralofte;
570. Þe stif mon steppez þeron, and þe stel hondelez,
571. Dubbed in a dublet of a dere tars,
572. And syþen a crafty capados, closed aloft,
573. Þat wyth a bry3t blaunner was bounden withinne.
574. Þenne set þay þe sabatounz vpon þe segge fotez,
575. His legez lapped in stel with luflych greuez,
576. With polaynez piched þerto, policed ful clene,
577. Aboute his knez knaged wyth knotez of golde;
578. Queme quyssewes þen, þat coyntlych closed
579. His thik þrawen þy3ez, with þwonges to tachched;
580. And syþen þe brawden bryné of bry3t stel ryngez
581. Vmbeweued þat wy3 vpon wlonk stuffe,
582. And wel bornyst brace vpon his boþe armes,
583. With gode cowters and gay, and glouez of plate,
584. And alle þe godlych gere þat hym gayn schulde

[bob]

585. þat tyde;

[wheel]

586. Wyth ryche cote-armure,

587. His gold sporez spend with pryde,
588. Gurde wyth a bront ful sure
589. With silk sayn vmbe his syde.

[stanza xxvi]

590. When he watz hasped in armes, his harnays watz ryche:
591. Þe lest lachet oþer loupe lemed of golde.
592. So harnayst as he watz he herknez his masse,
593. Offred and honoured at þe heȝe auter.
594. Syþen he comez to þe kyng and to his cort-ferez,
595. Lachez lufly his leue at lordez and ladyez;
596. And þay hym kyst and conueyed, bikende hym to Kryst.
597. Bi þat watz Gryngolet grayth, and gurde with a sadel
598. Þat glemed ful gayly with mony golde frenges,
599. Ayquere naylet ful nwe, for þat note ryched;
600. Þe brydel barred aboute, with bryȝt golde bounden;
601. Þe apparayl of þe payttrure and of þe proude skyrtez,
602. Þe cropore and þe couertor, acorded wyth þe arsounez;
603. And al watz rayled on red ryche golde naylez,
604. Þat al glytered and glent as glem of þe sunne.
605. Þenne hentes he þe helme, and hastily hit kysses,
606. Þat watz stapled stifly, and stoffed wythinne.
607. Hit watz hyȝe on his hede, hasped bihynde,
608. Wyth a lyȝtly vrysoun ouer þe auentayle,
609. Enbrawden and bounden wyth þe best gemmez
610. On brode sylkyn borde, and bryddez on semez,
611. As papiayez paynted peruyng bitwene,
612. Tortors and trulofez entayled so þyk
613. As mony burde þeraboute had ben seuen wynter

[bob]

614. in toune.

[wheel]

615. Þe cercle watz more o prys
616. Þat vmbeclypped hys croun,
617. Of diamauntez a deuys
618. Þat boþe were bryȝt and broun.

[stanza xxvii]

Then þay schewed hym þe schelde, þat was of schyr goulez
Wyth þe pentangel depaynt of pure golde hwez.
He braydez hit by þe bauderyk, aboute þe hals kestes,
Þat bisemed þe segge semlyly fayre.
And quy þe pentangel apendez to þat prynce noble
I am in tent yow to telle, þof tary hyt me schulde:
Hit is a syngne þat Salamon set sumquyle
In bytoknyng of trawþe, bi tytle þat hit habbez,
For hit is a figure þat haldez fyue poyntez,
And vche lyne vmbelappez and loukez in oþer,
And ayquere hit is endelez; and Englych hit callen
Oueral, as I here, þe endeles knot.
Forþy hit acordez to þis kny3t and to his cler armez,
For ay faythful in fyue and sere fyue syþez
Gawan watz for gode knawen, and as golde pured,
Voyded of vche vylany, wyth vertuez ennourned

[bob]

in mote;

[wheel]

Forþy þe pentangel nwe
He ber in schelde and cote,
As tulk of tale most trwe
And gentylest kny3t of lote.

[stanza xxviii]

Fyrst he watz funden fautlez in his fyue wyttez,
And efte fayled neuer þe freke in his fyue fyngres,
And alle his afyaunce vpon folde watz in þe fyue woundez
Þat Cryst ka3t on þe croys, as þe crede tellez;
And quere-so-euer þys mon in melly watz stad,
His þro þo3t watz in þat, þur3 alle oþer þyngez,
Þat alle his forsnes he feng at þe fyue joyez
Þat þe hende heuen-quene had of hir chylde;
At þis cause þe kny3t comlyche hade
In þe inore half of his schelde hir ymage depaynted,
Þat quen he blusched þerto his belde neuer payred.
Þe fyft fyue þat I finde þat þe frek vsed
Watz fraunchyse and fela3schyp forbe al þyng,

His clannes and his cortaysye croked were neuer,
And pité, þat passez alle poyntez, þyse pure fyue
Were harder happed on þat haþel þen on any oþer.
Now alle þese fyue syþez, for soþe, were fetled on þis kny3t,
And vchone halched in oþer, þat non ende hade,
And fyched vpon fyue poyntez, þat fayld neuer,
Ne samned neuer in no syde, ne sundred nouþer,
Withouten ende at any noke I oquere fynde,
Whereeuer þe gomen bygan, or glod to an ende.
Þerfore on his schene schelde schapen watz þe knot
Ryally wyth red golde vpon rede gowlez,
Þat is þe pure pentaungel wyth þe peple called

[bob]

with lore.

[wheel]

Now grayþed is Gawan gay,
And la3t his launce ry3t þore,
And gef hem alle goud day,
He wende for euermore.

[stanza xxix]

He sperred þe sted with þe spurez and sprong on his way,
So stif þat þe ston-fyr stroke out þerafter.
Al þat se3 þat semly syked in hert,
And sayde soþly al same segges til oþer,
Carande for þat comly: 'Bi Kryst, hit is scaþe
Þat þou, leude, schal be lost, þat art of lyf noble!
To fynde hys fere vpon folde, in fayth, is not eþe.
Warloker to haf wro3t had more wyt bene,
And haf dy3t 3onder dere a duk to haue worþed;
A lowande leder of ledez in londe hym wel semez,
And so had better haf ben þen britned to no3t,
Hadet wyth an aluisch mon, for angardez pryde.
Who knew euer any kyng such counsel to take
As kny3tez in cauelaciounz on Crystmasse gomnez!'
Wel much watz þe warme water þat waltered of y3en,
When þat semly syre so3t fro þo wonez

[bob]

686. þad daye.

[wheel]

687. He made non abode,
688. Bot wyȝtly went hys way;
689. Mony wylsum way he rode,
690. Þe bok as I herde say.

[stanza xxx]

691. Now ridez þis renk þurȝ þe ryalme of Logres,
692. Sir Gauan, on Godez halue, þaȝ hym no gomen þoȝt.
693. Oft leudlez alone he lengez on nyȝtez
694. Þer he fonde noȝt hym byfore þe fare þat he lyked.
695. Hade he no fere bot his fole bi frythez and dounez,
696. Ne no gome bot God bi gate wyth to karp,
697. Til þat he neȝed ful neghe into þe Norþe Walez.
698. Alle þe iles of Anglesay on lyft half he haldez,
699. And farez ouer þe fordez by þe forlondez,
700. Ouer at þe Holy Hede, til he hade eft bonk
701. In þe wyldrenesse of Wyrale; wonde þer bot lyte
702. Þat auþer God oþer gome wyth goud hert louied.
703. And ay he frayned, as he ferde, at frekez þat he met,
704. If þay hade herde any karp of a knyȝt grene,
705. In any grounde þeraboute, of þe grene chapel;
706. And al nykked hym wyth nay, þat neuer in her lyue
707. Þay seȝe neuer no segge þat watz of suche hwez

[bob]

708. of grene.

[wheel]

709. Þe knyȝt tok gates straunge
710. In mony a bonk vnbene,
711. His cher ful oft con chaunge
712. Þat chapel er he myȝt sene.

[stanza xxxi]

713. Mony klyf he ouerclambe in contrayez straunge,
714. Fer floten fro his frendez fremedly he rydez.
715. At vche warþe oþer water þer þe wyȝe passed

He fonde a foo hym byfore, bot ferly hit were,
And þat so foule and so felle þat feȝt hym byhode.
So mony meruayl bi mount þer þe mon fyndez,
Hit were to tore for to telle of þe tenþe dole.
Sumwhyle wyth wormez he werrez, and with wolues als,
Sumwhyle wyth wodwos, þat woned in þe knarrez,
Boþe wyth bullez and berez, and borez oþerquyle,
And etaynez, þat hym anelede of þe heȝe felle;
Nade he ben duȝty and dryȝe, and Dryȝtyn had serued,
Douteles he hade ben ded and dreped ful ofte.
For werre wrathed hym not so much þat wynter nas wors,
When þe colde cler water fro þe cloudez schadde,
And fres er hit falle myȝt to þe fale erþe;
Ner slayn wyth þe slete he sleped in his yrnes
Mo nyȝtez þen innoghe in naked rokkez,
Þer as claterande fro þe crest þe colde borne rennez,
And henged heȝe ouer his hede in hard iisse-ikkles.
Þus in peryl and payne and plytes ful harde
Bi contray cayrez þis knyȝt, tyl Krystmasse euen,

[bob]

al one;

[wheel]

Þe knyȝt wel þat tyde
To Mary made his mone,
Þat ho hym red to ryde
And wysse hym to sum wone.

[stanza xxxii]

Bi a mounte on þe morne meryly he rydes
Into a forest ful dep, þat ferly watz wylde,
Hiȝe hillez on vche a halue, and holtwodez vnder
Of hore okez ful hoge a hundreth togeder;
Þe hasel and þe haȝþorne were harled al samen,
With roȝe raged mosse rayled aywhere,
With mony bryddez vnblyþe vpon bare twyges,
Þat pitosly þer piped for pyne of þe colde.
Þe gome vpon Gryngolet glydez hem vnder,
Þurȝ mony misy and myre, mon al hym one,

750. Carande for his costes, lest he ne keuer schulde
751. To se þe seruyse of þat syre, þat on þat self nyȝt
752. Of a burde watz borne oure baret to quelle;
753. And þerfore sykyng he sayde, 'I beseche þe, lorde,
754. And Mary, þat is myldest moder so dere,
755. Of sum herber þer heȝly I myȝt here masse,
756. Ande þy matynez to-morne, mekely I ask,
757. And þerto prestly I pray my pater and aue

[bob]

758. and crede.'

[wheel]

759. He rode in his prayere,
760. And cryed for his mysdede,
761. He sayned hym in syþes sere,
762. And sayde 'Cros Kryst me spede!'

[stanza xxxiii]

763. Nade he sayned hymself, segge, bot þrye,
764. Er he watz war in þe wod of a won in a mote,
765. Abof a launde, on a lawe, loken vnder boȝez
766. Of mony borelych bole aboute bi þe diches:
767. A castel þe comlokest þat euer knyȝt aȝte,
768. Pyched on a prayere, a park al aboute,
769. With a pyked palays pyned ful þik,
770. Þat vmbeteȝe mony tre mo þen two myle.
771. Þat holde on þat on syde þe haþel auysed,
772. As hit schemered and schon þurȝ þe schyre okez;
773. Þenne hatz he hendly of his helme, and heȝly he þonkez
774. Jesus and sayn Gilyan, þat gentyle ar boþe,
775. Þat cortaysly had hym kydde, and his cry herkened.
776. 'Now bone hostel,' coþe þe burne, 'I beseche yow ȝette!'
777. Þenne gerdez he to Gryngolet with þe gilt helez,
778. And he ful chauncely hatz chosen to þe chef gate,
779. Þat broȝt bremly þe burne to þe bryge ende

[bob]

780. in haste.

[wheel]

Þe bryge watz breme vpbrayde,
Þe ȝatez wer stoken faste,
Þe wallez were wel arayed,
Hit dut no wyndez blaste.

[stanza xxxiv]

Þe burne bode on blonk, þat on bonk houed
Of þe depe double dich þat drof to þe place;
Þe walle wod in þe water wonderly depe,
Ande eft a ful huge heȝt hit haled vpon lofte
Of harde hewen ston vp to þe tablez,
Enbaned vnder þe abataylment in þe best lawe;
And syþen garytez ful gaye gered bitwene,
Wyth mony luflych loupe þat louked ful clene:
A better barbican þat burne blusched vpon neuer.
And innermore he behelde þat halle ful hyȝe,
Towres telded bytwene, trochet ful þik,
Fayre fylyolez þat fyȝed, and ferlyly long,
With coruon coprounes craftyly sleȝe.
Chalkwhyt chymnees þer ches he innoȝe
Vpon bastel rouez, þat blenked ful quyte;
So mony pynakle payntet watz poudred ayquere,
Among þe castel carnelez clambred so þik,
Þat pared out of papure purely hit semed.
Þe fre freke on þe fole hit fayr innoghe þoȝt,
If he myȝt keuer to com þe cloyster wythinne,
To herber in þat hostel whyl halyday lested,

[bob]

auinant.

[wheel]

He calde, and sone þer com
A porter pure plesaunt,
On þe wal his ernd he nome,
And haylsed þe knyȝt erraunt.

[stanza xxxv]

'Gode sir,' quoþ Gawan, 'woldez þou go myn ernde
To þe heȝ lorde of þis hous, herber to craue?'

'ȝe, Peter,' quoþ þe porter, 'and purely I trowee
Þat ȝe be, wyȝe, welcum to won quyle yow lykez.'
Þen ȝede þe wyȝe ȝerne and com aȝayn swyþe,
And folke frely hym wyth, to fonge þe knyȝt.
Þay let doun þe grete draȝt and derely out ȝeden,
And kneled doun on her knes vpon þe colde erþe
To welcum þis ilk wyȝ as worþy hom þoȝt;
Þay ȝolden hym þe brode ȝate, ȝarked vp wyde,
And he hem raysed rekenly, and rod ouer þe brygge.
Sere seggez hym sesed by sadel, quel he lyȝt,
And syþen stabeled his stede stif men innoȝe.
Knyȝtez and swyerez comen doun þenne
For to bryng þis buurne wyth blys into halle;
Quen he hef vp his helme, þer hiȝed innoghe
For to hent hit at his honde, þe hende to seruen;
His bronde and his blasoun boþe þay token.
Þen haylsed he ful hendly þo haþelez vchone,
And mony proud mon þer presed þat prynce to honour.
Alle hasped in his heȝ wede to halle þay hym wonnen,
Þer fayre fyre vpon flet fersly brenned.
Þenne þe lorde of þe lede loutez fro his chambre
For to mete wyth menske þe mon on þe flor;
He sayde, 'ȝe ar welcum to welde as yow lykez
Þat here is; al is yowre awen, to haue at yowre wylle

[bob]

and welde.'

[wheel]

'Graunt mercy,' quoþ Gawayn,
'Þer Kryst hit yow forȝelde.'
As frekez þat semed fayn
Ayþer oþer in armez con felde.

[stanza xxxvi]

Gawayn glyȝt on þe gome þat godly hym gret,
And þuȝt hit a bolde burne þat þe burȝ aȝte,
A hoge haþel for þe nonez, and of hyghe eldee;
Brode, bryȝt, watz his berde, and al beuer-hwed,
Sturne, stif on þe stryþþe on stalworth schonkez,

847. Felle face as þe fyre, and fre of hys speche;
848. And wel hym semed, for soþe, as þe segge þuȝt,
849. To lede a lortschyp in lee of leudez ful gode.
850. Þe lorde hym charred to a chambre, and chefly cumaundez
851. To delyuer hym a leude, hym loȝly to serue;
852. And þere were boun at his bode burnez innoȝe,
853. Þat broȝt hym to a bryȝt boure, þer beddyng watz noble,
854. Of cortynes of clene sylk wyth cler golde hemmez,
855. And couertorez ful curious with comlych panez
856. Of bryȝt blaunner aboue, enbrawded bisydez,
857. Rudelez rennande on ropez, red golde ryngez,
858. Tapitez tyȝt to þe woȝe of tuly and tars,
859. And vnder fete, on þe flet, of folȝande sute.
860. Þer he watz dispoyled, wyth spechez of myerþe,
861. Þe burn of his bruny and of his bryȝt wedez.
862. Ryche robes ful rad renkkez hym broȝten,
863. For to charge, and to chaunge, and chose of þe best.
864. Sone as he on hent, and happed þerinne,
865. Þat sete on hym semly wyth saylande skyrtez,
866. Þe ver by his uisage verayly hit semed
867. Welneȝ to vche haþel, alle on hwes
868. Lowande and lufly alle his lymmez vnder,
869. Þat a comloker knyȝt neuer Kryst made

[bob]

870. hem þoȝt.

[wheel]

871. Wheþen in worlde he were,
872. Hit semed as he moȝt
873. Be prynce withouten pere
874. In felde þer felle men foȝt.

[stanza xxxvii]

875. A cheyer byfore þe chemné, þer charcole brenned,
876. Watz grayþed for Sir Gawan grayþely with cloþez,
877. Whyssynes vpon queldepoyntes þat koynt wer boþe;
878. And þenne a meré mantyle watz on þat mon cast
879. Of a broun bleeaunt, enbrauded ful ryche
880. And fayre furred wythinne with fellez of þe best,

Alle of ermyn in erde, his hode of þe same;
And he sete in þat settel semlych ryche,
And achaufed hym chefly, and þenne his cher mended.
Sone watz telded vp a tabil on trestez ful fayre,
Clad wyth a clene cloþe þat cler quyt schewed,
Sanap, and salure, and syluerin sponez.
Þe wyȝe wesche at his wylle, and went to his mete.
Seggez hym serued semly innoȝe
Wyth sere sewes and sete, sesounde of þe best,
Double-felde, as hit fallez, and fele kyn fischez,
Summe baken in bred, summe brad on þe gledez,
Summe soþen, summe in sewe sauered with spyces,
And ay sawes so sleȝe þat þe segge lyked.
Þe freke calde hit a fest ful frely and ofte
Ful hendely, quen alle þe haþeles rehayted hym at onez,

[bob]

'As hende,

[wheel]

Þis penaunce now ȝe take,
And eft hit schal amende.'
Þat mon much merþe con make,
For wyn in his hed þat wende.

[stanza xxxviii]

Þenne watz spyed and spured vpon spare wyse
Bi preué poyntez of þat prynce, put to hymseluen,
Þat he beknew cortaysly of þe court þat he were
Þat aþel Arthure þe hende haldez hym one,
Þat is þe ryche ryal kyng of þe Rounde Table,
And hit watz Wawen hymself þat in þat won syttez,
Comen to þat Krystmasse, as case hym þen lymped.
When þe lorde hade lerned þat he þe leude hade,
Loude laȝed he þerat, so lef hit hym þoȝt,
And alle þe men in þat mote maden much joye
To apere in his presense prestly þat tyme,
Þat alle prys and prowes and pured þewes
Apendes to hys persoun, and praysed is euer;
Byfore alle men vpon molde his mensk is þe most.

Vch segge ful softly sayde to his fere:
'Now schal we semlych se sleȝtez of þewez
And þe teccheles termes of talkyng noble,
Wich spede is in speche vnspurd may we lerne,
Syn we haf fonged þat fyne fader of nurture.
God hatz geuen vus his grace godly for soþe,
Þat such a gest as Gawan grauntez vus to haue,
When burnez blyþe of his burþe schal sitte

[bob]

and synge.

[wheel]

In menyng of manerez mere
Þis burne now schal vus bryng,
I hope þat may hym here
Schal lerne of luf-talkyng.'

[stanza xxxix]

Bi þat þe diner watz done and þe dere vp
Hit watz neȝ at þe niyȝt neȝed þe tyme.
Chaplaynez to þe chapeles chosen þe gate,
Rungen ful rychely, ryȝt as þay schulden,
To þe hersum euensong of þe hyȝe tyde.
Þe lorde loutes þerto, and þe lady als,
Into a cumly closet coyntly ho entrez.
Gawan glydez ful gay and gos þeder sone;
Þe lorde laches hym by þe lappe and ledez hym to sytte,
And couþly hym knowez and callez hym his nome,
And sayde he watz þe welcomest wyȝe of þe worlde;
And he hym þonkked þroly, and ayþer halched oþer,
And seten soberly samen þe seruise quyle.
Þenne lyst þe lady to loke on þe knyȝt,
Þenne com ho of hir closet with mony cler burdez.
Ho watz þe fayrest in felle, of flesche and of lyre,
And of compas and colour and costes, of alle oþer,
And wener þen Wenore, as þe wyȝe þoȝt.
Ho ches þurȝ þe chaunsel to cheryche þat hende.
An oþer lady hir lad bi þe lyft honde,
Þat watz alder þen ho, an auncian hit semed,

949. And heȝly honowred with haþelez aboute.
950. Bot vnlyke on to loke þo ladyes were,
951. For if þe ȝonge watz ȝep, ȝolȝe watz þat oþer;
952. Riche red on þat on rayled ayquere,
953. Rugh ronkled chekez þat oþer on rolled;
954. Kerchofes of þat on, wyth mony cler perlez,
955. Hir brest and hir bryȝt þrote bare displayed,
956. Schon schyrer þen snawe þat schedez on hillez;
957. Þat oþer wyth a gorger watz gered ouer þe swyre,
958. Chymbled ouer hir blake chyn with chalkquyte vayles,
959. Hir frount folden in sylk, enfoubled ayquere,
960. Toreted and treleted with tryflez aboute,
961. Þat noȝt watz bare of þat burde bot þe blake broȝes,
962. Þe tweyne yȝen and þe nase, þe naked lyppez,
963. And þose were soure to se and sellyly blered;
964. A mensk lady on molde mon may hir calle,

[bob]

965. for Gode!

[wheel]

966. Hir body watz schort and þik,
967. Hir buttokez balȝ and brode,
968. More lykkerwys on to lyk
969. Watz þat scho hade on lode.

[stanza xl]

970. When Gawayn glyȝt on þat gay, þat graciously loked,
971. Wyth leue laȝt of þe lorde he lent hem aȝaynes;
972. Þe alder he haylses, heldande ful lowe,
973. Þe loueloker he lappez a lyttel in armez,
974. He kysses hir comlyly, and knyȝtly he melez.
975. Þay kallen hym of aquoyntaunce, and he hit quyk askez
976. To be her seruaunt sothly, if hemself lyked.
977. Þay tan hym bytwene hem, wyth talkyng hym leden
978. To chambre, to chemné, and chefly þay asken
979. Spycez, þat vnsparely men speded hom to bryng,
980. And þe wynnelych wyne þerwith vche tyme.
981. Þe lorde luflych aloft lepez ful ofte,
982. Mynned merthe to be made vpon mony syþez,

Hent heȝly of his hode, and on a spere henged,
And wayned hom to wynne þe worchip þerof,
Þat most myrþe myȝt meue þat Crystenmas whyle—
'And I schal fonde, bi my fayth, to fylter wyth þe best
Er me wont þe wede, with help of my frendez.'
Þus wyth laȝande lotez þe lorde hit tayt makez,
For to glade Sir Gawayn with gomnez in halle

[bob]

þat nyȝt,

[wheel]

Til þat hit watz tyme
Þe lord comaundet lyȝt;
Sir Gawen his leue con nyme
And to his bed hym diȝt.

[stanza xli]

On þe morne, as vch mon mynez þat tyme
Þat Dryȝtyn for oure destyné to deȝe watz borne,
Wele waxez in vche a won in worlde for his sake;
So did hit þere on þat day þurȝ dayntés mony:
Boþe at mes and at mele messes ful quaynt
Derf men vpon dece drest of þe best.
Þe olde auncian wyf heȝest ho syttez,
Þe lorde lufly her by lent, as I trowe;
Gawan and þe gay burde togeder þay seten,
Euen inmyddez, as þe messe metely come,
And syþen þurȝ al þe sale as hem best semed.
Bi vche grome at his degré grayþely watz serued
Þer watz mete, þer watz myrþe, þer watz much ioye,
Þat for to telle þerof hit me tene were,
And to poynte hit ȝet I pyned me parauenture.
Bot ȝet I wot þat Wawen and þe wale burde
Such comfort of her compaynye caȝten togeder
Þurȝ her dere dalyaunce of her derne wordez,
Wyth clene cortays carp closed fro fylþe,
Þat hor play watz passande vche prynce gomen,

[bob]

in vayres.

[wheel]

1016. Trumpez and nakerys,
1017. Much pypyng þer repayres;
1018. Vche mon tented hys,
1019. And þay two tented þayres.

[stanza xlii]

1020. Much dut watz þer dryuen þat day and þat oþer,
1021. And þe þryd as þro þronge in þerafter;
1022. Þe ioye of sayn Jonez day watz gentyle to here,
1023. And watz þe last of þe layk, leudez þer þoȝten.
1024. Þer wer gestes to go vpon þe gray morne,
1025. Forþy wonderly þay woke, and þe wyn dronken,
1026. Daunsed ful dreȝly wyth dere carolez.
1027. At þe last, when hit watz late, þay lachen her leue,
1028. Vchon to wende on his way þat watz wyȝe stronge.
1029. Gawan gef hym god day, þe godmon hym lachchez,
1030. Ledes hym to his awen chambre, þe chymné bysyde,
1031. And þere he draȝez hym on dryȝe, and derely hym þonkkez
1032. Of þe wynne worschip þat he hym wayued hade,
1033. As to honour his hous on þat hyȝe tyde,
1034. And enbelyse his burȝ with his bele chere:
1035. 'Iwysse sir, quyl I leue, me worþez þe better
1036. Þat Gawayn hatz ben my gest at Goddez awen fest.'
1037. 'Grant merci, sir,' quoþ Gawayn, 'in god fayth hit is yowrez,
1038. Al þe honour is your awen—þe heȝe kyng yow ȝelde!
1039. And I am wyȝe at your wylle to worch youre hest,
1040. As I am halden þerto, in hyȝe and in loȝe,

[bob]

1041. bi riȝt.'

[wheel]

1042. Þe lorde fast can hym payne
1043. To holde lenger þe knyȝt;
1044. To hym answarez Gawayn
1045. Bi non way þat he myȝt.

[stanza xliii]

1046. Then frayned þe freke ful fayre at himseluen

1047. Quat derue dede had hym dryuen at þat dere tyme
1048. So kenly fro þe kyngez kourt to kayre al his one,
1049. Er þe halidayez holly were halet out of toun.
1050. 'For soþe, sir,' quoþ þe segge, 'ȝe sayn bot þe trawþe,
1051. A heȝe ernde and a hasty me hade fro þo wonez,
1052. For I am sumned myselfe to sech to a place,
1053. I ne wot in worlde whederwarde to wende hit to fynde.
1054. I nolde bot if I hit negh myȝt on Nw Ȝeres morne
1055. For alle þe londe inwyth Logres, so me oure lorde help!
1056. Forþy, sir, þis enquest I require yow here,
1057. Þat ȝe me telle with trawþe if euer ȝe tale herde
1058. Of þe grene chapel, quere hit on grounde stondez,
1059. And of þe knyȝt þat hit kepes, of colour of grene.
1060. Þer watz stabled bi statut a steuen vus bytwene
1061. To mete þat mon at þat mere, ȝif I myȝt last;
1062. And of þat ilk Nw Ȝere bot neked now wontez,
1063. And I wolde loke on þat lede, if God me let wolde,
1064. Gladloker, bi Goddez sun, þen any god welde!
1065. Forþi, iwysse, bi ȝowre wylle, wende me bihoues,
1066. Naf I now to busy bot bare þre dayez,
1067. And me als fayn to falle feye as fayly of myyn ernde.'
1068. Þenne laȝande quoþ þe lorde, 'Now leng þe byhoues,
1069. For I schal teche yow to þat terme bi þe tymez ende,
1070. Þe grene chapayle vpon grounde greue yow no more;
1071. Bot ȝe schal be in yowre bed, burne, at þyn ese,
1072. Quyle forth dayez, and ferk on þe fyrst of þe ȝere,
1073. And cum to þat merk at mydmorn, to make quat yow likez

[bob]

1074. in spenne.

[wheel]

1075. Dowellez whyle New Ȝeres daye,
1076. And rys, and raykez þenne,
1077. Mon schal yow sette in waye,
1078. Hit is not two myle henne.'

[stanza xliv]

1079. Þenne watz Gawan ful glad, and gomenly he laȝed:
1080. 'Now I þonk yow þryuandely þurȝ alle oþer þynge,

1081. Now acheued is my chaunce, I schal at your wylle
1082. Dowelle, and ellez do quat ȝe demen.'
1083. Þenne sesed hym þe syre and set hym bysyde,
1084. Let þe ladiez be fette to lyke hem þe better.
1085. Þer watz seme solace by hemself stille;
1086. Þe lorde let for luf lotez so myry,
1087. As wyȝ þat wolde of his wyte, ne wyst quat he myȝt.
1088. Þenne he carped to þe knyȝt, criande loude,
1089. 'Ȝe han demed to do þe dede þat I bidde;
1090. Wyl ȝe halde þis hes here at þys onez?'
1091. 'Ȝe, sir, for soþe,' sayd þe segge trwe,
1092. 'Whyl I byde in yowre borȝe, be bayn to ȝowre hest.'
1093. 'For ȝe haf trauayled,' quoþ þe tulk, 'towen fro ferre,
1094. And syþen waked me wyth, ȝe arn not wel waryst
1095. Nauþer of sostnaunce ne of slepe, soþly I knowe;
1096. Ȝe schal lenge in your lofte, and lyȝe in your ese
1097. To-morn quyle þe messequyle, and to mete wende
1098. When ȝe wyl, wyth my wyf, þat wyth yow schal sitte
1099. And comfort yow with compayny, til I to cort torne;

[bob]

1100. ȝe lende,

[wheel]

1101. And I schal erly ryse,
1102. On huntyng wyl I wende.'
1103. Gauayn grantez alle þyse,
1104. Hym heldande, as þe hende.

[stanza xlv]

1105. 'Ȝet firre,' quoþ þe freke, 'a forwarde we make:
1106. Quat-so-euer I wynne in þe wod hit worþez to yourez,
1107. And quat chek so ȝe acheue chaunge me þerforne.
1108. Swete, swap we so, sware with trawþe,
1109. Queþer, leude, so lymp, lere oþer better.'
1110. 'Bi God,' quoþ Gawayn þe gode, 'I grant þertylle,
1111. And þat yow lyst for to layke, lef hit me þynkes.'
1112. 'Who bryngez vus þis beuerage, þis bargayn is maked':
1113. So sayde þe lorde of þat lede; þay laȝed vchone,
1114. Þay dronken and daylyeden and dalten vntyȝtel,

Þise lordez and ladyez, quyle þat hem lyked;
And syþen with Frenkysch fare and fele fayre lotez
Þay stoden and stemed and stylly speken,
Kysten ful comlyly and kaȝten her leue.
With mony leude ful lyȝt and lemande torches
Vche burne to his bed watz broȝt at þe laste,

[bob]

ful softe.

[wheel]

To bed ȝet er þay ȝede,
Recorded couenauntez ofte;
Þe olde lorde of þat leude
Cowþe wel halde layk alofte.

PASSUS III

[stanza xlvi]

Ful erly bifore þe day þe folk vprysen,
Gestes þat go wolde hor gromez þay calden,
And þay busken vp bilyue blonkkez to sadel,
Tyffen her takles, trussen her males,
Richen hem þe rychest, to ryde alle arayde,
Lepen vp lyȝtly, lachen her brydeles,
Vche wyȝe on his way þer hym wel lyked.
Þe leue lorde of þe londe watz not þe last
Arayed for þe rydyng, with renkkez ful mony;
Ete a sop hastyly, when he hade herde masse,
With bugle to bent-felde he buskez bylyue.
By þat any daylyȝt lemed vpon erþe
He with his haþeles on hyȝe horsses weren.
Þenne þise cacheres þat couþe cowpled hor houndez,
Vnclosed þe kenel dore and calde hem þeroute,
Blwe bygly in buglez þre bare mote;
Braches bayed þerfore and breme noyse maked;
And þay chastysed and charred on chasyng þat went,
A hundreth of hunteres, as I haf herde telle,

[bob]

1145. of þe best.

[wheel]

1146. To trystors vewters ȝod,
1147. Couples huntes of kest;
1148. Þer ros for blastez gode
1149. Gret rurd in þat forest.

[stanza xlvii]

1150. At þe fyrst quethe of þe quest quaked þe wylde;
1151. Der drof in þe dale, doted for drede,
1152. Hiȝed to þe hyȝe, bot heterly þay were
1153. Restayed with þe stablye, þat stoutly ascryed.
1154. Þay let þe herttez haf þe gate, with þe hyȝe hedes,
1155. Þe breme bukkez also with hor brode paumez;
1156. For þe fre lorde hade defende in fermysoun tyme
1157. Þat þer schulde no mon meue to þe male dere.
1158. Þe hindez were halden in with hay! and war!
1159. Þe does dryuen with gret dyn to þe depe sladez;
1160. Þer myȝt mon se, as þay slypte, slentyng of arwes—
1161. At vche wende vnder wande wapped a flone—
1162. Þat bigly bote on þe broun with ful brode hedez.
1163. What! þay brayen, and bleden, bi bonkkez þay deȝen,
1164. And ay rachches in a res radly hem folȝes,
1165. Hunterez wyth hyȝe horne hasted hem after
1166. Wyth such a crakkande kry as klyffes haden brusten.
1167. What wylde so atwaped wyȝes þat schotten
1168. Watz al toraced and rent at þe resayt,
1169. Bi þay were tened at þe hyȝe and taysed to þe wattrez;
1170. Þe ledez were so lerned at þe loȝe trysteres,
1171. And þe grehoundez so grete, þat geten hem bylyue
1172. And hem tofylched, as fast as frekez myȝt loke,

[bob]

1173. þer-ryȝt.

[wheel]

1174. Þe lorde for blys abloy
1175. Ful oft con launce and lyȝt,
1176. And drof þat day wyth joy
1177. Thus to þe derk nyȝt.

[stanza xlviii]

1178. Þus laykez þis lorde by lynde-wodez euez,
1179. And Gawayn þe god mon in gay bed lygez,
1180. Lurkkez quyl þe daylyȝt lemed on þe wowes,
1181. Vnder couertour ful clere, cortyned aboute;
1182. And as in slomeryng he slode, sleȝly he herde
1183. A littel dyn at his dor, and dernly vpon;
1184. And he heuez vp his hed out of þe cloþes,
1185. A corner of þe cortyn he caȝt vp a lyttel,
1186. And waytez warly þiderwarde quat hit be myȝt.
1187. Hit watz þe ladi, loflyest to beholde,
1188. Þat droȝ þe dor after hir ful dernly and stylle,
1189. And boȝed towarde þe bed; and þe burne schamed,
1190. And layde hym doun lystyly, and let as he slepte;
1191. And ho stepped stilly and stel to his bedde,
1192. Kest vp þe cortyn and creped withinne,
1193. And set hir ful softly on þe bed-syde,
1194. And lenged þere selly longe to loke quen he wakened.
1195. Þe lede lay lurked a ful longe quyle,
1196. Compast in his concience to quat þat cace myȝt
1197. Meue oþer amount—to meruayle hym þoȝt,
1198. Bot ȝet he sayde in hymself, 'More semly hit were
1199. To aspye wyth my spelle in space quat ho wolde.'
1200. Þen he wakenede, and wroth, and to hir warde torned,
1201. And vnlouked his yȝe-lyddez, and let as hym wondered,
1202. And sayned hym, as bi his saȝe þe sauer to worthe,

[bob]

1203. with hande.

[wheel]

1204. Wyth chynne and cheke ful swete,
1205. Boþe quit and red in blande,
1206. Ful lufly con ho lete
1207. Wyth lyppez smal laȝande.

[stanza xlix]

1208. 'God moroun, Sir Gawayn,' sayde þat gay lady,
1209. 'Ȝe ar a sleper vnslyȝe, þat mon may slyde hider;
1210. Now ar ȝe tan as-tyt! Bot true vus may schape,

1211. I schal bynde yow in your bedde, þat be ȝe trayst':
1212. Al laȝande þe lady lanced þo bourdez.
1213. 'Goud moroun, gay,' quoþ Gawayn þe blyþe,
1214. 'Me schal worþe at your wille, and þat me wel lykez,
1215. For I ȝelde me ȝederly, and ȝeȝe after grace,
1216. And þat is þe best, be my dome, for me byhouez nede':
1217. And þus he bourded aȝayn with mony a blyþe laȝter.
1218. 'Bot wolde ȝe, lady louely, þen leue me grante,
1219. And deprece your prysoun, and pray hym to ryse,
1220. I wolde boȝe of þis bed, and busk me better;
1221. I schulde keuer þe more comfort to karp yow wyth.'
1222. 'Nay for soþe, beau sir,' sayd þat swete,
1223. 'Ȝe schal not rise of your bedde, I rych yow better,
1224. I schal happe yow here þat oþer half als,
1225. And syþen karp wyth my knyȝt þat I kaȝt haue;
1226. For I wene wel, iwysse, Sir Wowen ȝe are,
1227. Þat alle þe worlde worchipez quere-so ȝe ride;
1228. Your honour, your hendelayk is hendely praysed
1229. With lordez, wyth ladyes, with alle þat lyf bere.
1230. And now ȝe ar here, iwysse, and we bot oure one;
1231. My lorde and his ledez ar on lenþe faren,
1232. Oþer burnez in her bedde, and my burdez als,
1233. Þe dor drawen and dit with a derf haspe;
1234. And syþen I haue in þis hous hym þat al lykez,
1235. I schal ware my whyle wel, quyl hit lastez,

[bob]

1236. with tale.

[wheel]

1237. Ȝe ar welcum to my cors,
1238. Yowre awen won to wale,
1239. Me behouez of fyne force
1240. Your seruaunt be, and schale.'

[stanza l]

1241. 'In god fayth,' quoþ Gawayn, 'gayn hit me þynkkez,
1242. Þaȝ I be not now he þat ȝe of speken;
1243. To reche to such reuerence as ȝe reherce here
1244. I am wyȝe vnworþy, I wot wel myseluen.

Bi God, I were glad, and yow god þoȝt,
At saȝe oþer at seruyce þat I sette myȝt
To þe plesaunce of your prys—hit were a pure ioye.'
'In god fayth, Sir Gawayn,' quoþ þe gay lady,
'Þe prys and þe prowes þat plesez al oþer,
If I hit lakked oþer set at lyȝt, hit were littel daynté;
Bot hit ar ladyes innoȝe þat leuer wer nowþe
Haf þe, hende, in hor holde, as I þe habbe here,
To daly with derely your daynté wordez,
Keuer hem comfort and colen her carez,
Þen much of þe garysoun oþer golde þat þay hauen.
Bot I louue þat ilk lorde þat þe lyfte haldez,
I haf hit holly in my honde þat al desyres,

[bob]

þurȝe grace.'

[wheel]

Scho made hym so gret chere,
Þat watz so fayr of face,
Þe knyȝt with speches skere
Answared to vche a cace.

[stanza li]

'Madame,' quoþ þe myry mon, 'Mary yow ȝelde,
For I haf founden, in god fayth, yowre fraunchis nobele,
And oþer ful much of oþer folk fongen bi hor dedez,
Bot þe daynté þat þay delen, for my disert nys euen,
Hit is þe worchyp of yourself, þat noȝt bot wel connez.'
'Bi Mary,' quoþ þe menskful, 'me þynk hit an oþer;
For were I worth al þe wone of wymmen alyue,
And al þe wele of þe worlde were in my honde,
And I schulde chepen and chose to cheue me a lorde,
For þe costes þat I haf knowen vpon þe, knyȝt, here,
Of bewté and debonerté and blyþe semblaunt,
And þat I haf er herkkened and halde hit here trwee,
Þer schulde no freke vpon folde bifore yow be chosen.'
'Iwysse, worþy,' quoþ þe wyȝe, 'ȝe haf waled wel better,
Bot I am proude of þe prys þat ȝe put on me,
And, soberly your seruaunt, my souerayn I holde yow,

1279. And yowre knyȝt I becom, and Kryst yow forȝelde.'
1280. Þus þay meled of muchquat til mydmorn paste,
1281. And ay þe lady let lyk as hym loued mych;
1282. Þe freke ferde with defence, and feted ful fayre—
1283. 'Þaȝ I were burde bryȝtest', þe burde in mynde hade.
1284. Þe lasse luf in his lode for lur þat he soȝt

[bob]

1285. boute hone,

[wheel]

1286. Þe dunte þat schulde hym deue,
1287. And nedez hit most be done.
1288. Þe lady þenn spek of leue,
1289. He granted hir ful sone.

[stanza lii]

1290. Þenne ho gef hym god day, and wyth a glent laȝed,
1291. And as ho stod, ho stonyed hym wyth ful stor wordez:
1292. 'Now he þat spedez vche spech þis disport ȝelde yow!
1293. Bot þat ȝe be Gawan, hit gotz in mynde.'
1294. 'Querfore?' quoþ þe freke, and freschly he askez,
1295. Ferde lest he hade fayled in fourme of his castes;
1296. Bot þe burde hym blessed, and 'Bi þis skyl' sayde:
1297. 'So god as Gawayn gaynly is halden,
1298. And cortaysye is closed so clene in hymseluen,
1299. Couth not lyȝtly haf lenged so long wyth a lady,
1300. Bot he had craued a cosse, bi his courtaysye,
1301. Bi sum towch of summe tryfle at sum talez ende.'
1302. Þen quoþ Wowen: 'Iwysse, worþe as yow lykez;
1303. I schal kysse at your comaundement, as a knyȝt fallez,
1304. And fire, lest he displese yow, so plede hit no more.'
1305. Ho comes nerre with þat, and cachez hym in armez,
1306. Loutez luflych adoun and þe leude kyssez.
1307. Þay comly bykennen to Kryst ayþer oþer;
1308. Ho dos hir forth at þe dore withouten dyn more;
1309. And he ryches hym to ryse and rapes hym sone,
1310. Clepes to his chamberlayn, choses his wede,
1311. Boȝez forth, quen he watz boun, blyþely to masse;
1312. And þenne he meued to his mete þat menskly hym keped,

1313. And made myry al day, til þe mone rysed,

[bob]

1314. with game.

[wheel]

1315. Watz neuer freke fayrer fonge
1316. Bitwene two so dyngne dame,
1317. Þe alder and þe ȝonge;
1318. Much solace set þay same.

[stanza liii]

1319. And ay þe lorde of þe londe is lent on his gamnez,
1320. To hunt in holtez and heþe at hyndez barayne;
1321. Such a sowme he þer slowe bi þat þe sunne heldet,
1322. Of dos and of oþer dere, to deme were wonder.
1323. Þenne fersly þay flokked in folk at þe laste,
1324. And quykly of þe quelled dere a querré þay maked.
1325. Þe best boȝed þerto with burnez innoghe,
1326. Gedered þe grattest of gres þat þer were,
1327. And didden hem derely vndo as þe dede askez;
1328. Serched hem at þe asay summe þat þer were,
1329. Two fyngeres þay fonde of þe fowlest of alle.
1330. Syþen þay slyt þe slot, sesed þe erber,
1331. Schaued wyth a scharp knyf, and þe schyre knitten;
1332. Syþen rytte þay þe foure lymmes, and rent of þe hyde,
1333. Þen brek þay þe balé, þe bowelez out token
1334. Lystily for laucyng þe lere of þe knot;
1335. Þay gryped to þe gargulun, and grayþely departed
1336. Þe wesaunt fro þe wynt-hole, and walt out þe guttez;
1337. Þen scher þay out þe schulderez with her scharp knyuez,
1338. Haled hem by a lyttel hole to haue hole sydes.
1339. Siþen britned þay þe brest and brayden hit in twynne,
1340. And eft at þe gargulun bigynez on þenne,
1341. Ryuez hit vp radly ryȝt to þe byȝt,
1342. Voydez out þe avanters, and verayly þerafter
1343. Alle þe rymez by þe rybbez radly þay lance;
1344. So ryde þay of by resoun bi þe rygge bonez,
1345. Euenden to þe haunche, þat henged alle samen,
1346. And heuen hit vp al hole, and hwen hit of þere,

1347. And þat þay neme for þe noumbles bi nome, as I trowe,

[bob]

1348. bi kynde;

[wheel]

1349. Bi þe by3t al of þe þy3es
1350. Þe lappez þay lance bihynde;
1351. To hewe hit in two þay hy3es,
1352. Bi þe bakbon to vnbynde.

[stanza liv]

1353. Boþe þe hede and þe hals þay hwen of þenne,
1354. And syþen sunder þay þe sydez swyft fro þe chyne,
1355. And þe corbeles fee þay kest in a greue;
1356. Þenn þurled þay ayþer þik side þur3 bi þe rybbe,
1357. And henged þenne ayþer bi ho3ez of þe fourchez,
1358. Vche freke for his fee, as fallez for to haue.
1359. Vpon a felle of þe fayre best fede þay þayr houndes
1360. Wyth þe lyuer and þe ly3tez, þe leþer of þe paunchez,
1361. And bred baþed in blod blende þeramongez.
1362. Baldely þay blw prys, bayed þayr rachchez,
1363. Syþen fonge þay her flesche, folden to home,
1364. Strakande ful stoutly mony stif motez.
1365. Bi þat þe dayly3t watz done þe douthe watz al wonen
1366. Into þe comly castel, þer þe kny3t bidez

[bob]

1367. ful stille,

[wheel]

1368. Wyth blys and bry3t fyr bette.
1369. Þe lorde is comen þertylle;
1370. When Gawayn wyth hym mette
1371. Þer watz bot wele at wylle.

[stanza lv]

1372. Thenne comaunded þe lorde in þat sale to samen alle þe meny,
1373. Boþe þe ladyes on loghe to ly3t with her burdes
1374. Bifore alle þe folk on þe flette, frekez he beddez
1375. Verayly his venysoun to fech hym byforne,

And al godly in gomen Gawayn he called,
Techez hym to þe tayles of ful tayt bestes,
Schewez hym þe schyree grece schorne vpon rybbes.
'How payez yow þis play? Haf I prys wonnen?
Haue I þryuandely þonk þurȝ my craft serued?'
'Ȝe iwysse,' quoþ þat oþer wyȝe, 'here is wayth fayrest
Þat I seȝ þis seuen ȝere in sesoun of wynter.'
'And al I gif yow, Gawayn,' quoþ þe gome þenne,
'For by acorde of couenaunt ȝe craue hit as your awen.'
'Þis is soth,' quoþ þe segge, 'I say yow þat ilke:
Þat I haf worthyly wonnen þis wonez wythinne,
Iwysse with as god wylle hit worþez to ȝourez.'
He hasppez his fayre hals his armez wythinne,
And kysses hym as comlyly as he couþe awyse:
'Tas yow þere my cheuicaunce, I cheued no more;
I wowche hit saf fynly, þaȝ feler hit were.'
'Hit is god,' quoþ þe godmon, 'grant mercy þerfore.
Hit may be such hit is þe better, and ȝe me breue wolde
Where ȝe wan þis ilk wele bi wytte of yorseluen.'
'Þat watz not forward,' quoþ he, 'frayst me no more.
For ȝe haf tan þat yow tydez, trawe non oþer

[bob]

ȝe mowe.'

[wheel]

Þay laȝed, and made hem blyþe
Wyth lotez þat were to lowe;
To soper þay ȝede as-swyþe,
Wyth dayntés nwe innowe.

[stanza lvi]

And syþen by þe chymné in chamber þay seten,
Wyȝez þe walle wyn weȝed to hem oft,
And efte in her bourdyng þay bayþen in þe morn
To fylle þe same forwardez þat þay byfore maden:
Wat chaunce so bytydez hor cheuysaunce to chaunge,
What nwez so þay nome, at naȝt quen þay metten.
Þay acorded of þe couenauntez byfore þe court alle;
Þe beuerage watz broȝt forth in bourde at þat tyme,

Þenne þay louelych leȝten leue at þe last,
Vche burne to his bedde busked bylyue.
Bi þat þe coke hade crowen and cakled bot þryse,
Þe lorde watz lopen of his bedde, þe leudez vchone;
So þat þe mete and þe masse watz metely delyuered,
Þe douthe dressed to þe wod, er any day sprenged,

[bob]

to chace;

[wheel]

Heȝ with hunte and hornez
Þurȝ playnez þay passe in space,
Vncoupled among þo þornez
Rachez þat ran on race.

[stanza lvii]

Sone þay calle of a quest in a ker syde,
Þe hunt rehayted þe houndez þat hit fyrst mynged,
Wylde wordez hym warp wyth a wrast noyce;
Þe howndez þat hit herde hastid þider swyþe,
And fellen as fast to þe fuyt, fourty at ones;
Þenne such a glauer ande glam of gedered rachchez
Ros, þat þe rocherez rungen aboute;
Hunterez hem hardened with horne and wyth muthe.
Þen al in a semblé sweyed togeder,
Bitwene a flosche in þat fryth and a foo cragge;
In a knot bi a clyffe, at þe kerre syde,
Þer as þe rogh rocher vnrydely watz fallen,
Þay ferden to þe fyndyng, and frekez hem after;
Þay vmbekesten þe knarre and þe knot boþe,
Wyȝez, whyl þay wysten wel wythinne hem hit were,
Þe best þat þer breued watz wyth þe blodhoundez.
Þenne þay beten on þe buskez, and bede hym vpryse,
And he vnsoundyly out soȝt seggez ouerþwert;
On þe sellokest swyn swenged out þere,
Long sythen fro þe sounder þat siȝed for olde,
For he watz breme, bor alþer-grattest,
Ful grymme quen he gronyed; þenne greued mony,
For þre at þe fyrst þrast he þryȝt to þe erþe,

And sparred forth good sped boute spyt more.
Þise oþer halowed hyghe! ful hyȝe, and hay! hay! cryed,
Haden hornez to mouþe, heterly rechated;
Mony watz þe myry mouthe of men and of houndez
Þat buskkez after þis bor with bost and wyth noyse

[bob]

to quelle.

[wheel]

Ful oft he bydez þe baye,
And maymez þe mute inn melle;
He hurtez of þe houndez, and þay
Ful ȝomerly ȝaule and ȝelle.

[stanza lviii]

Schalkez to schote at hym schowen to þenne,
Haled to hym of her arewez, hitten hym oft;
Bot þe poyntez payred at þe pyth þat pyȝt in his scheldez,
And þe barbez of his browe bite non wolde—
Þaȝ þe schauen schaft schyndered in pecez,
Þe hede hypped aȝayn were-so-euer hit hitte.
Bot quen þe dyntez hym dered of her dryȝe strokez,
Þen, braynwod for bate, on burnez he rasez,
Hurtez hem ful heterly þer he forth hyȝez,
And mony arȝed þerat, and on lyte droȝen.
Bot þe lorde on a lyȝt horce launces hym after,
As burne bolde vpon bent his bugle he blowez,
He rechated, and rode þurȝ ronez ful þyk,
Suande þis wylde swyn til þe sunne schafted.
Þis day wyth þis ilk dede þay dryuen on þis wyse,
Whyle oure luflych lede lys in his bedde,
Gawayn grayþely at home, in gerez ful ryche

[bob]

of hewe.

[wheel]

Þe lady noȝt forȝate,
Com to hym to salue;
Ful erly ho watz hym ate

1475. His mode for to remwe.

[stanza lix]

1476. Ho commes to þe cortyn, and at þe kny3t totes.
1477. Sir Wawen her welcumed worþy on fyrst,
1478. And ho hym 3eldez a3ayn ful 3erne of hir wordez,
1479. Settez hir softly by his syde, and swyþely ho la3ez,
1480. And wyth a luflych loke ho layde hym þyse wordez:
1481. 'Sir, 3if 3e be Wawen, wonder me þynkkez,
1482. Wy3e þat is so wel wrast alway to god,
1483. And connez not of compaynye þe costez vndertake,
1484. And if mon kennes yow hom to knowe, 3e kest hom of your mynde;
1485. Þou hatz for3eten 3ederly þat 3isterday I ta3tte
1486. Bi alder-truest token of talk þat I cowþe.'
1487. 'What is þat?' quoþ þe wyghe, 'Iwysse I wot neuer;
1488. If hit be sothe þat 3e breue, þe blame is myn awen.'
1489. '3et I kende yow of kyssyng,' quoþ þe clere þenne,
1490. 'Quere-so countenaunce is couþe quikly to clayme;
1491. Þat bicumes vche a kny3t þat cortaysy vses.'
1492. 'Do way,' quoþ þat derf mon, 'my dere, þat speche,
1493. For þat durst I not do, lest I deuayed were;
1494. If I were werned, I were wrang, iwysse, 3if I profered.'
1495. 'Ma fay,' quoþ þe meré wyf, '3e may not be werned,
1496. 3e ar stif innoghe to constrayne wyth strenkþe, 3if yow lykez,
1497. 3if any were so vilanous þat yow devaye wolde.'
1498. '3e, be God,' quoþ Gawayn, 'good is your speche,
1499. Bot þrete is vnþryuande in þede þer I lende,
1500. And vche gift þat is geuen not with goud wylle.
1501. I am at your comaundement, to kysse quen yow lykez,
1502. 3e may lach quen yow lyst, and leue quen yow þynkkez,

[bob]

1503. in space.'

[wheel]

1504. Þe lady loutez adoun,
1505. And comlyly kysses his face,
1506. Much speche þay þer expoun
1507. Of druryes greme and grace.

[stanza lx]

'I woled wyt at yow, wyȝe,' þat worþy þer sayde,
'And yow wrathed not þerwyth, what were þe skylle
Þat so ȝong and so ȝepe as ȝe at þis tyme,
So cortayse, so knyȝtyly, as ȝe ar knowen oute—
And of alle cheualry to chose, þe chef þyng alosed
Is þe lel layk of luf, þe lettrure of armes;
For to telle of þis teuelyng of þis trwe knyȝtez,
Hit is þe tytelet token and tyxt of her werkkez,
How ledes for her lele luf hor lyuez han auntered,
Endured for her drury dulful stoundez,
And after wenged with her walour and voyded her care,
And broȝt blysse into boure with bountees hor awen—
And ȝe ar knyȝt comlokest kyd of your elde,
Your worde and your worchip walkez ayquere,
And I haf seten by yourself here sere twyes,
Ȝet herde I neuer of your hed helde no wordez
Þat euer longed to luf, lasse ne more;
And ȝe, þat ar so cortays and coynt of your hetes,
Oghe to a ȝonke þynk ȝern to schewe
And teche sum tokenez of trweluf craftes.
Why! ar ȝe lewed, þat alle þe los weldez?
Oþer elles ȝe demen me to dille your dalyaunce to herken?

[bob]

For schame!

[wheel]

I com hider sengel, and sitte
To lerne at yow sum game;
Dos, techez me of your wytte,
Whil my lorde is fro hame.'

[stanza lxi]

'In goud fayþe,' quoþ Gawayn, 'God yow forȝelde!
Gret is þe gode gle, and gomen to me huge,
Þat so worþy as ȝe wolde wynne hidere,
And pyne yow with so pouer a mon, as play wyth your knyȝt
With anyskynnez countenaunce, hit keuerez me ese;
Bot to take þe toruayle to myself to trwluf expoun,

1541. And towche þe temez of tyxt and talez of armez
1542. To yow þat, I wot wel, weldez more sly3t
1543. Of þat art, bi þe half, or a hundreth of seche
1544. As I am, oþer euer schal, in erde þer I leue,
1545. Hit were a folé felefolde, my fre, by my trawþe.
1546. I wolde yowre wylnyng worche at my my3t,
1547. As I am hy3ly bihalden, and euermore wylle
1548. Be seruaunt to yourseluen, so saue me Dry3tyn!'
1549. Þus hym frayned þat fre, and fondet hym ofte,
1550. For to haf wonnen hym to wo3e, what-so scho þo3t ellez;
1551. Bot he defended hym so fayr þat no faut semed,
1552. Ne non euel on nawþer halue, nawþer þay wysten

[bob]

1553. bot blysse.

[wheel]

1554. Þay la3ed and layked longe;
1555. At þe last scho con hym kysse,
1556. Hir leue fayre con scho fonge
1557. And went hir waye, iwysse.

[stanza lxii]

1558. Then ruþes hym þe renk and ryses to þe masse,
1559. And siþen hor diner watz dy3t and derely serued.
1560. Þe lede with þe ladyez layked alle day,
1561. Bot þe lorde ouer þe londez launced ful ofte,
1562. Swez his vncely swyn, þat swyngez bi þe bonkkez
1563. And bote þe best of his brachez þe bakkez in sunder
1564. Þer he bode in his bay, tel bawemen hit breken,
1565. And madee hym mawgref his hed for to mwe vtter,
1566. So felle flonez þer flete when þe folk gedered.
1567. Bot 3et þe styffest to start bi stoundez he made,
1568. Til at þe last he watz so mat he my3t no more renne,
1569. Bot in þe hast þat he my3t he to a hole wynnez
1570. Of a rasse bi a rokk þer rennez þe boerne.
1571. He gete þe bonk at his bak, bigynez to scrape,
1572. Þe froþe femed at his mouth vnfayre bi þe wykez,
1573. Whettez his whyte tuschez; with hym þen irked
1574. Alle þe burnez so bolde þat hym by stoden

To nye hym on-ferum, bot neȝe hym non durst
[bob]
for woþe;
[wheel]
He hade hurt so mony byforne
Þat al þuȝt þenne ful loþe
Be more wyth his tusches torne,
Þat breme watz and braynwod bothe,

[stanza lxiii]

Til þe knyȝt com hymself, kachande his blonk,
Syȝ hym byde at þe bay, his burnez bysyde;
He lyȝtes luflych adoun, leuez his corsour,
Braydez out a bryȝt bront and bigly forth strydez,
Foundez fast þurȝ þe forth þer þe felle bydez.
Þe wylde watz war of þe wyȝe with weppen in honde,
Hef hyȝly þe here, so hetterly he fnast
Þat fele ferde for þe freke, lest felle hym þe worre.
Þe swyn settez hym out on þe segge euen,
Þat þe burne and þe bor were boþe vpon hepez
In þe wyȝtest of þe water; þe worre hade þat oþer,
For þe mon merkkez hym wel, as þay mette fyrst,
Set sadly þe scharp in þe slot euen,
Hit hym vp to þe hult, þat þe hert schyndered,
And he ȝarrande hym ȝelde, and ȝedoun þe water
[bob]
ful tyt.
[wheel]
A hundreth houndez hym hent,
Þat bremely con hym bite,
Burnez him broȝt to bent,
And doggez to dethe endite.

[stanza lxiv]

There watz blawyng of prys in mony breme horne,
Heȝe halowing on hiȝe with haþelez þat myȝt;
Brachetes bayed þat best, as bidden þe maysterez

1604. Of þat chargeaunt chace þat were chef huntes.
1605. Þenne a wyȝe þat watz wys vpon wodcraftez
1606. To vnlace þis bor lufly bigynnez.
1607. Fyrst he hewes of his hed and on hiȝe settez,
1608. And syþen rendez him al roghe bi þe rygge after,
1609. Braydez out þe boweles, brennez hom on glede,
1610. With bred blent þerwith his braches rewardez.
1611. Syþen he britnez out þe brawen in bryȝt brode cheldez,
1612. And hatz out þe hastlettez, as hiȝtly bisemez;
1613. And ȝet hem halchez al hole þe haluez togeder,
1614. And syþen on a stif stange stoutly hem henges.
1615. Now with þis ilk swyn þay swengen to home;
1616. Þe bores hed watz borne bifore þe burnes seluen
1617. Þat him forferde in þe forþe þurȝ forse of his honed

[bob]

1618. so stronge.

[wheel]

1619. Til he seȝ Sir Gawayne
1620. In halle hym poȝt ful longe;
1621. He calde, and he com gayn
1622. His feez þer for to fonge.

[stanza lxv]

1623. Þe lorde ful lowde with lote and laȝter myry,
1624. When he seȝe Sir Gawayn, with solace he spekez;
1625. Þe goude ladyez were geten, and gedered þe meyny,
1626. He schewez hem þe scheldez, and schapes hem þe tale
1627. Of þe largesse and þe lenþe, þe liþernez alse
1628. Of þe were of þe wylde swyn in wod þer he fled.
1629. Þat oþer knyȝt ful comly comended his dedez,
1630. And praysed hit as gret prys þat he proued hade,
1631. For suche a brawne of a best, þe bolde burne sayde,
1632. Ne such sydes of a swyn segh he neuer are.
1633. Þenne hondeled þay þe hoge hed, þe hende mon hit praysed,
1634. And let lodly þerat þe lorde for to here.
1635. 'Now, Gawayn,' quoþ þe godmon, 'þis gomen is your awen
1636. Bi fyn forwarde and faste, faythely ȝe knowe.'
1637. 'Hit is sothe,' quoþ þe segge, 'and as siker trwe

1638. Alle my get I schal yow gif agayn, bi my trawþe.'
1639. He hent þe haþel aboute þe halse, and hendely hym kysses,
1640. And eftersones of þe same he serued hym þere.
1641. 'Now ar we euen,' quoþ þe haþel, 'in þis euentide
1642. Of alle þe couenauntes þat we knyt, syþen I com hider,

[bob]

1643. bi lawe.'

[wheel]

1644. Þe lorde sayde, 'Bi saynt Gile,
1645. Ʒe ar þe best þat I knowe!
1646. Ʒe ben ryche in a whyle,
1647. Such chaffer and ȝe drowe.'

[stanza lxvi]

1648. Þenne þay teldet tablez trestes alofte,
1649. Kesten cloþen vpon; clere lyȝt þenne
1650. Wakned bi woȝez, waxen torches;
1651. Seggez sette and serued in sale al aboute;
1652. Much glam and gle glent vp þerinne
1653. Aboute þe fyre vpon flet, and on fele wyse
1654. At þe soper and after, mony aþel songez,
1655. As coundutes of Krystmasse and carolez newe
1656. With al þe manerly merþe þat mon may of telle,
1657. And euer oure luflych knyȝt þe lady bisyde.
1658. Such semblaunt to þat segge semly ho made
1659. Wyth stille stollen countenaunce, þat stalworth to plese,
1660. Þat al forwondered watz þe wyȝe, and wroth with hymseluen,
1661. Bot he nolde not for his nurture nurne hir aȝaynez,
1662. Bot dalt with hir al in daynté, how-se-euer þe dede turned

[bob]

1663. towrast.

[wheel]

1664. Quen þay hade played in halle
1665. As longe as hor wylle hom last,
1666. To chambre he con hym calle,
1667. And to þe chemné þay past.

[stanza lxvii]

1668. Ande þer þay dronken, and dalten, and demed eft nwe
1669. To norne on þe same note on Nwe 3erez euen;
1670. Bot þe kny3t craued leue to kayre on þe morn,
1671. For hit watz ne3 at þe terme þat he to schulde.
1672. Þe lorde hym letted of þat, to lenge hym resteyed,
1673. And sayde, 'As I am trwe segge, I siker my trawþe
1674. Þou schal cheue to þe grene chapel þy charres to make,
1675. Leude, on Nw 3erez ly3t, longe bifore pryme.
1676. Forþy þow lye in þy loft and lach þyn ese,
1677. And I schal hunt in þis holt, and halde þe towchez,
1678. Chaunge wyth þe cheuisaunce, bi þat I charre hider;
1679. For I haf fraysted þe twys, and faythful I fynde þe.
1680. Now "þrid tyme þrowe best" þenk on þe morne,
1681. Make we mery quyl we may and mynne vpon joye,
1682. For þe lur may mon lach when-so mon lykez.'
1683. Þis watz grayþely graunted, and Gawayn is lenged,
1684. Bliþe bro3t watz hym drynk, and þay to bedde 3eden

[bob]

1685. with li3t.

[wheel]

1686. Sir Gawayn lis and slepes
1687. Ful stille and softe al ni3t;
1688. Þe lorde þat his craftez kepes,
1689. Ful erly he watz di3t.

[stanza lxviii]

1690. After messe a morsel he and his men token;
1691. Miry watz þe mornyng, his mounture he askes.
1692. Alle þe haþeles þat on horse schulde helden hym after
1693. Were boun busked on hor blonkkez bifore þe halle 3atez.
1694. Ferly fayre watz þe folde, for þe forst clenged;
1695. In rede rudede vpon rak rises þe sunne,
1696. And ful clere costez þe clowdes of þe welkyn.
1697. Hunteres vnhardeled bi a holt syde,
1698. Rocheres roungen bi rys for rurde of her hornes;
1699. Summe fel in þe fute þer þe fox bade,
1700. Traylez ofte a traueres bi traunt of her wyles;

1701. A kenet kyres þerof, þe hunt on hym calles;
1702. His felaȝes fallen hym to, þat fnasted ful þike,
1703. Runnen forth in a rabel in his ryȝt fare,
1704. And he fyskez hem byfore; þay founden hym sone,
1705. And quen þay seghe hym with syȝt þay sued hym fast,
1706. Wreȝande hym ful weterly with a wroth noyse;
1707. And he trantes and tornayeez þurȝ mony tene greue,
1708. Hauilounez, and herkenez bi heggez ful ofte.
1709. At þe last bi a littel dich he lepez ouer a spenne,
1710. Stelez out ful stilly bi a strothe rande,
1711. Went haf wylt of þe wode with wylez fro þe houndes;
1712. Þenne watz he went, er he wyst, to a wale tryster,
1713. Þer þre þro at a þrich þrat hym at ones,

[bob]

1714. al graye.

[wheel]

1715. He blenched aȝayn bilyue
1716. And stifly start on-stray,
1717. With alle þe wo on lyue
1718. To þe wod he went away.

[stanza lxix]

1719. Thenne watz hit list vpon lif to lyþen þe houndez,
1720. When alle þe mute hade hym met, menged togeder:
1721. Suche a sorȝe at þat syȝt þay sette on his hede
1722. As alle þe clamberande clyffes hade clatered on hepes;
1723. Here he watz halawed, when haþelez hym metten,
1724. Loude he watz ȝayned with ȝarande speche;
1725. Þer he watz þreted and ofte þef called,
1726. And ay þe titleres at his tayl, þat tary he ne myȝt;
1727. Ofte he watz runnen at, when he out rayked,
1728. And ofte reled in aȝayn, so Reniarde watz wylé.
1729. And ȝe he lad hem bi lagmon, þe lorde and his meyny,
1730. On þis maner bi þe mountes quyle myd-ouer-vnder,
1731. Whyle þe hende knyȝt at home holsumly slepes
1732. Withinne þe comly cortynes, on þe colde morne.
1733. Bot þe lady for luf let not to slepe,
1734. Ne þe purpose to payre þat pyȝt in hir hert,

1735. Bot ros hir vp radly, rayked hir þeder
1736. In a mery mantyle, mete to þe erþe,
1737. Þat watz furred ful fyne with fellez wel pured,
1738. No hwef goud on hir hede bot þe haȝer stones
1739. Trased aboute hir tressour be twenty in clusteres;
1740. Hir þryuen face and hir þrote þrowen al naked,
1741. Hir brest bare bifore, and bihinde eke.
1742. Ho comez withinne þe chambre dore, and closes hit hir after,
1743. Wayuez vp a wyndow, and on þe wyȝe callez,
1744. And radly þus rehayted hym with hir riche wordes,

[bob]

1745. with chere:

[wheel]

1746. 'A! mon, how may þou slepe,
1747. Þis morning is so clere?'
1748. He watz in drowping depe,
1749. Bot þenne he con hir here.

[stanza lxx]

1750. In dreȝ droupyng of dreme draueled þat noble,
1751. As mon þat watz in mornyng of mony þro þoȝtes,
1752. How þat destiné schulde þat day dele hym his wyrde
1753. At þe grene chapel, when he þe gome metes,
1754. And bihoues his buffet abide withoute debate more;
1755. Bot quen þat comly com he keuered his wyttes,
1756. Swenges out of þe sweuenes, and swarez with hast.
1757. Þe lady luflych com laȝande swete,
1758. Felle ouer his fayre face, and fetly hym kyssed;
1759. He welcumez hir worþily with a wale chere.
1760. He seȝ hir so glorious and gayly atyred,
1761. So fautles of hir fetures and of so fyne hewes,
1762. Wiȝt wallande joye warmed his hert.
1763. With smoþe smylyng and smolt þay smeten into merþe,
1764. Þat al watz blis and bonchef þat breke hem bitwene,

[bob]

1765. and wynne.

[wheel]

1766. Þay lanced wordes gode,
1767. Much wele þen watz þerinne;
1768. Gret perile bitwene hem stod,
1769. Nif Maré of hir kny3t mynne.

[stanza lxxi]

1770. For þat prynces of pris depresed hym so þikke,
1771. Nurned hym so ne3e þe þred, þat nede hym bihoued
1772. Oþer lach þer hir luf, oþer lodly refuse.
1773. He cared for his cortaysye, lest craþayn he were,
1774. And more for his meschef 3if he schulde make synne,
1775. And be traytor to þat tolke þat þat telde a3t.
1776. 'God schylde,' quoþ þe schalk, 'þat schal not befalle!'
1777. With luf-la3yng a lyt he layd hym bysyde
1778. Alle þe spechez of specialté þat sprange of her mouthe.
1779. Quoþ þat burde to þe burne, 'Blame 3e disserue,
1780. 3if 3e luf not þat lyf þat 3e lye nexte,
1781. Bifore alle þe wy3ez in þe worlde wounded in hert,
1782. Bot if 3e haf a lemman, a leuer, þat yow lykez better,
1783. And folden fayth to þat fre, festned so harde
1784. Þat yow lausen ne lyst—and þat I leue nouþe;
1785. And þat 3e telle me þat now trwly I pray yow,
1786. For alle þe lufez vpon lyue layne not þe soþe

[bob]

1787. for gile.'

[wheel]

1788. Þe kny3t sayde, 'Be sayn Jon,'
1789. And smeþely con he smyle,
1790. 'In fayth I welde ri3t non,
1791. Ne non wil welde þe quile.'

[stanza lxxii]

1792. 'Þat is a worde,' quoþ þat wy3t, 'þat worst is of alle,
1793. Bot I am swared for soþe, þat sore me þinkkez.
1794. Kysse me now comly, and I schal cach heþen,
1795. I may bot mourne vpon molde, as may þat much louyes.'
1796. Sykande ho swe3e doun and semly hym kyssed,
1797. And siþen ho seueres hym fro, and says as ho stondes,

1798. 'Now, dere, at þis departyng do me þis ese,
1799. Gif me sumquat of þy gifte, þi gloue if hit were,
1800. Þat I may mynne on þe, mon, my mournyng to lassen.'
1801. 'Now iwysse,' quoþ þat wyȝe, 'I wolde I hade here
1802. Þe leuest þing for þy luf þat I in londe welde,
1803. For ȝe haf deserued, for soþe, sellyly ofte
1804. More rewarde bi resoun þen I reche myȝt;
1805. Bot to dele yow for drurye þat dawed bot neked,
1806. Hit is not your honour to haf at þis tyme
1807. A gloue for a garysoun of Gawaynez giftez,
1808. And I am here an erande in erdez vncouþe,
1809. And haue no men wyth no malez with menskful þingez;
1810. Þat mislykez me, ladé, for luf at þis tyme,
1811. Iche tolke mon do as he is tan, tas to non ille

[bob]

1812. ne pine.'

[wheel]

1813. 'Nay, hende of hyȝe honours,'
1814. Quoþ þat lufsum vnder lyne,
1815. 'Þaȝ I hade noȝt of yourez,
1816. ȝet schulde ȝe haue of myne.'

[stanza lxxiii]

1817. Ho raȝt hym a riche rynk of red golde werkez,
1818. Wyth a starande ston stondande alofte
1819. Þat bere blusschande bemez as þe bryȝt sunne;
1820. Wyt ȝe wel, hit watz worth wele ful hoge.
1821. Bot þe renk hit renayed, and redyly he sayde,
1822. 'I wil no giftez, for Gode, my gay, at þis tyme;
1823. I haf none yow to norne, ne noȝt wyl I take.'
1824. Ho bede hit hym ful bysily, and he hir bode wernes,
1825. And swere swyfte by his sothe þat he hit sese nolde,
1826. And ho soré þat he forsoke, and sayde þerafter,
1827. 'If ȝe renay my rynk, to ryche for hit semez,
1828. ȝe wolde not so hyȝly halden be to me,
1829. I schal gif yow my girdel, þat gaynes yow lasse.'
1830. Ho laȝt a lace lyȝtly þat leke vmbe hir sydez,
1831. Knit vpon hir kyrtel vnder þe clere mantyle,

1832. Gered hit watz with grene sylke and with golde schaped,
1833. Noȝt bot arounde brayden, beten with fyngrez;
1834. And þat ho bede to þe burne, and blyþely bisoȝt,
1835. Þaȝ hit vnworþi were, þat he hit take wolde.
1836. And he nay þat he nolde neghe in no wyse
1837. Nauþer golde ne garysoun, er God hym grace sende
1838. To acheue to þe chaunce þat he hade chosen þere.
1839. 'And þerfore, I pray yow, displese yow noȝt,
1840. And lettez be your bisinesse, for I bayþe hit yow neuer

[bob]

1841. to graunte;

[wheel]

1842. I am derely to yow biholde
1843. Bicause of your sembelaunt,
1844. And euer in hot and colde
1845. To be your trwe seruaunt.'

[stanza lxxiv]

1846. 'Now forsake ȝe þis silke,' sayde þe burde þenne,
1847. 'For hit is symple in hitself? And so hit wel semez.
1848. Lo! so hit is littel, and lasse hit is worþy;
1849. Bot who-so knew þe costes þat knit ar þerinne,
1850. He wolde hit prayse at more prys, parauenture;
1851. For quat gome so is gorde with þis grene lace,
1852. While he hit hade hemely halched aboute,
1853. Þer is no haþel vnder heuen tohewe hym þat myȝt,
1854. For he myȝt not be slayn for slyȝt vpon erþe.'
1855. Þen kest þe knyȝt, and hit come to his hert
1856. Hit were a juel for þe jopardé þat hym iugged were:
1857. When he acheued to þe chapel his chek for to fech,
1858. Myȝt he haf slypped to be vnslayn, þe sleȝt were noble.
1859. Þenne he þulged with hir þrepe and þoled hir to speke,
1860. And ho bere on hym þe belt and bede hit hym swyþe—
1861. And he granted and hym gafe with a goud wylle—
1862. And bisoȝt hym, for hir sake, disceuer hit neuer,
1863. Bot to lelly layne fro hir lorde; þe leude hym acordez
1864. Þat neuer wyȝe schulde hit wyt, iwysse, bot þay twayne

[bob]

1865. for noȝte;

[wheel]

1866. He þonkked hir oft ful swyþe,
1867. Ful þro with hert and þoȝt.
1868. Bi þat on þrynne syþe
1869. Ho hatz kyst þe knyȝt so toȝt.

[stanza lxxv]

1870. Thenne lachchez ho hir leue, and leuez hym þere,
1871. For more myrþe of þat mon moȝt ho not gete.
1872. When ho watz gon, Sir Gawayn gerez hym sone,
1873. Rises and riches hym in araye noble,
1874. Lays vp þe luf-lace þe lady hym raȝt,
1875. Hid hit ful holdely, þer he hit eft fonde.
1876. Syþen cheuely to þe chapel choses he þe waye,
1877. Preuély aproched to a prest, and prayed hym þere
1878. Þat he wolde lyste his lyf and lern hym better
1879. How his sawle schulde be saued when he schuld seye heþen.
1880. Þere he schrof hym schyrly and schewed his mysdedez,
1881. Of þe more and þe mynne, and merci besechez,
1882. And of absolucioun he on þe segge calles;
1883. And he asoyled hym surely and sette hym so clene
1884. As domezday schulde haf ben diȝt on þe morn.
1885. And syþen he mace hym as mery among þe fre ladyes,
1886. With comlych caroles and alle kynnes ioye,
1887. As neuer he did bot þat daye, to þe derk nyȝt,

[bob]

1888. with blys.

[wheel]

1889. Vche mon hade daynté þare
1890. Of hym, and sayde, 'Iwysse,
1891. Þus myry he watz neuer are,
1892. Syn he com hider, er þis.'

[stanza lxxvi]

1893. Now hym lenge in þat lee, þer luf hym bityde!
1894. Ȝet is þe lorde on þe launde ledande his gomnes.

He hatz forfaren þis fox þat he folȝed longe;
As he sprent ouer a spenne to spye þe schrewe,
Þer as he herd þe howndes þat hasted hym swyþe,
Renaud com richchande þurȝ a roȝe greue,
And alle þe rabel in a res ryȝt at his helez.
Þe wyȝe watz war of þe wylde, and warly abides,
And braydez out þe bryȝt bronde, and at þe best castez.
And he schunt for þe scharp, and schulde haf arered;
A rach rapes hym to, ryȝt er he myȝt,
And ryȝt bifore þe hors fete þay fel on hym alle,
And woried me þis wyly wyth a wroth noyse.
Þe lorde lyȝtez bilyue, and lachez hym sone,
Rased hym ful radly out of þe rach mouþes,
Haldez heȝe ouer his hede, halowez faste,
And þer bayen hym mony braþ houndez.
Huntes hyȝed hem þeder with hornez ful mony,
Ay rechatande aryȝt til þay þe renk seȝen.
Bi þat watz comen his compeyny noble,
Alle þat euer ber bugle blowed at ones,
And alle þise oþer halowed þat hade no hornes;
Hit watz þe myriest mute þat euer men herde,
Þe rich rurd þat þer watz raysed for Renaude saule

[bob]

with lote.

[wheel]

Hor houndez þay þer rewarde,
Her hedez þay fawne and frote,
And syþen þay tan Reynarde,
And tyruen of his cote.

[stanza lxxvii]

And þenne þay helden to home, for hit watz nieȝ nyȝt,
Strakande ful stoutly in hor store hornez.
Þe lorde is lyȝt at þe laste at hys lef home,
Fyndez fire vpon flet, þe freke þer-byside,
Sir Gawayn þe gode, þat glad watz withalle,
Among þe ladies for luf he ladde much ioye;
He were a bleaunt of blwe þat bradde to þe erþe,

1929. His surkot semed hym wel þat softe watz forred,
1930. And his hode of þat ilke henged on his schulder,
1931. Blande al of blaunner were boþe al aboute.
1932. He metez me þis godmon inmyddez þe flore,
1933. And al with gomen he hym gret, and goudly he sayde,
1934. 'I schal fylle vpon fyrst oure forwardez nouþe,
1935. Þat we spedly han spoken, þer spared watz no drynk.'
1936. Þen acoles he þe kny3t and kysses hym þryes,
1937. As sauerly and sadly as he hem sette couþe.
1938. 'Bi Kryst,' quoþ þat oþer kny3t, '3e cach much sele
1939. In cheuisaunce of þis chaffer, 3if 3e hade goud chepez.'
1940. '3e, of þe chepe no charg,' quoþ chefly þat oþer,
1941. 'As is pertly payed þe chepez þat I a3te.'
1942. 'Mary,' quoþ þat oþer mon, 'myn is bihynde,
1943. For I haf hunted al þis day, and no3t haf I geten
1944. Bot þis foule fox felle—þe fende haf þe godez!—
1945. And þat is ful pore for to pay for suche prys þinges
1946. As 3e haf þry3t me here þro, suche þre cosses

[bob]

1947. so gode.'

[wheel]

1948. 'Ino3,' quoþ Sir Gawayn,
1949. 'I þonk yow, bi þe rode',
1950. And how þe fox watz slayn
1951. He tolde hym as þay stode.

[stanza lxxviii]

1952. With merþe and mynstralsye, with metez at hor wylle,
1953. Þay maden as mery as any men mo3ten—
1954. With la3yng of ladies, with lotez of bordes
1955. Gawayn and þe godemon so glad were þay boþe—
1956. Bot if þe douthe had doted, oþer dronken ben oþer.
1957. Boþe þe mon and þe meyny maden mony iapez,
1958. Til þe sesoun watz se3en þat þay seuer moste;
1959. Burnez to hor bedde behoued at þe laste.
1960. Þenne lo3ly his leue at þe lorde fyrst
1961. Fochchez þis fre mon, and fayre he hym þonkkez:
1962. 'Of such a selly soiorne as I haf hade here,

1963. Your honour at þis hyȝe fest, þe hyȝe kyng yow ȝelde!
1964. I ȝef yow me for on of yourez, if yowreself lykez,
1965. For I mot nedes, as ȝe wot, meue to-morne,
1966. And ȝe me take sum tolke to teche, as ȝe hyȝt,
1967. Þe gate to þe grene chapel, as God wyl me suffer
1968. To dele on Nw Ȝerez day þe dome of my wyrdes.'
1969. 'In god fayþe,' quoþ þe godmon, 'wyth a goud wylle
1970. Al þat euer I yow hyȝt halde schal I redé.'
1971. Þer asyngnes he a seruaunt to sett hym in þe waye,
1972. And coundue hym by þe downez, þat he no drechch had,
1973. For to ferk þurȝ þe fryth and fare at þe gaynest

[bob]

1974. bi greue.

[wheel]

1975. Þe lorde Gawayn con þonk,
1976. Such worchip he wolde hym weue.
1977. Þen at þo ladyez wlonk
1978. Þe knyȝt hatz tan his leue.

[stanza lxxix]

1979. With care and wyth kyssyng he carppez hem tille,
1980. And fele þryuande þonkkez he þrat hom to haue,
1981. And þay ȝelden hym aȝayn ȝeply þat ilk;
1982. Þay bikende hym to Kryst with ful colde sykyngez.
1983. Syþen fro þe meyny he menskly departes;
1984. Vche mon þat he mette, he made hem a þonke
1985. For his seruyse and his solace and his sere pyne,
1986. Þat þay wyth busynes had ben aboute hym to serue;
1987. And vche segge as soré to seuer with hym þere
1988. As þay hade wonde worþyly with þat wlonk euer.
1989. Þen with ledes and lyȝt he watz ladde to his chambre
1990. And blyþely broȝt to his bedde to be at his rest.
1991. Ȝif he ne slepe soundyly say ne dar I,
1992. For he hade muche on þe morn to mynne, ȝif he wolde,

[bob]

1993. in þoȝt.

[wheel]

1994. Let hym lyȝe þere stille,
1995. He hatz nere þat he soȝt;
1996. And ȝe wyl a whyle be stylle
1997. I schal telle yow how þay wroȝt.

PASSUS IV

[stanza lxxx]

1998. Now neȝez þe Nw Ȝere, and þe nyȝt passez,
1999. Þe day dryuez to þe derk, as Dryȝtyn biddez;
2000. Bot wylde wederez of þe worlde wakned þeroute,
2001. Clowdes kesten kenly þe colde to þe erþe,
2002. Wyth nyȝe innoghe of þe norþe, þe naked to tene;
2003. Þe snawe snitered ful snart, þat snayped þe wylde;
2004. Þe werbelande wynde wapped fro þe hyȝe,
2005. And drof vche dale ful of dryftes ful grete.
2006. Þe leude lystened ful wel þat leȝ in his bedde,
2007. Þaȝ he lowkez his liddez, ful lyttel he slepes;
2008. Bi vch kok þat crue he knwe wel þe steuen.
2009. Deliuerly he dressed vp, er þe day sprenged,
2010. For þere watz lyȝt of a laumpe þat lemed in his chambre;
2011. He called to his chamberlayn, þat cofly hym swared,
2012. And bede hym bryng hym his bruny and his blonk sadel;
2013. Þat oþer ferkez hym vp and fechez hym his wedez,
2014. And grayþez me Sir Gawayn vpon a grett wyse.
2015. Fyrst he clad hym in his cloþez þe colde for to were,
2016. And syþen his oþer harnays, þat holdely watz keped,
2017. Boþe his paunce and his platez, piked ful clene,
2018. Þe ryngez rokked of þe roust of his riche bruny;
2019. And al watz fresch as vpon fyrst, and he watz fayn þenne

[bob]

2020. to þonk;

[wheel]

2021. He hade vpon vche pece,
2022. Wypped ful wel and wlonk;
2023. Þe gayest into Grece,
2024. Þe burne bede bryng his blonk.

[stanza lxxxi]

Whyle þe wlonkest wedes he warp on hymseluen—
His cote wyth þe conysaunce of þe clere werkez
Ennurned vpon veluet, vertuus stonez
Aboute beten and bounden, enbrauded semez,
And fayre furred withinne wyth fayre pelures—
Ȝet laft he not þe lace, þe ladiez gifte,
Þat forgat not Gawayn for gode of hymseluen.
Bi he hade belted þe bronde vpon his balȝe haunchez,
Þenn dressed he his drurye double hym aboute,
Swyþe sweþled vmbe his swange swetely þat knyȝt
Þe gordel of þe grene silke, þat gay wel bisemed,
Vpon þat ryol red cloþe þat ryche watz to schewe.
Bot wered not þis ilk wyȝe for wele þis gordel,
For pryde of þe pendauntez, þaȝ polyst þay were,
And þaȝ þe glyterande golde glent vpon endez,
Bot for to sauen hymself, when suffer hym byhoued,
To byde bale withoute dabate of bronde hym to were

[bob]

oþer knyffe.

[wheel]

Bi þat þe bolde mon boun
Wynnez þeroute bilyue,
Alle þe meyny of renoun
He þonkkez ofte ful ryue.

[stanza lxxxii]

Thenne watz Gryngolet grayþe, þat gret watz and huge,
And hade ben soiourned sauerly and in a siker wyse,
Hym lyst prik for poynt, þat proude hors þenne.
Þe wyȝe wynnez hym to and wytez on his lyre,
And sayde soberly hymself and by his soth swerez:
'Here is a meyny in þis mote þat on menske þenkkez,
Þe mon hem maynteines, ioy mot þay haue;
Þe leue lady on lyue luf hir bityde;
Ȝif þay for charyté cherysen a gest,
And halden honour in her honde, þe haþel hem ȝelde
Þat haldez þe heuen vpon hyȝe, and also yow alle!

2058. And ȝif I myȝt lyf vpon londe lede any quyle,
2059. I schuld rech yow sum rewarde redyly, if I myȝt.'
2060. Þenn steppez he into stirop and strydez alofte;
2061. His schalk schewed hym his schelde, on schulder he hit laȝt,
2062. Gordez to Gryngolet with his gilt helez,
2063. And he startez on þe ston, stod he no lenger

[bob]

2064. to praunce.

[wheel]

2065. His haþel on hors watz þenne,
2066. Þat bere his spere and launce.
2067. 'Þis kastel to Kryst I kenne':
2068. He gef hit ay god chaunce.

[stanza lxxxiii]

2069. The brygge watz brayde doun, and þe brode ȝatez
2070. Vnbarred and born open vpon boþe halue.
2071. Þe burne blessed hym bilyue, and þe bredez passed—
2072. Prayses þe porter bifore þe prynce kneled,
2073. Gef hym God and goud day, þat Gawayn he saue—
2074. And went on his way with his wyȝe one,
2075. Þat schulde teche hym to tourne to þat tene place
2076. Þer þe ruful race he schulde resayue.
2077. Þay boȝen bi bonkkez þer boȝez ar bare,
2078. Þay clomben bi clyffez þer clengez þe colde.
2079. Þe heuen watz vphalt, bot vgly þer-vnder;
2080. Mist muged on þe mor, malt on þe mountez,
2081. Vch hille hade a hatte, a myst-hakel huge.
2082. Brokez byled and breke bi bonkkez aboute,
2083. Schyre schaterande on schorez, þer þay doun schowued.
2084. Wela wylle watz þe way þer þay bi wod schulden,
2085. Til hit watz sone sesoun þat þe sunne ryses

[bob]

2086. þat tyde.

[wheel]

2087. Þay were on a hille ful hyȝe,
2088. Þe quyte snaw lay bisyde;

Þe burne þat rod hym by
Bede his mayster abide.

[stanza lxxxiv]

'For I haf wonnen yow hider, wyȝe, at þis tyme,
And now nar ȝe not fer fro þat note place
Þat ȝe han spied and spuryed so specially after;
Bot I schal say yow for soþe, syþen I yow knowe,
And ȝe ar a lede vpon lyue þat I wel louy,
Wolde ȝe worch bi my wytte, ȝe worþed þe better.
Þe place þat ȝe prece to ful perelous is halden;
Þer wonez a wyȝe in þat waste, þe worst vpon erþe,
For he is stiffe and sturne, and to strike louies,
And more he is þen any mon vpon myddelerde,
And his body bigger þen þe best fowre
Þat ar in Arþurez hous, Hestor, oþer oþer.
He cheuez þat chaunce at þe chapel grene,
Þer passes non bi þat place so proude in his armes
Þat he ne dyngez hym to deþe with dynt of his honde;
For he is a mon methles, and mercy non vses,
For be hit chorle oþer chaplayn þat bi þe chapel rydes,
Monk oþer masseprest, oþer any mon elles,
Hym þynk as queme hym to quelle as quyk go hymseluen.
Forþy I say þe, as soþe as ȝe in sadel sitte,
Com ȝe þere, ȝe be kylled, may þe knyȝt rede,
Trawe ȝe me þat trwely, þaȝ ȝe had twenty lyues

[bob]

to spende.

[wheel]

He hatz wonyd here ful ȝore,
On bent much baret bende,
Aȝayn his dyntez sore
Ȝe may not yow defende.

[stanza lxxxv]

'Forþy, goude Sir Gawayn, let þe gome one,
And gotz away sum oþer gate, vpon Goddez halue!
Cayrez bi sum oþer kyth, þer Kryst mot yow spede,

2121. And I schal hyʒ me hom aʒayn, and hete yow fyrre
2122. Þat I schal swere bi God and alle his gode halʒez,
2123. As help me God and þe halydam, and oþez innoghe,
2124. Þat I schal lelly yow layne, and lance neuer tale
2125. Þat euer ʒe fondet to fle for freke þat I wyst.'
2126. 'Grant merci', quoþ Gawayn, and gruchyng he sayde:
2127. 'Wel worth þe, wyʒe, þat woldez my gode,
2128. And þat lelly me layne I leue wel þou woldez.
2129. Bot helde þou hit neuer so holde, and I here passed,
2130. Founded for ferde for to fle, in fourme þat þou tellez,
2131. I were a knyʒt kowarde, I myʒt not be excused.
2132. Bot I wyl to þe chapel, for chaunce þat may falle,
2133. And talk wyth þat ilk tulk þe tale þat me lyste,
2134. Worþe hit wele oþer wo, as þe wyrde lykez

[bob]

2135. hit hafe.

[wheel]

2136. Þaʒe he be a sturn knape
2137. To stiʒtel, and stad with staue,
2138. Ful wel con Dryʒtyn schape
2139. His seruauntez for to saue.'

[stanza lxxxvi]

2140. 'Mary!' quoþ þat oþer mon, 'now þou so much spellez,
2141. Þat þou wylt þyn awen nye nyme to þyseluen,
2142. And þe lyst lese þy lyf, þe lette I ne kepe.
2143. Haf here þi helme on þy hede, þi spere in þi honde,
2144. And ryde me doun þis ilk rake bi ʒon rokke syde,
2145. Til þou be broʒt to þe boþem of þe brem valay;
2146. Þenne loke a littel on þe launde, on þi lyfte honde,
2147. And þou schal se in þat slade þe self chapel,
2148. And þe borelych burne on bent þat hit kepez.
2149. Now farez wel, on Godez half, Gawayn þe noble!
2150. For alle þe golde vpon grounde I nolde go wyth þe,
2151. Ne bere þe felaʒschip þurʒ þis fryth on fote fyrre.'
2152. Bi þat þe wyʒe in þe wod wendez his brydel,
2153. Hit þe hors with þe helez as harde as he myʒt,
2154. Lepez hym ouer þe launde, and leuez þe knyʒt þere

[bob]

al one.

[wheel]

'Bi Goddez self,' quoþ Gawayn,
'I wyl nauþer grete ne grone;
To Goddez wylle I am ful bayn,
And to hym I haf me tone.'

[stanza lxxxvii]

Thenne gyrdez he to Gryngolet, and gederez þe rake,
Schowuez in bi a schore at a schaȝe syde,
Ridez þurȝ þe roȝe bonk ryȝt to þe dale;
And þenne he wayted hym aboute, and wylde hit hym þoȝt,
And seȝe no syngne of resette bisydez nowhere,
Bot hyȝe bonkkez and brent vpon boþe halue,
And ruȝe knokled knarrez with knorned stonez;
Þe skwez of þe scowtes skayned hym þoȝt.
Þenne he houed, and wythhylde his hors at þat tyde,
And ofte chaunged his cher þe chapel to seche:
He seȝ non suche in no syde, and selly hym þoȝt,
Saue, a lyttel on a launde, a lawe as hit were;
A balȝ berȝ bi a bonke þe brymme bysyde,
Bi a forȝ of a flode þat ferked þare;
Þe borne blubred þerinne as hit boyled hade.
Þe knyȝt kachez his caple, and com to þe lawe,
Liȝtez doun luflyly, and at a lynde tachez
Þe rayne and his riche with a roȝe braunche.
Þenne he boȝez to þe berȝe, aboute hit he walkez,
Debatande with hymself quat hit be myȝt.
Hit hade a hole on þe ende and on ayþer syde,
And ouergrowen with gresse in glodes aywhere,
And al watz holȝ inwith, nobot an olde caue,
Or a creuisse of an olde cragge, he couþe hit noȝt deme

[bob]

with spelle.

[wheel]

'We! Lorde,' quoþ þe gentyle knyȝt,

2186. 'Wheþer þis be þe grene chapelle?
2187. Here my3t aboute mydny3t
2188. Þe dele his matynnes telle!

[stanza lxxxviii]

2189. 'Now iwysse,' quoþ Wowayn, 'wysty is here;
2190. Þis oritore is vgly, with erbez ouergrowen;
2191. Wel bisemez þe wy3e wruxled in grene
2192. Dele here his deuocioun on þe deuelez wyse.
2193. Now I fele hit is þe fende, in my fyue wyttez,
2194. Þat hatz stoken me þis steuen to strye me here.
2195. Þis is a chapel of meschaunce, þat chekke hit bytyde!
2196. Hit is þe corsedest kyrk þat euer I com inne!'
2197. With he3e helme on his hede, his launce in his honde,
2198. He romez vp to þe roffe of þe ro3 wonez.
2199. Þene herde he of þat hy3e hil, in a harde roche
2200. Bi3onde þe broke, in a bonk, a wonder breme noyse,
2201. Quat! hit clatered in þe clyff, as hit cleue schulde,
2202. As one vpon a gryndelston hade grounden a syþe.
2203. What! hit wharred and whette, as water at a mulne;
2204. What! hit rusched and ronge, rawþe to here.
2205. Þenne 'Bi Godde,' quoþ Gawayn, 'þat gere, as I trowe,
2206. Is ryched at þe reuerence me, renk, to mete

[bob]

2207. bi rote.

[wheel]

2208. Let God worche! "We loo"—
2209. Hit helppez me not a mote.
2210. My lif þa3 I forgoo,
2211. Drede dotz me no lote.'

[stanza lxxxix]

2212. Thenne þe kny3t con calle ful hy3e:
2213. 'Who sti3tlez in þis sted me steuen to holde?
2214. For now is gode Gawayn goande ry3t here.
2215. If any wy3e o3t wyl, wynne hider fast,
2216. Oþer now oþer neuer, his nedez to spede.'
2217. 'Abyde', quoþ on on þe bonke abouen ouer his hede,

'And þou schal haf al in hast þat I þe hyȝt ones.'
Ȝet he rusched on þat rurde rapely a þrowe.
And wyth quettyng awharf, er he wolde lyȝt;
And syþen he keuerez bi a cragge, and comez of a hole,
Whyrlande out of a wro wyth a felle weppen,
A denez ax nwe dyȝt, þe dynt with to ȝelde,
With a borelych bytte bende by þe halme,
Fyled in a fylor, fowre fote large—
Hit watz no lasse bi þat lace þat lemed ful bryȝt—
And þe gome in þe grene gered as fyrst,
Boþe þe lyre and þe leggez, lokkez and berde,
Saue þat fayre on his fote he foundez on þe erþe,
Sette þe stele to þe stone, and stalked bysyde.
When he wan to þe watter, þer he wade nolde,
He hypped ouer on hys ax, and orpedly strydez,
Bremly broþe on a bent þat brode watz aboute,

[bob]

on snawe.

[wheel]

Sir Gawayn þe knyȝt con mete,
He ne lutte hym noþyng lowe;
Þat oþer sayde, 'Now, sir swete,
Of steuen mon may þe trowe.'

[stanza xc]

'Gawayn,' quoþ þat grene gome, 'God þe mot loke!
Iwysse þou art welcom, wyȝe, to my place,
And þou hatz tymed þi trauayl as truee mon schulde,
And þou knowez þe couenauntez kest vus bytwene:
At þis tyme twelmonyth þou toke þat þe falled,
And I schulde at þis Nwe Ȝere ȝeply þe quyte.
And we ar in þis valay verayly oure one;
Here ar no renkes vs to rydde, rele as vus likez.
Haf þy helme of þy hede, and haf here þy pay.
Busk no more debate þen I þe bede þenne
When þou wypped of my hede at a wap one.'
'Nay, bi God,' quoþ Gawayn, 'þat me gost lante,
I schal gruch þe no grwe for grem þat fallez.

Bot sty3tel þe vpon on strok, and I schal stonde stylle
And warp þe no wernyng to worch as þe lykez,

[bob]

nowhare.'

[wheel]

He lened with þe nek, and lutte,
And schewed þat schyre al bare,
And lette as he no3t dutte;
For drede he wolde not dare.

[stanza xci]

Then þe gome in þe grene grayþed hym swyþe,
Gederez vp hys grymme tole Gawayn to smyte;
With alle þe bur in his body he ber hit on lofte,
Munt as ma3tyly as marre hym he wolde;
Hade hit dryuen adoun as dre3 as he atled,
Þer hade ben ded of his dynt þat do3ty watz euer.
Bot Gawayn on þat giserne glyfte hym bysyde,
As hit com glydande adoun on glode hym to schende,
And schranke a lytel with þe schulderes for þe scharp yrne.
Þat oþer schalk wyth a schunt þe schene wythhaldez,
And þenne repreued he þe prynce with mony prowde wordez:
'Þou art not Gawayn,' quoþ þe gome, 'þat is so goud halden,
Þat neuer ar3ed for no here by hylle ne be vale,
And now þou fles for ferde er þou fele harmez!
Such cowardise of þat kny3t cowþe I neuer here.
Nawþer fyked I ne fla3e, freke, quen þou myntest,
Ne kest no kauelacion in kyngez hous Arthor.
My hede fla3 to my fote, and 3et fla3 I neuer;
And þou, er any harme hent, ar3ez in hert;
Wherfore þe better burne me burde be called

[bob]

þerfore.'

[wheel]

Quoþ Gawayn, 'I schunt onez,
And so wyl I no more;
Bot þa3 my hede falle on þe stonez,

I con not hit restore.

[stanza xcii]

'Bot busk, burne, bi þi fayth, and bryng me to þe poynt.
Dele to me my destiné, and do hit out of honde,
For I schal stonde þe a strok, and start no more
Til þyn ax haue me hitte: haf here my trawþe.'
'Haf at þe þenne!' quoþ þat oþer, and heuez hit alofte,
And waytez as wroþely as he wode were.
He myntez at hym maȝtyly, bot not þe mon rynez,
Withhelde heterly his honde, er hit hurt myȝt.
Gawayn grayþely hit bydez, and glent with no membre,
Bot stode stylle as þe ston, oþer a stubbe auþer
Þat raþeled is in roché grounde with rotez a hundreth.
Þen muryly efte con he mele, þe mon in þe grene:
'So, now þou hatz þi hert holle, hitte me bihous.
Halde þe now þe hyȝe hode þat Arþur þe raȝt,
And kepe þy kanel at þis kest, ȝif hit keuer may.'
Gawayn ful gryndelly with greme þenne sayde:
'Wy! þresch on, þou þro mon, þou þretez to longe;
I hope þat þi hert arȝe wyth þyn awen seluen.'
'For soþe,' quoþ þat oþer freke, 'so felly þou spekez,
I wyl no lenger on lyte lette þin ernde

[bob]

riȝt nowe.'

[wheel]

Þenne tas he hym stryþe to stryke,
And frounsez boþe lyppe and browe;
No meruayle þaȝ hym myslyke
Þat hoped of no rescowe.

[stanza xciii]

He lyftes lyȝtly his lome, and let hit doun fayre
With þe barbe of þe bitte bi þe bare nek;
Þaȝ he homered heterly, hurt hym no more
Bot snyrt hym on þat on syde, þat seuered þe hyde.
Þe scharp schrank to þe flesche þurȝ þe schyre grece,
Þat þe schene blod ouer his schulderes schot to þe erþe;

2315. And quen þe burne seȝ þe blode blenk on þe snawe,
2316. He sprit forth spenne-fote more þen a spere lenþe,
2317. Hent heterly his helme, and on his hed cast,
2318. Schot with his schulderez his fayre schelde vnder,
2319. Braydez out a bryȝt sworde, and bremely he spekez—
2320. Neuer syn þat he watz burne borne of his moder
2321. Watz he neuer in þis worlde wyȝe half so blyþe—
2322. 'Blynne, burne, of þy bur, bede me no mo!
2323. I haf a stroke in þis sted withoute stryf hent,
2324. And if þow rechez me any mo, I redyly schal quyte,
2325. And ȝelde ȝederly aȝayn—and þerto ȝe tryst—

[bob]

2326. and foo.

[wheel]

2327. Bot on stroke here me fallez—
2328. Þe couenaunt schop ryȝt so,
2329. Fermed in Arþurez hallez—
2330. And þerfore, hende, now hoo!'

[stanza xciv]

2331. The haþel heldet hym fro, and on his ax rested,
2332. Sette þe schaft vpon schore, and to þe scharp lened,
2333. And loked to þe leude þat on þe launde ȝede,
2334. How þat doȝty, dredles, deruely þer stondez
2335. Armed, ful aȝlez: in hert hit hym lykez.
2336. Þenn he melez muryly wyth a much steuen,
2337. And wyth a rynkande rurde he to þe renk sayde:
2338. 'Bolde burne, on þis bent be not so gryndel.
2339. No mon here vnmanerly þe mysboden habbez,
2340. Ne kyd bot as couenaunde at kyngez kort schaped.
2341. I hyȝt þe a strok and þou hit hatz, halde þe wel payed;
2342. I relece þe of þe remnaunt of ryȝtes alle oþer.
2343. Iif I deliuer had bene, a boffet paraunter
2344. I couþe wroþeloker haf waret, to þe haf wroȝt anger.
2345. Fyrst I mansed þe muryly with a mynt one,
2346. And roue þe wyth no rof-sore, with ryȝt I þe profered
2347. For þe forwarde þat we fest in þe fyrst nyȝt,
2348. And þou trystyly þe trawþe and trwly me haldez,

2349. Al þe gayne þow me gef, as god mon schulde.
2350. Þat oþer munt for þe morne, mon, I þe profered,
2351. Þou kyssedes my clere wyf—þe cossez me raȝtez.
2352. For boþe two here I þe bede bot two bare myntes

[bob]

2353. boute scaþe.

[wheel]

2354. Trwe mon trwe restore,
2355. Þenne þar mon drede no waþe.
2356. At þe þrid þou fayled þore,
2357. And þerfor þat tappe ta þe.

[stanza xcv]

2358. 'For hit is my wede þat þou werez, þat ilke wouen girdel,
2359. Myn owen wyf hit þe weued, I wot wel for soþe.
2360. Now know I wel þy cosses, and þy costes als,
2361. And þe wowyng of my wyf: I wroȝt hit myseluen.
2362. I sende hir to asay þe, and sothly me þynkkez
2363. On þe fautlest freke þat euer on fote ȝede;
2364. As perle bi þe quite pese is of prys more,
2365. So is Gawayn, in god fayth, bi oþer gay knyȝtez.
2366. Bot here yow lakked a lyttel, sir, and lewté yow wonted;
2367. Bot þat watz for no wylyde werke, ne wowyng nauþer,
2368. Bot for ȝe lufed your lyf; þe lasse I yow blame.'
2369. Þat oþer stif mon in study stod a gret whyle,
2370. So agreued for greme he gryed withinne;
2371. Alle þe blode of his brest blende in his face,
2372. Þat al he schrank for schome þat þe schalk talked.
2373. Þe forme worde vpon folde þat þe freke meled:
2374. 'Corsed worth cowarddyse and couetyse boþe!
2375. In yow is vylany and vyse þat vertue disstryez.'
2376. Þenne he kaȝt to þe knot, and þe kest lawsez,
2377. Brayde broþely þe belt to þe burne seluen:
2378. 'Lo! þer þe falssyng, foule mot hit falle!
2379. For care of þy knokke cowardyse me taȝt
2380. To acorde me with couetyse, my kynde to forsake,
2381. Þat is larges and lewté þat longez to knyȝtez.
2382. Now am I fawty and falce, and ferde haf ben euer

Of trecherye and vntrawþe: boþe bityde sorȝe

[bob]

and care!

[wheel]

I biknowe yow, knyȝt, here stylle,
Al fawty is my fare;
Letez me ouertake your wylle
And efte I schal be ware.'

[stanza xcvi]

Thenn loȝe þat oþer leude and luflyly sayde:
'I halde hit hardily hole, þe harme þat I hade.
Þou art confessed so clene, beknowen of þy mysses,
And hatz þe penaunce apert of þe poynt of myn egge,
I halde þe polysed of þat plyȝt, and pured as clene
As þou hadez neuer forfeted syþen þou watz fyrst borne;
And I gif þe, sir, þe gurdel þat is golde-hemmed,
For hit is grene as my goune. Sir Gawayn, ȝe maye
Þenk vpon þis ilke þrepe, þer þou forth þryngez
Among prynces of prys, and þis a pure token
Of þe chaunce of þe grene chapel at cheualrous knyȝtez.
And ȝe schal in þis Nwe Ȝer aȝayn to my wonez,
And we schyn reuel þe remnaunt of þis ryche fest

[bob]

ful bene.'

[wheel]

Þer laþed hym fast þe lorde
And sayde: 'With my wyf, I wene,
We schal yow wel acorde,
Þat watz your enmy kene.'

[stanza xcvii]

'Nay, for soþe,' quoþ þe segge, and sesed hys helme,
And hatz hit of hendely, and þe haþel þonkkez,
'I haf soiorned sadly; sele yow bytyde,
And he ȝelde hit yow ȝare þat ȝarkkez al menskes!
And comaundez me to þat cortays, your comlych fere,

Boþe þat on and þat oþer, myn honoured ladyez,
Þat þus hor kny3t wyth hor kest han koyntly bigyled.
Bot hit is no ferly þa3 a fole madde,
And þur3 wyles of wymmen be wonen to sor3e,
For so watz Adam in erde with one bygyled,
And Salamon with fele sere, and Samson eftsonez—
Dalyda dalt hym hys wyrde—and Dauyth þerafter
Watz blended with Barsabe, þat much bale þoled.
Now þese were wrathed wyth her wyles, hit were a wynne huge
To luf hom wel, and leue hem not, a leude þat couþe.
For þes wer forne þe freest, þat fol3ed alle þe sele
Exellently of alle þyse oþer, vnder heuenryche

[bob]

þat mused;

[wheel]

And alle þay were biwyled
With wymmen þat þay vsed.
Þa3 I be now bigyled,
Me þink me burde be excused.

[stanza xcviii]

'Bot your gordel', quoþ Gawayn, 'God yow for3elde!
Þat wyl I welde wyth guod wylle, not for þe wynne golde,
Ne þe saynt, ne þe sylk, ne þe syde pendaundes,
For wele ne for worchyp, ne for þe wlonk werkkez,
Bot in syngne of my surfet I schal se hit ofte,
When I ride in renoun, remorde to myseluen
Þe faut and þe fayntyse of þe flesche crabbed,
How tender hit is to entyse teches of fylþe;
And þus, quen pryde schal me pryk for prowes of armes,
Þe loke to þis luf-lace schal leþe my hert.
Bot on I wolde yow pray, displeses yow neuer:
Syn 3e be lorde of þe 3onder londe þer I haf lent inne
Wyth yow wyth worschyp—þe wy3e hit yow 3elde
Þat vphaldez þe heuen and on hy3 sittez—
How norne 3e yowre ry3t nome, and þenne no more?'
'Þat schal I telle þe trwly,' quoþ þat oþer þenne,
'Bertilak de Hautdesert I hat in þis londe.

2446. Þurȝ myȝt of Morgne la Faye, þat in my hous lenges,
2447. And koyntyse of clergye, bi craftes wel lerned,
2448. Þe maystrés of Merlyn mony hatz taken—
2449. For ho hatz dalt drwry ful dere sumtyme
2450. With þat conable klerk, þat knowes alle your knyȝtez

[bob]

2451. at hame;

[wheel]

2452. Morgne þe goddes
2453. Þerfore hit is hir name:
2454. Weldez non so hyȝe hawtesse
2455. Þat ho ne con make ful tame—

[stanza xcix]

2456. 'Ho wayned me vpon þis wyse to your wynne halle
2457. For to assay þe surquidré, ȝif hit soth were
2458. Þat rennes of þe grete renoun of þe Rounde Table;
2459. Ho wayned me þis wonder your wyttez to reue,
2460. For to haf greued Gaynour and gart hir to dyȝe
2461. With glopnyng of þat ilke gome þat gostlych speked
2462. With his hede in his honde bifore þe hyȝe table.
2463. Þat is ho þat is at home, þe auncian lady;
2464. Ho is euen þyn aunt, Arþurez half-suster,
2465. Þe duches doȝter of Tyntagelle, þat dere Vter after
2466. Hade Arþur vpon, þat aþel is nowþe.
2467. Þerfore I eþe þe, haþel, to com to þyn aunt,
2468. Make myry in my hous; my meny þe louies,
2469. And I wol þe as wel, wyȝe, bi my faythe,
2470. As any gome vnder God for þy grete trauþe.'
2471. And he nikked hym naye, he nolde bi no wayes.
2472. Þay acolen and kyssen and kennen ayþer oþer
2473. To þe prynce of paradise, and parten ryȝt þere

[bob]

2474. on coolde;

[wheel]

2475. Gawayn on blonk ful bene
2476. To þe knygez burȝ buskez bolde,

And þe kny3t in þe enker-grene
Whiderwarde-so-euer he wolde.

[stanza c]

Wylde wayez in þe worlde Wowen now rydez
On Gryngolet, þat þe grace hade geten of his lyue;
Ofte he herbered in house and ofte al þeroute,
And mony aventure in vale, and venquyst ofte,
Þat I ne ty3t at þis tyme in tale to remene.
Þe hurt watz hole þat he hade hent in his nek,
And þe blykkande belt he bere þeraboute
Abelef as a bauderyk bounden bi his syde,
Loken vnder his lyfte arme, þe lace, with a knot,
In tokenyng he watz tane in tech of a faute.
And þus he commes to þe court, kny3t al in sounde.
Þer wakned wele in þat wone when wyst þe grete
Þat gode Gawayn watz commen; gayn hit hym þo3t.
Þe kyng kyssez þe kny3t, and þe whene alce,
And syþen mony syker kny3t þat so3t hym to haylce,
Of his fare þat hym frayned; and ferlyly he telles,
Biknowez alle þe costes of care þat he hade,
Þe chaunce of þe chapel, þe chere of þe kny3t,
Þe luf of þe ladi, þe lace at þe last.
Þe nirt in þe nek he naked hem schewed
Þat he la3t for his vnleuté at þe leudes hondes

[bob]

for blame.

[wheel]

He tened quen he schulde telle,
He groned for gref and grame;
Þe blod in his face con melle,
When he hit schulde schewe, for schame.

[stanza ci]

'Lo! lorde,' quoþ þe leude, and þe lace hondeled,
'Þis is þe bende of þis blame I bere in my nek,
Þis is þe laþe and þe losse þat I la3t haue
Of couardise and couetyse þat I haf ca3t þare;

Þis is þe token of vntrawþe þat I am tan inne,
And I mot nedez hit were wyle I may last;
For mon may hyden his harme, bot vnhap ne may hit,
For þer hit onez is tachched twynne wil hit neuer.'
Þe kyng comfortez þe kny3t, and alle þe court als
La3en loude þerat, and luflyly acorden
Þat lordes and ladis þat longed to þe Table,
Vche burne of þe broþerhede, a bauderyk schulde haue,
A bende abelef hym aboute of a bry3t grene,
And þat, for sake of þat segge, in swete to were.
For þat watz acorded þe renoun of þe Rounde Table,
And he honoured þat hit hade euermore after,
As hit is breued in þe best boke of romaunce.
Þus in Arthurus day þis aunter bitidde,
Þe Brutus bokez þerof beres wyttenesse;
Syþhen Brutus, þe bolde burne, bo3ed hider fyrst,
After þe segge and þe asaute watz sesed at Troye,

[bob]

iwysse,

[wheel]

Mony aunterez here-biforne
Haf fallen suche er þis.
Now þat here þe croun of þorne,
He bryng vus to his blysse! AMEN.

HONY SOYT QUI MAL PENCE.

SIR GAWAIN AND THE DARK KNIGHT: WHY HEROES MUST BE REBORN (AN AFTERWORD)

BY JASON S. RIDLER, PHD

NO AUTHOR CAN ESCAPE THEIR PLACE AND TIME. They are products of their era, and this imbues even timeless tales with the language, culture, vice, virtues, cares, and disdains of a specific place in history. And whenever that work is transcribed, translated, interpreted, recast, even stolen, the work undergoes a rebirth, including its heroes. Consider the journey you just took with Sir Gawain, written by an unknown poet of the fourteenth century. It is a collection of folklore and stories from others but also reflects the tastes and choices of an author of the Middle Ages who lived at the same time as Chaucer in a world of raids and sieges, of knights, pikes, and long bows, where wars were won on the physical strength of soldiers. This is not the industrial world of steam, smog, and imperialism that Jessie L. Weston called home, let alone the high-paced world of social media, drones, and hybrid warfare of writer and soldier Weston Ochse.

Purists often lament primary-source stories breeding new versions of itself. The original work, they surmise, has an integrity denied its brood: The genius is in the original, not these replicants traced by foreign hands and languages from eras they could never truly understand.

Which is class bias and simple-minded worship of origin stories in literary history. The original was best. Trust us. You can't read it.

At a recent literary convention, I was asked: Should Batman change or revert to earlier iterations? In other words, was old Batman more legit?

My minority voice shouted, "Batman *should* change, he *must* change, and *has* changed, otherwise he'd become a juvenile fossil. Bill Finger and Bob

Kane's 1939 Batman was a New Deal power fantasy about a rich man who could save us with punches and gadgets and enjoyed scaring bad guys who looked an awful like the gangs of New York City and the hungry violence that stalked its streets. And Batman was largely stolen from the Shadow, Doc Savage, and Zorro, so much for originality. It's when he is reborn, we get a new Batman for a new age instead of a vestigial hero out of time (regardless of how much Batman would time travel). In the '60s he got groovy, then dead serious, and in the 1980s, my Batman was a noirish detective that toyed with libertarian and fascist thinking as the Cold War screamed its final nuclear threats. None are as childlike and naïve as the 1939 world of dark adventure for kids raised through the Depression. We capture the essence of the character and make him our own. And that is the only reason Batman is a billion-dollar media machine. Not because of Bob Kane's artwork." (Or words to that effect).

In *Death Is No Obstacle,* award-winning fiction author Michael Moorcock advised any author working in heroic fiction to go past the Inklings, George McDonald, and William Morris. Run by Samuel Taylor Coleridge's translation of the *Iliad*, though never forget his English words in the mouth of Achilles, "Let me, this instant, rush into the fields, And reap what glory life's short harvest yields." Follow their footnotes until there are no precedents. Read the "primary sources" of this literature, ancient epic poems, fables, German Romantics and more. Understand how they worked in their time and why nowadays their mores and views might seem insane. For much of his "sword and sorcery work," Moorcock found models, modes and ideas in these primary sources, especially in Sir Walter Scott's *Ivanhoe.* For him, this was the birth of "adventure fiction," one with deep roots. Many of Moorcock's fantasy novels are lifted from these sources and made fresh to speak to readers in the '60s and '70s, even today—especially his Elric of Melniboné series. Here religious morality and authority, good and evil, and a sense of just and orderly Christian universe has become the domain of chaos fighting order, morals corrupted by power, where heroes cannot be trusted. Especially Elric.

By such means are ancient heroes reborn through recreation, innovation, translation, and modernization. The last two are most critical for survival, as most were not granted generational wealth to learn ancient languages as part of our caste. Which is why translation and modernization robs the privileged class of their monopoly of the past.

Now consider again your journey through *Sir Gawain and the Green Knight.* Authors Jessie L. Weston and Weston Ochse were given this epic story and the enduring mythology that lived far past the days of Vauban. While technically both these authors write in Modern English, they are not the same. The English of the late nineteenth century was filled with the flair of the Romantic Age, holding on to visions of nature, god, and beauty that spoke to the Edwardians rejecting the industrial vocabulary of "those Satanic Mills." And with the Great War's hammer strike on European civilization, the old words and phrases that inspired chivalry shattered against the horrors of the Somme. As Paul Fussell noted in *The Great War and Modern Memory*, warriors were now soldiers, chargers were horses, and where once a warrior's wounds unleashed the "red wine of youth," there was now only *blood*. Consider the journey you have taken with Gawain, not just toward his battle with the Green Knight but through the hundred years gulf between authors—when English has gone from dratted to *DAAAMMMMNNNN*.

Time and place separate Jessie L. Weston and Weston Ochse. One was a trailblazing and independent scholar, who wanted one of the great pieces of Arthurian lore to endure. The other provides a new layer to the story through the lens of creative writing as an artistic act, and with that perspective casts light in new windows of both versions. Yet both are united in purpose: to have one of the earliest known Arthurian tales made accessible to their own era, she on the shoulders of the essential and lost poet, he on the shoulders of her trailblazing work.

So long as we continue to find meaning in the story and language of the unknown poet, Gawain is reborn. And in this fashion he evolves in the minds of new generations, against new context, so that his evolution refuses to die.

(Sources available upon request.)

JASON S. RIDLER holds a PhD in war studies from the Royal Military College of Canada and is a former visiting scholar at the University of California, Berkeley. He has published numerous articles on special forces, unconventional warfare, counterinsurgency, and military history. Additionally he has taught the skills of education, history, and writing to students of all ages for over twenty years. His students have found passions for learning, sold novels, stories, and memoirs, and thrived in education from high school to grad school. He currently teaches creative writing at Google and History at Johns Hopkins University. For more, visit: www.jasonridler.com.

A SELECTED READING LIST FOR WORKS OF SIMILAR FICTION

FOR READERS WHO ENJOYED *SIR GAWAIN AND THE Green Knight* and wish to explore similar stories, consider the following list, which comprises only a small sampling of wonderful works relating to Arthurian Legend; Middle English-Based Romance; Medieval Historic Fiction; British Questing Knights; and/or other themes centered around Chivalry and Adventure.

The Acts of King Arthur and His Noble Knights by John Steinbeck (1976): A modernized retelling of the Arthurian legend based on Sir Thomas Malory's text, *Le Morte d'Arthur*.

Beowulf (author unknown) (circa 700–1000 A.D.): An epic poem, considered one of the most important works of Old English literature, in which a heroic future king battles dragons and monsters until his death, while in protection of the realm.

Beowulf: A New Translation by Maria Dahvana Headley (2020): A modernized retelling of the classic *Beowulf* tale, viewed through a lens of 21st-century culture and social progressiveness.

The Canterbury Tales by Geoffrey Chaucer (1392): A collection of twenty-four stories from pilgrims as they travel to Canterbury Cathedral to visit the shrine of Saint Thomas Becket.

A Connecticut Yankee in King Arthur's Court by Mark Twain (1889): An 1800s-American engineer is sent back in time to the reign of King Arthur where he tries to modernize the past.

The Crystal Cave (***Arthurian Saga*** series, #1) by Mary Stewart (1970): A coming-of-age story about young Merlin as he travels throughout England, learns magic, and reaches toward a great destiny.

The Faerie Queene by Edmund Spenser (1590–1596): One of the longest poems in the English language, this work follows the exploits of several knights as an allegorical means to examine "gentlemanly" virtues.

The Ghosts of Sherwood by Carrie Vaughn (2020): Twenty years after the adventures of Robin Hood left off, his and wife Marian's children are kidnapped, and a motley group of new characters assemble to help find them.

Gwenhwyfar by Mercedes Lackey (2009): A contemporary vision of an additional future-wife to King Arthur, princess Gwenhwyfar prefers to have her own heroic adventures rather than placate gender expectations.

Havelok the Dane (attributed to Geffrei Gaimar) (13th century): One of the great Middle English romance works that comprise the "Matter of England," this epic poem follows several ruling families in England and Denmark as they intermarry and battle one another for thrones.

The History of the Kings of Britain (Latin: ***Historia regum Britanniae***) by Geoffrey of Monmouth (circa 1136): A pseudohistorical account covering over 2,000 years of British history, it includes the earliest known story of *King Lear* and also helped popularize the legend of King Arthur.

The Hobbit by J. R. R. Tolkien (1937): A hobbit, in company of dwarves and a wizard, finds a magic ring and participates in epic battle against many evil things, including goblins and a marauding dragon.

Ivanhoe by Walter Scott (1819): A three-volume epic in which the heroic Saxon knight Ivanhoe fights for love and honor, and also allies with Robin Hood while caught in the struggle between royal brothers Richard the Lion-Hearted and Prince John over the throne.

King Horn (author unknown) (1225): The oldest extant romance in Middle English, this chivalric tale follows a young price who is captured by invading forces, has many adventures in foreign lands, and then returns to claim his English throne and beloved bride.

Lancelot, the Knight of the Cart (French: ***Lancelot, le Chevalier de la Charrette***) by Chrétien de Troyes (circa 12th century): One of the first stories to feature Sir Lancelot of Arthurian fame, this poem tells of the rescue and love affair with Guinevere.

The Last Kingdom (***The Saxon Chronicles*** series, #1) by Bernard Cornwell (2006): One final kingdom remains standing in England against invading Dane forces, and its king must do whatever he can not to fall.

The Lord of the Rings (trilogy) by J. R. R. Tolkien (1954): An epic high-fantasy trilogy set in imagined lands in which a hobbit becomes part of a raging war between forces of good and those of evil and dark magic.

The Merry Adventures of Robin Hood by Howard Pyle (1883): A series of interconnected tales relating to the English outlaw Robin Hood and his band of Merry Men as they resist the crooked Sheriff of Nottingham.

The Mists of Avalon by Marion Zimmer Bradley (1982): A series of Arthurian legends told from the perspective of female characters.

Le Morte d'Arthur by Sir Thomas Malory (1485): A collection of tales relating to King Arthur and Camelot, this book is considered the best known work of Arthurian literature.

The Once and Future King by T. H. White (1958): A modernization, with additional stories, to compliment Sir Thomas Malory's text, *Le Morte d'Arthur*.

The Pearl (author unknown, attributed to same author who wrote ***Sir Gawain and the Green Knight***) (14th century): Considered one of the most important surviving Middle English works, this poem relates the dream-vision of a mourning father who encounters an angelic woman and the Heavenly City.

The Princess Bride by William Goldman (1973): A beautiful, grieving young woman is kidnapped, and to her rescue comes her "true love" a swashbuckling farm boy she thought died years before.

Sword at Sunset by Rosemary Sutcliff (1963): An epic retelling of the Arthurian legend in which an "authentic" warrior-king saves civilization against barbarian hordes without the use of magic or shining chivalric code.

THOUGHTS FROM THE EDITOR

ONE DAY, A KING WILL COME, AND THE SWORD WILL rise again . . . Or, in this case, an author will come, and the pen will leap again to paper!

. . . And see, herein, the event that has occurred as foretold . . .

Haha. A bit vainglorious perhaps. But Weston Ochse deserves it. As does Jessie L. Weston before him. For as scholar Jason S. Ridler wrote in his afterword, each author has expertly recast this Arthurian tale in the language and context of a new generation. And in the case of Weston Ochse, brought along myself and publisher Dark Moon Books for this literary journey.

I'm absolutely thrilled to play a small role in the latest modernization of this epic work, and just in time for the theatrical release of A24 Studio's 2021 film *The Green Knight*. Serendipitous, indeed.

I've known Wes since early 2012 when he mentored me into the writers' industry through the organization Horror Writers Association (the largest organization dedicated to horror and dark fantasy literature). Everything Wes touches becomes elevated to the highest of esteem so, needless to say, it was an honor to have him approach me about helping to develop this concept, bringing into existence the most comprehensive edition available for *Sir Gawain and the Green Knight*. By building one reworking upon another, readers are able to appreciate the passage of language and voice in a tale so timeless it still appeals to audiences of all ages, across a span of nearly seven hundred years.

So thank you. To Wes, and to you, dear reader, for your interest in this tale. I hope you enjoyed it and/or found value in its treatment. I hope also that this edition will still be found enjoyable and of value seven hundred years more into the future.

HONY SOYT QUI MAL PENCE.

—Eric J. Guignard
Chino Hills, California
June 10, 2021

ACKNOWLEDGEMENTS

NO BOOK OF ANY QUALITY IS CREATED IN A VACUUM. Too many folks along the way have contributed to my love of fiction and my appreciation for *Sir Gawain and the Green Knight* for me to count. I've already outed my father and thanked my mother, who were my earliest influences. In the preface, you will learn about J.R.R. Tolkien's contribution. But for now, let me give a moment to Ms. Spurling, my senior year high school English teacher at Tyner High School in Chattanooga, Tennessee.

I chose her because she was also the head of the drama department. A lot of my friends were in Advanced Placement classes, and while I qualified, I didn't want the workload. I was already taking Trig and other silly classes that a budding Master of Fine Arts would never use in his lifetime, plus I was a senior and had discovered girls and had a car and could almost drink legally. Because she was the drama teacher, she was very vivacious and always encouraging. Back then, for some reason, I'd developed an intermittent stutter. It was purely psychological, but it was there nevertheless, and she was always patient with me, even when I was mortified about how other students looked at me.

And I was a different student. I played Victor Velasco in Neil Simon's *Barefoot in the Park.*

When other students wrote their papers on Abortion or Marriage or Gas Prices, I wrote mine on *The Affects of* 19th *Century Commune Societies on* 20th *Century American Values.* And she stimulated me. She was always encouraging. I'd approach her and tell her that I felt I was doing too much, and she said to me, too much for some people isn't too much for you. And that stuck with me.

Trust a teacher to do the right thing.

Trust a teacher to change my world.

I'd also like to thank the contributors to this book. As a longtime member of the Horror Writers Association, I was one of the first mentors they had in their then-nascent mentor program. I had no less than ten young souls who I was able to work with and be my version of Ms. Spurling to. Several of them still write. Several of them moved away. But the two who are part of this work are luminaries.

The editor, Eric J. Guignard, is one of those polymaths who puts as much love into building furniture as he does piecing together an anthology. He's always tremendous at everything he does, so deciding to ask him if he wanted to publish and edit this work was a no-brainer. Plus, he's a multiple Bram Stoker Award-winning author and editor. I couldn't be more proud of him or in better hands.

The scholar who wrote the afterword was also a person I mentored. He wrote some magnificent fiction, but moved on to obtain his PhD in Unconventional Warfare, which makes his contribution all the more powerful, when you consider the unconventionality of the Green Knight.

Then of course there is my wife, Yvonne Navarro. An author of astounding significance, she is also an incredible artist. The pieces you see in this book are all hers and I was delighted when I approached her and asked her to be a part of this long-time pet project and she jumped at the opportunity.

I would also like to acknowledge, you, the reader. Approaching such a work as *Sir Gawain and the Green Knight* is not something done gently. Although I've included the original Middle English (good luck with that), and the Jessie L. Weston 1898 translation, my hope is that you will spend most of your time in the first sixty or so pages where I've worked magnificently hard in trying to produce a story that is accessible and something that will be remembered.

So, thank you. This book is dedicated to your spirit.

—Weston Ochse

PUBLISHER'S REQUEST

DEAR READER, FAN, OR SUPPORTER,

It's a dreadful commentary that the worth of indie publications is measured by online 5-star reviews, but such is the state of current commerce.

Should you have enjoyed this book, gratitude is most appreciated by posting a brief and honest online review at Amazon.com, Goodreads.com, and/or a highly-visible blog.

With sincerest thanks,

Eric J. Guignard
Publisher, Dark Moon Books

ALSO FROM DARK MOON BOOKS:

A World of Horror

Every nation of the globe has unique tales to tell, whispers that settle in through the land, creatures or superstitions that enliven the night, but rarely do readers get to experience such a diversity of these voices in one place as in ***A WORLD OF HORROR***, the latest anthology book created by award-winning editor Eric J. Guignard, and beautifully illustrated by artist Steve Lines.

Enclosed within its pages are twenty-two all-new dark and speculative fiction stories written by authors from around the world that explore the myths and monsters, fables and fears of their homelands.

Encounter the haunting things that stalk those radioactive forests outside Chernobyl in Ukraine; sample the curious dishes one may eat in Canada; beware the veldt monster that mirrors yourself in Uganda; or simply battle mountain trolls alongside Alfred Nobel in Sweden. These stories and more are found within *A World of Horror*: Enter and discover, truly, there's no place on the planet devoid of frights, thrills, and wondrous imagination.

"This breath of fresh air for horror readers shows the limitless possibilities of the genre."
—*Publishers Weekly* (starred review)

"This is the book we need right now!"
—*Becky Spratford; librarian, reviewer,* RA for All: Horror

"A fresh collection of horror authors exploring monsters and myths from their homelands."
—*Library Journal*

Order your copy at www.darkmoonbooks.com or www.amazon.com
ISBN-13: 978-0-9989383-1-8

ALSO FROM DARK MOON BOOKS:

POP THE CLUTCH: THRILLING TALES OF ROCKABILLY, MONSTERS, AND HOT ROD HORROR

Welcome to the cool side of the 1950s, where the fast cars and revved-up movie monsters peel out in the night. Where outlaw vixens and jukebox tramps square off with razorblades and lead pipes. Where rockers rock, cool cats strut, and hot rods roar. Where you howl to the moon as the tiki drums pound and the electric guitar shrieks and that spit-and-holler jamboree ain't gonna stop for a long, long time . . . maybe never.

This is the '50s where ghost shows still travel the back roads of the south, and rockabilly has a hold on the nation's youth; where lucky hearts tell the tale, and maybe that fella in the Shriners' fez ain't so square after all. Where exist noir detectives of the supernatural, tattoo artists of another kind, Hollywood fix-it men, and a punk kid with grasshopper arms under his chain-studded jacket and an icy stare on his face.

This is the '50s of *Pop the Clutch: Thrilling Tales of Rockabilly, Monsters, and Hot Rod Horror*. This is your ticket to the dark side of American kitsch . . . the fun and frightful side!

"A fitting tribute to the 1950s with this 18-story compendium of hot rods, rock 'n' roll, and creature features come to life."

—*Publishers Weekly*

Order your copy at www.darkmoonbooks.com or www.amazon.com

ISBN-13: 978-0-9834335-9-0

ALSO FROM DARK MOON BOOKS:

The Five Senses of Horror

Hearing, sight, touch, smell, and taste: Our impressions of the world are formed by our five senses, and so too are our fears, our imaginations, and our captivation in reading fiction stories that embrace these senses.

Whether hearing the song of infernal caverns, tasting the erotic kiss of treachery, or smelling the lush fragrance of a fiend, enclosed within this anthology are fifteen horror and dark fantasy tales that will quicken the beat of fear, sweeten the flavor of wonder, sharpen the spike of thrills, and otherwise brighten the marvel of storytelling that is found resonant!

Editor Eric J. Guignard and psychologist Jessica Bayliss, PhD also include companion discourse throughout, offering academic and literary insight as well as psychological commentary examining the physiology of our senses, why each of our senses are engaged by dark fiction stories, and how it all inspires writers to continually churn out ideas in uncommon and invigorating ways.

Featuring stunning interior illustrations by Nils Bross, and including fiction short stories by such world-renowned authors as John Farris, Ramsey Campbell, Poppy Z. Brite, Darrell Schweitzer, Lisa Morton, and Richard Christian Matheson, amongst others.

Intended for readers, writers, and students alike, explore ***THE FIVE SENSES OF HORROR***!

Order your copy at www.darkmoonbooks.com or www.amazon.com

ISBN-13: 978-0-9988275-0-6

ALSO FROM DARK MOON BOOKS:

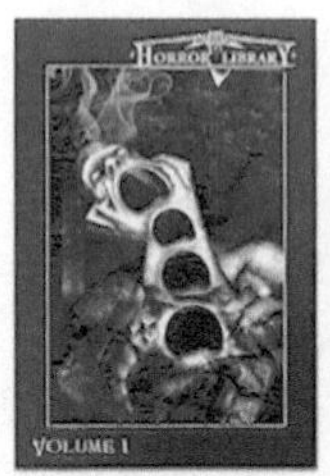

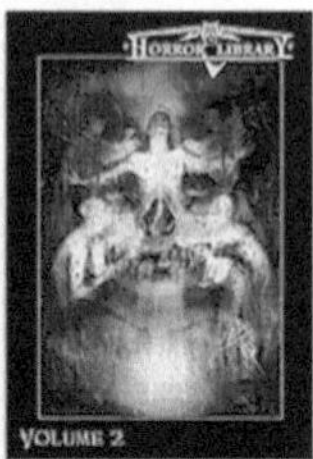

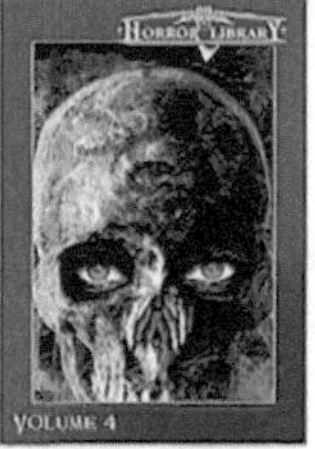

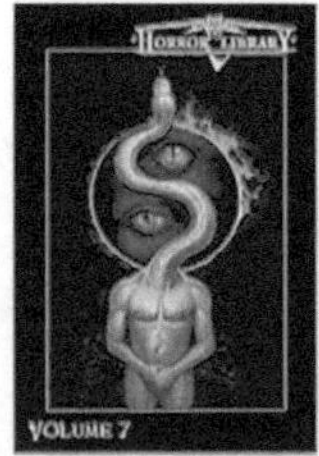

+HORROR LIBRARY+ ANTHOLOGY SERIES

Since 2006, the +Horror Library+ series of anthologies has been internationally praised as a groundbreaking source of contemporary horror short fiction stories—relevant to the moment and stunning in impact—from leading authors of the macabre and darkly imaginative.

Filled with Fears and Fantasy. Death and Dark Dreams. Monsters and Mayhem. Literary Vision and Wonder. Managed by award-winning author Eric J. Guignard, each volume of the +Horror Library+ series is packed with heart-pounding thrills and creepy contemplations as to what truly lurks among the shadows of the world(s) we live in.

Read each volume, and watch for more forthcoming.

Shamble no longer through the banal humdrum of normalcy, but ENTER THE HORROR LIBRARY!

"Excellent stories of the highest caliber." —*Dread Central*

"Uniformly well-crafted and original." —*Rue Morgue Magazine*

"A mixture of surprising treats: Stark, livid, engaging." —*SFRreader.com*

"Impactful tales that throw the rules of both reality and genre fiction out the window." —*Fearnet* (*Chiller TV*)

Order your copy at www.darkmoonbooks.com or www.amazon.com

ALSO FROM DARK MOON BOOKS:

EXPLORING DARK SHORT FICTION PRIMER SERIES

An exploration of modern masters of literary short fiction, where horror is celebrated as literary, beautiful, and emotionally-resonant.

Cited as "visionary," this series of Primers include short stories, along with their light analysis, of progressive and outstanding authors who deserve wider recognition amongst readers.

Volumes in this series include:

#1: A Primer to Steve Rasnic Tem (2017)
#2: A Primer to Kaaron Warren (2018)
#3: A Primer to Nisi Shawl (2018)
#4: A Primer to Jeffrey Ford (2019)
#5: A Primer to Han Song (2020)
#6: A Primer to Ramsey Campbell (2021)
#7: A Primer to Gemma Files (2022)
. . . and more coming!

In a world of fast-changing tastes and values, there is one constant: Extraordinary writing carries on.

"A fascinating study for fans seeking new reads and for librarians developing wide-ranging collections." —*Library Journal*

"Refreshing and much-needed . . . Addresses significant themes and figures within the horror field." —*Locus Magazine*

"Dark and exquisite . . . Wonderful exposition about authors and selections of their stories." —*The Big Thrill Magazine*

Order your copy at www.darkmoonbooks.com or www.amazon.com

ABOUT AUTHOR
WESTON OCHSE

WESTON OCHSE's love for *Sir Gawain and the Green Knight* began when he was ten years old. Not only did it inspire him to join the military in order to become a knight of the red, white, and blue, but also to seek higher education so he could more readily understand the great works that came before him. He holds a Master of Fine Arts from National University and has been published all over the world.

The American Library Association calls Weston "one of the major horror authors of the 21st Century." His work has won the Bram Stoker Award, been nominated for the Pushcart Prize, won four New Mexico-Arizona Book Awards, and been a USA Today Bestseller. His military supernatural series *SEAL Team 666* has been optioned to be a movie starring Dwayne Johnson. His shorter work has appeared in DC Comics, IDW Comics, *Soldier of Fortune Magazine*, and *Weird Tales*. His franchise work includes the *X-Files*, *Predator*, *Aliens*, *Hellboy*, *Clive Barker's Midian*, and *V-Wars*. Weston is also a veteran of the US military, serving thirty-five years in the Army, special operations, and various agencies.

ABOUT AUTHOR

JESSIE L. WESTON

JESSIE LAIDLAY WESTON (Dec. 1850–Sept. 1928) was an English author, poet, scholar, and translator. She was born in Surrey, England to a wealthy tea merchant and his second wife, and given wide-ranging and excellent formal education at Brighton, Paris; Hildesheim, Germany; and also in art at London's Crystal Palace School.

In 1890, at the urging of publisher Alfred Nutt (whose family's publishing house eventually became part of what is today Hachette Book Group, one of the largest publishers in the world), Jessie began translating and "modernizing" ancient works in order to make them more widely known, first with German composer Richard Wagner, and then, most famously, with Arthurian legends. She translated many of the ancient tales, as those of Sir Gawain, Sir Lancelot du Lac, Sir Perceval, et. al., and additionally added scholarly commentary into the canon. Her works have since been commended as "valuable translations" by Arthurian scholar Juliette Wood, PhD. She was further acknowledged by poet T. S. Eliot as an inspiration as well as crucial to understanding books of another era.

Jessie L. Weston passed away in London in 1928, at the age of 77. She never married nor had children. Her writing has continued to attract readers interested in ancient religion, myth, and especially Arthurian legend for over a century.

ABOUT ILLUSTRATOR

YVONNE NAVARRO

YVONNE NAVARRO is the author of twenty-three published novels and a lot of short stories, articles and a reference dictionary. Her most recently published book is *Supernatural: The Usual Sacrifices* (based in the Supernatural Universe). Her writing has won numerous awards, including a Bram Stoker Award. Lately she's been really getting into painting and artwork. She lives way down in the southeastern corner of Arizona, fifteen miles from the Mexican border, is married to author Weston Ochse, and dotes on their rescued Great Danes. She has an "I Want To Do" list. It has about 4,274 projects on it and won't stop growing. Her latest addition to that list is the completion of the Hummingbird Triathlon in Sierra Vista. She figured she'd would crawl over the finish line, then she read the rules don't allow that. Check her Facebook page for updates.

www.ingramcontent.com/pod-product-compliance
Lightning Source LLC
Chambersburg PA
CBHW021139190726
48288CB00008B/2733

* 9 7 8 1 9 4 9 4 9 1 4 2 5 *